"NOW IT'S YOUR TURN," LAURENS SAID

Confidently Mayi held the wine bag at arm's length and squeezed gently. She gasped as a thin stream of red wine soared past her ear. A few drops splashed over her naked breasts, her stomach and onto her thigh.

"I'll have to take a dip in the pool now," she said ruefully.

"I have a better idea," Laurens said, his eyes gleaming. He picked her up and carried her to a large sunny patch of moss in the grotto. Mayi felt a sharp thrill as he captured the drops of wine on her breast with his tongue, and she stretched her arms over her head in mute invitation.

As if mesmerized, Laurens watched her, and the flame in his eyes told her he would wait no longer. Their love would be consummated in this peaceful and beautiful place in the forest.

Dear Reader:

We are very excited to announce a change to Harlequin Superromances effective with the February releases, title numbers 150–153. As you know, romance publishing is never static, but is always growing and innovative. After extensive market research, we have decided to slightly shorten the length of the four Superromances published each month, guaranteeing a faster-paced story.

You will still receive that "something extra" in plot and character development that has made these longer romance novels so popular. A strong well-written love story will remain at the heart of a Harlequin Superromance, but with the tighter format, drama will be heightened from start to finish.

Our authors are delighted with and challenged by this change, and they have been busy writing some wonderful new stories for you. Enjoy!

Laurie Bauman

Laurie Bauman,
Superromance Senior Editor

Irma Walker
THROUGH NIGHT AND DAY

Harlequin Books

TORONTO • NEW YORK • LONDON
AMSTERDAM • PARIS • SYDNEY • HAMBURG
STOCKHOLM • ATHENS • TOKYO • MILAN

Published January 1985

First printing November 1984

ISBN 0-373-70147-0

Printed in Canada

White snow dove, whither are you flying?
All the passes into Spain are full of snow.
Tonight you will take refuge in our house.

I am not afraid of the snow or of the darkness,
My beloved; for you I would pass through night
   and day.
Through night and day and through deserted
   forests.

Basque Folk Song

CHAPTER ONE

MAYI HURRIED ALONG THE PATH that cut through one of the groves of Tahoe pines dotting the University of Nevada campus. She was headed for the Arts and Science Building, the place where she was to meet Pio Aquirre. A rootless happiness, a feeling that all was well with her world, lightened her step and made her want to burst out singing. Even the realization that she had little to sing about wasn't enough to ruin her lighthearted mood. The afternoon sun was too warm, the day too perfect—and she was young. She felt certain she could handle anything life threw at her, including the problem of finding the kind of job she wanted after graduation, which was just a few weeks away.

Graduation....

Another chapter of her life was fast coming to an end, something she both welcomed and dreaded. For one thing, even with her high grades, she still hadn't been able to find a teaching job, and time was running out. The few teaching slots available in Reno and in the sparsely populated area that surrounded the city were already filled for the fall. She had known the odds against walking right into a position, but becoming a teacher had been the whole point of these past five years of struggle and sacrifice, and she couldn't help being disappointed. After all, being a teacher was something she wanted more than anything else in the world—

No, not really, Mayi. More than anything else in the world you want someone to love—someone who will love you, care for you, stand up with you against the world. . . .

The thought had come out of her deepest sub-conscious, slipping through her defenses so unex-pectedly that she stopped in the middle of the path, her breath escaping in a long sigh. What on earth was the matter with her? Was she going crazy? Why would she think such an absurd thing? Everybody was always saying how practical and down-to-earth she was. What would her friends think if they knew that for a moment she'd had a mental image of her-self standing shoulder to shoulder with a man, a faceless man, who was strong and tender and so loving to her?

As she started on her way again, the crisp spring wind, fresh off the Sierra Nevada, tossed her hair in the air and whirled it around her face until she felt as if she was looking at the world through a red veil. Although she liked to think of her hair as auburn, she was all too aware that it was much redder. One of her foster mothers had once remarked, "I swear, that child looks as if her head is on fire!"

The gray-haired man who was walking along the path toward Mayi stopped to smile at her, his eyes quizzical. "If ever there's anyone who is the embodiment of spring, it's you, Mayi Jenners," he said, shaking his head. "It won't seem the same around here next year without you asking the kinds of questions that keep an old prof on his toes. Are you certain you don't want to do some postgrad work?"

Mayi threw off her troubled thoughts and smiled back. She had taken French and Spanish classes from Professor Montaigne since her freshman year, and a casual friendship had developed between them. "No, it's already taken me five years to get my diploma," she said. "I'm afraid I can't indulge myself with an extra year."

"You could have applied for a scholarship. I offered to recommend you several times, you know."

Mayi stiffened. "I didn't need it, Professor Montaigne. I've done okay by myself."

"Well, I do understand your feelings, but accepting a scholarship isn't the same as charity, you know."

Mayi winced. *Charity.* She hated that word, hated the feeling of helplessness, hated knowing that the very food in your mouth had been put there through the charity of other people, and that they now had the power to tell you what to do and how to live.

She and her grandmother had been forced to go on welfare for four years after her grandmother fell and shattered her hip so badly. The misery of listening while her grandmother was badgered by the humiliating questions of an indifferent and insensitive social worker was still too vivid, as were memories of her later years as a foster child in numerous foster homes after her grandmother's death. These experiences had left her with the burning determination never to take charity again, as long as she lived, from anyone, no matter what.

"I do think you should get your master's," Professor Montaigne was going on, "but even an old academic like me understands the practicalities of life. Any luck with your job résumés yet?"

"Not yet," she told him. "Maybe in the fall I can work as a substitute teacher in Reno and eventually get a full-time position. Luckily, I still have my job at the casino."

The professor nodded his understanding. Many of the students at the University of Nevada put themselves through school by working at Reno's gambling casinos as cocktail waitresses, blackjack dealers or keno runners, the job Mayi had held since she'd turned twenty-one two years earlier.

"Well, don't stay too long at the fair," he advised. "It could be too tempting. I'm sure the pay of a blackjack dealer is twice what a teacher earns."

"I won't." Mayi smiled suddenly. "Of course, I could always get a job as a show girl. The casino manager, Mr. Rourke, asked me again if I wanted a job dancing in the Sherwood Forest Room."

"Uh-huh. Well, with that flaming red hair, you'd probably be a sensation, though—well, I'm glad you turned him down."

"Why are you so sure that I did?" she teased. "Maybe I told him I'd be delighted."

"Oh, I know you pretty well. Of course, you do dance like an angel. I still remember watching you during that program on ethnic dancing, doing the—what is that Basque dance called?"

"The *jota*. It's a dance my grandmother taught me, though I'm sure I must've made a lot of mistakes. It's been so many years since—" She broke off, suddenly fighting the old grief. It had been so many years since her grandmother's death, but the pain was still there, just below the surface. After all, Grammy had been her only relative, the anchor of her life.

"Your grandmother was Basque, wasn't she? You must have inherited your brown eyes from her. But where on earth did you get your unusual coloring? Most Basques are dark, aren't they?"

"My grandmother had dark hair and skin, and so did my mother. Maybe I look like my father's side of the family. I think he was Irish. My grandmother didn't speak much English and he didn't speak Spanish or Basque, so she knew very little about him."

She stopped, wondering again what was wrong with her today. She seldom talked about her past. In fact, she was adept at evading personal questions. The years she'd lived in foster homes had left deep emotional scars, and she didn't like to think about them, much less talk about them.

She realized that Professor Montaigne was answering her and she forced herself to listen. "You're a sensible young woman, Mayi. You'll do all right. Just don't let your heart rule your head."

She hid her surprise behind a smile. Although she had known Professor Montaigne for five years, theirs had always been a teacher-student relationship. He had never given her any personal advice other than to urge her to get her master's in languages.

As if he sensed her surprise, he added, "Sorry, that was uncalled for. You're perfectly capable of managing your own life. It's just that—well, in some ways you seem naive, even though you have so much determination. I just hope—" His smile was rueful. "I apologize again. My daughter would say that I'm doing my 'mother-hen thing.' In any case, I'd better get along home before Mrs. Montaigne's scallopini is ruined."

He nodded, glanced down at his watch, then hurried off, looking like the White Rabbit in *Alice's Adventures in Wonderland*, Mayi thought absently. She stood there for a moment, staring after him, before she went on. She couldn't help wondering about their strange conversation. Professor Montaigne was noted for being a rather standoffish man who never became personally involved with students. Well, spring did that to people. It made you feel as if you were in tune with the rest of the world, she thought, and suddenly the rootless happiness was back.

Up ahead she saw the Arts and Science Building

and hastened her step. Was she late? No, Pio still wasn't there, and he was always on time. She smiled to herself, thinking about her friend. Although she knew so many people on campus, most of her relationships were casual. Holding down a full-time job in addition to a packed school schedule meant she had little time for a social life. She seldom dated, and then only for a few school affairs that were important to her. But she had made room in her busy life for Pio, because at last she had found someone who could satisfy her hunger to know more about her grandmother's people, the Basques.

She had always been fascinated by the things her grandmother had told her about Navarra, the Spanish province she'd emigrated from when she was a young woman. Those stories about a village set in the high Pyrenees were still vivid in Mayi's mind, even after thirteen years, and during the time when she'd had nothing else to give her a sense of her own identity, she'd found out all she could about Navarra from books. She had clung to the knowledge that she did have a heritage, however tentative, and had considered herself Basque, even though she was only part Basque. She knew nothing at all about her father's family except like her, her father had been an orphan.

Then, six months ago, she had enrolled in a Basque language course taught by Pio Aquirre, a young exchange professor from Navarra, and a whole new world had opened up for her. Although their relationship was purely as friends, she felt a deep affection for him and was sad that he would soon be returning to his homeland.

"Hi, Mayi." It was Peggy Logan, Mayi's former roommate, and Dick Croft, Peggy's live-in boyfriend.

As she returned her friends' greeting, Mayi reflected that soon their paths would part. Both of her friends were going to New York to try their wings—Peggy in media communications and Dick in commercial art. It saddened Mayi, and yet she too would be moving away from Reno if she couldn't find work there as a teacher. She was determined to use her teaching degree. No one in her family had ever gone to college, much less graduated. Her maternal grandfather had been a sheepherder and her father an itinerant truck driver. Her grandmother had been in awe of teachers and had told her so many times that a teacher could always find work—and respect. If working as a teacher meant moving away from a place Mayi was familiar with, so be it. She wasn't going to compromise now that she was finally within reach of her dream.

"Are you waiting for that gorgeous Basque prof?" Peggy asked. At Mayi's nod, she sighed and rolled her eyes. "He's something else. Talk about soulful eyes—sort of a modern-day Byron. Just my weakness."

"Down, girl," Dick said sternly. "He only has eyes for Mayi."

"We're just friends," Mayi said with a tinge of regret. It would be so convenient if she could fall in love with Pio and he with her. But there was no chemistry between them, and she would never settle for less than the real thing.

"Well, you could have fooled me. He looks at you like he wants to put you in his pocket and walk off with you," Peggy said.

Mayi laughed. "And you're a hopeless romantic, Peg."

"You're not? If you ask me, you're the romantic here. What is it you want, Mayi? Some knight on a white horse? You hardly ever date, and yet half the boys in school are drooling over you."

"Including me," Dick said, his eyes laughing.

Peggy slapped him playfully. "Down, boy! Mayi isn't interested in a crazy guy like you. I think she's holding out for Sir Lancelot."

The two left, still bantering, and Mayi looked after them with wistful eyes. They were so obviously in love. She wondered if their love would last outside the cloistered world of the university. And what about herself? Would she ever find someone who really loved her? Maybe she should have settled for less, taken up with one of the boys who tried to date her. It could be dangerous, having so little experience with men.

"Why so pensive?" a familiar voice said behind her. "Are you getting—I think one of my students calls it 'graduation jitters'?"

Mayi turned and smiled at Pio. Although he was

only a few inches taller than her own five-four, he gave the illusion of a greater height, possibly because his body was so well proportioned and he carried himself so proudly. His hair was black, very thick, his features regular, and his brown eyes were fringed with dark lashes.

Mayi smiled to herself, remembering Peggy's description of Pio. He did look like a young Byron, but she was sure his appearance was deceptive. Pio was a pragmatic person, with a reserve that even she hadn't been able to penetrate completely. Sometimes she felt as if there were hidden fires behind that reserve, or was it an innate sadness she sensed sometimes when his guard was down?

"Am I late?" he asked. "One of my students had a question—or more like a dozen questions."

"A female student, right?"

"As it happened, yes." Although his accent was marked, Pio spoke perfect English. Once he had told her that it was his knack for languages that had opened doors for him and allowed him to escape from the prison of his own narrow world. She had started to question him, but it had been so early in their friendship that she hadn't wanted to offend him, especially since she'd been told so often by her grandmother that the Basques dislike personal questions.

But now her curiosity stirred, and before she had time to reconsider she asked, "What did you mean when you told me once that your knack for languages opened the doors of your prison?"

Pio was silent a moment. "I shouldn't have put it that way. What I meant was, without my English, I wouldn't have been chosen as an exchange professor in your university's Basque Studies Program. As for the prison—sometimes the walls seem to close in on you when you have responsibilities not of your own choosing. So this is a respite to my real life. I only wish it could be—" He broke off and smiled at her. "And you don't want to hear about my problems, not on a day like this. Your name is appropriate, Mayi. You remind me of a spring day, of all the good, happy things of life."

"I'm going to be so vain I won't be able to get my head through a door," Mayi said ruefully. "First Professor Montaigne tells me I'm the embodiment of spring, and now you say I remind you of a spring day."

"It's that radiant smile and that hair. I believe a person could read by the light of your hair, Mayi."

"If you had to put up with this mop, you'd understand why I'm tempted so often to have it cut off," Mayi said. "When it's wet, it clings to the brush and drives me out of my mind. I can't wear it any way except plain and hanging loose."

He touched her hair, brushing a loose strand away from her face. There was a strange look in his eyes, as if his thoughts were somewhere else. "It looks like a cloud that has been charged with electricity."

"It's the altitude here in Reno and the lack of moisture in the air. It creates static electricity, you know. If I have to move to California to get a job, maybe living at sea level will have its advantages.''

"Still nothing in the way of a teaching position?''

"Nothing is right. A big fat zero. There just isn't much demand for teachers in this area at any grade level, especially for language teachers. Too few schools and too many recent grads.''

As they walked toward Pio's car, which was parked in the faculty lot, both of them were silent. Pio seemed lost in his own thoughts, and Mayi didn't feel the urge for conversation. As always, when he helped her into his car, she wanted to shake her head in disbelief, not only because of his old-world courtesy, which seemed so out of place in Reno, but because of the car, a small, sleek Porsche.

Even before Pio had asked her out to dinner that first time, so diffidently that she hadn't had the heart to say no, she had suspected from the impeccable tailoring of his suits that he didn't have to depend for a living on his salary as an associate professor. Even so, the Porsche had been a surprise, and so had his apartment, the time she'd been there for a party he'd given for his students.

He lived in one of the most expensive buildings in town, and his own apartment was furnished with a quiet luxury that was totally beyond the range of an associate professor's pay. Her surprise must have been apparent, because he'd said something about the generosity of his brother and then had changed the subject, letting her know that this was one of the private places where she shouldn't intrude. Mayi had her own private areas and had respected his obvious reluctance to talk about himself. Since then she'd never inquired further about his brother, or even whether he had any more family.

"Where are we going this evening?" she asked now. It was one of her nights off at the casino, and they'd made arrangements to go out to dinner.

"The Continental Room. Our reservation is for seven o'clock. I thought we could stay and dance awhile after we've had dinner."

Mayi resisted an impulse to whistle softly. The Continental Room was Reno's finest, and so expensive she'd never eaten there. Usually Pio took her to one of the local Basque restaurants so she could practice her Basque, and both of them favored the plain but excellent Basque food. "Is this a celebration?" she asked.

"It could be," he said, then added quickly before she could ask the obvious question, "What happened when you had your interview with the Topah City school board?"

She told him about that disappointing interview, making it sound like a comical experience, which it hadn't been. She didn't add that after she'd left the conference room where the interview had taken place she'd had a good—and rare—cry in her car.

The questions about her personal life had been so pointed, and it became obvious to her that there was no way in the world these upright public servants would give the job to someone who looked as if she might be a bad influence on the students. For a while, until her sense of humor had asserted itself, she'd found herself wishing that her hair was some drab color, that her lips were thin and her skin muddy. Well, she was what she was, and if people were foolish enough to judge her by such superficial things as her appearance, that was *their* problem, not hers.

"You're looking pensive again, Mayi," Pio said softly, and she realized that he'd been watching her as they drove along the highway, heading toward town. "What really happened at that school-board meeting?"

She gave him a rueful look. "You're a mind reader, aren't you? Well, you're right. It was a disaster from the beginning. The two women members of the board looked at me as if I were some kind of—of call girl, and one of the men followed me outside afterward and tried to get me to have a drink with him at a local bar. What is there about me that makes people misunderstand where I'm coming from?"

"There's nothing wrong with you, Mayi. You're a friendly, warm, uncomplicated person, but those are the things that also make you vulnerable. You must learn to protect yourself, you know."

She gave him a surprised look. "Is that how you see me? As vulnerable? I'm not—not at all. I've been on my own since I was seventeen. I can take care of myself. Anyone who works in a casino, even one as respectable as the Robin Hood, learns how to handle—well, things like men coming on to you. I'm no innocent, you know. But I certainly do nothing to invite the wrong kind of attention. And yet—'' She broke off, suddenly regretting that she'd revealed so much of herself to him.

''And yet you are sometimes bewildered by the reaction you have on men?''

Mayi shrugged, wishing he would change the subject. Ever since she had turned fifteen and had matured, seemingly overnight, she had received unwelcome male attention. As a result she had become wary of men, and she'd learned to play down her exotic appearance. Even at work she used no makeup, and away from work she was conscious of how she dressed and usually wore loose-fitting casual clothes. But it hadn't always helped.

''There is a solution,'' Pio said. ''You could get married. A husband would end that kind of harassment.''

''Uh-huh. Married to whom? Are you proposing?'' she said.

She had been teasing him, and when he didn't answer immediately with his own quip, she turned her head to stare at him. ''Yes, that's just what I am doing, Mayi,'' he said finally.

''Don't joke about it, Pio,'' she said, laughing. ''It isn't safe. Some girl just might take you up on it.''

''But I am serious. When I return home after graduation week is over, I want to take you with me, as my wife. There's a reason why you're so fascinated by my stories about Zubilibia. I believe it's because you belong there, not here. If you marry me and come back with me to Navarra, you'll be with your own kind. We Basques are difficult to know sometimes, but you already speak Eskuara with the Navarra dialect, and the rarity of an American girl who speaks our language would open doors—and hearts—to you. As my wife you would have respect, the kind of respect you so often don't get here.''

He went on talking, listing more reasons why she should marry him and return with him to Navarra, and Mayi listened with a growing discomfort.

Yes, she did speak Pio's language, almost as well as a native. One of the reasons she'd enrolled at the University of Nevada instead of remaining in her native Idaho was their famous Basque Studies Program. She'd majored in French and Spanish but had managed to work into her program several courses on the Basque people and history, as well as a few semesters of Eskuara, the language of the Basque people. She had used the justification that the knowledge of Basque might be useful someday, but she'd known such a possibility was remote.

The Basque language had a reputation for being almost impossible for an outsider to learn, but her determined and systematic assault upon it, aided by a childhood familiarity with the language, had proven effective. Although Eskuara sounded a little like Spanish, it was totally different and had unusual verb and word-order irregularities, and complicated morphology.

It was obvious to her now that Pio believed it was fate that she'd learned his language, but why was he speaking so doggedly, as if he were presenting her with a business proposition? She knew, her heart told her, that Pio didn't love her, so why did he want her to become his wife? Like her he was Catholic and regarded marriage as a sacred and permanent compact between two people. Yet he seemed determined to return to Zubilibia with her as his wife.

"What's this really all about, Pio?" she burst out, interrupting his description of the wild beauty of the mountains that surrounded his village. "You don't love me, and you must know that I don't love you. How could we possibly have a happy marriage?"

"But I do love you, Mayi. I guess I'm not very romantic. Perhaps I should have waited for the right moment and proposed after dinner, while we were dancing. But you do see that marriage to me is the answer to all your problems, don't you? You've told me so often how you long for—how was it you put it?—for roots? And what better place to find them than in the mountains of your ancestors? You could have a home and children, and if you want to use your education, there is always a need for teachers in our valley. We're so isolated that it's almost impossible for us to get outside teachers to live there. My brother hopes to encourage tourism because the village desperately needs additional sources of income. You could teach English to our people so they could better deal with the tourists that do find their way into Zubilibia.''

Mayi relaxed a little. So this was the reason for Pio's proposal—he thought she needed his protection and she could also be useful to his people.

''You're not in love with me, Pio,'' she said gently. ''And I couldn't marry without love. I appreciate your friendship, but it isn't enough to build a marriage on. You deserve more, and so do I.''

''But you're twenty-three and you still haven't formed a permanent relationship with a man. I do love you. I'm just not a—a demonstrative man. The thought of leaving you fills me with great sadness. I know I'm saying this all wrong, but I'm being honest with you.'' For a second there was a bitter edge in his voice. ''I think marriage based on mutual respect would be much safer than the fireworks of a romantic love, the kind that burns out so quickly, leaving heartache behind. I could make you happy. You'd be safe with me. I want you very much.''

''You only want a wife,'' Mayi said. ''I'm flattered and very tempted, but I—I can't take advantage of your loneliness. When you get back among your own people, you'll feel differently. You'll see that this was a mistake.''

''I asked the university to extend my term,'' he said. ''Doesn't that prove to you that I'm not homesick?''

"Are you saying that you asked for an extension and the university refused?"

"Oh, they were very agreeable. But my brother has ordered me to return to Zubilibia, and of course I must obey."

"Why must you obey? You're a free agent."

"He's afraid that I might be contaminated by any more foreign culture. I must have been too enthusiastic about my life here in my letters." Again there was a tinge of bitterness in his voice.

"Do you always do what he says?"

He shrugged. "He is *etcheko jauna* of our house, and I am his *etcheko primu*," he said, as if that explained everything.

Mayi bit her lips. She wanted to blurt out that some of the old customs were unworkable in a modern world where individuality was so important. Pio had explained to her the significance of the relationship of the *etcheko jauna*, who is head and virtual ruler of the family, and the person he has chosen to be *etcheko primu*, his heir. Along with the power, the *etcheko jauna* had the responsibility for seeing to the welfare of the family, and individual happiness ran a poor second.

"But I don't want to leave without you," Pio said. "I need you, Mayi, and I think you need me."

Mayi fought against sudden temptation. She had been fascinated by Pio's stories of his childhood in a remote Pyrenees village. What would it be like to be part of a culture so ancient that its beginnings were buried in time? To put down her roots in a foreign land that didn't really seem foreign to her at all? What would it be like to raise her children in a place where they would never know the agony of belonging to no one, no place, of being totally alone in the world?

And what would it be like to be married to Pio, to share his bed, his life, to bear his children? She looked at Pio, who had fallen silent. His wedge-shaped face, his dark hair and eyes and his sensitive mouth were so familiar to her now, and she knew in her heart that no amount of time could change the friendship she felt for him to love, not the kind she'd longed for all her adult life. The love she felt for Pio was the kind that one human being feels for another, but he didn't stir her senses when he kissed her good-night after they'd been out for the evening. She felt no thrill when he put his arm around her on the dance floor, and she knew she couldn't settle for less. She couldn't spend her life with a man who didn't set her on fire with his kiss.

"I'm sorry, Pio," she said. Tears filled her eyes and her voice was uneven. "I want to love you, but I don't, and I'm sure you don't really love me, either."

"I'll change your mind," he said fiercely. He brought the car to a stop on the shoulder of the road and turned to her suddenly, pulling her into his arms. His kiss was gentle at first, then hard and rough, as if he meant to impose his will upon her, but when she didn't struggle, when she didn't respond at all, his arms slipped away. They sat in silence for a while, and then he started up the car again.

"I'm very tired, and I'm not really hungry," Mayi said softly. "Why don't you take me home?"

Pio didn't answer, but he turned the car around and drove back toward the university. She had noted that speed was one of Pio's few weaknesses, though when she was in the car he usually restrained himself. Tonight a devil seemed to be riding him. The speedometer reached eighty and then climbed even higher. Mayi bit her lip but she didn't say anything. The road was clear, the car was in perfect running condition and Pio was a superb driver.

But she was glad, fifteen minutes later, when they pulled up in front of the shabby apartment building where she lived. Pio turned off the engine, then looked at her. "You sure you won't change your mind?"

"I can't. I'm very tempted—you know that I care for you a lot, Pio. But it would be wrong, and dangerous. What if you fell in love with someone else after we were married? You're a devout Catholic. You would be trapped with a wife you don't love. And when I marry, I want it to be for life."

"It would be for life. I promise you that. If you marry me, you'll have 'a husband, a home, and, God willing, children. Even if something should happen to me, my brother would be your protector. That's the Basque way."

Again, some strong emotion seemed to color his voice. Mayi fought off the desire to get out of the

car and run into her apartment. Was it possible that
Pio did love her? Perhaps it was his reserve that
kept him from showing it—no, she *couldn't* be mistaken. When he'd kissed her a few minutes ago, she
was sure that it meant as little to him as it had to
her. He must understand that this idea of his was
all wrong. To be married to someone you didn't
love would be hell, a living hell.

"I'm sorry," she said. "I don't want to lose your
friendship. Can't we go on being friends?"

After a long pause Pio nodded, but his face was
in shadow and she couldn't see his expression. He
made no move to kiss her good-night, but she
leaned toward him and brushed his cheek with her
lips. "I'll see you tomorrow in class," she said.

"Tomorrow?" he repeated, as if it was a strange
word to him.

"The day after today," she said lightly.

"Yes, of course. And get some sleep. Don't
study too late," he said, and Mayi had to be satisfied with the normalcy of his words, the casualness
of his tone, as she got out of the car and ran lightly
up the front steps of her apartment building.

CHAPTER TWO

THE WARM SPRINGLIKE WEATHER had been premature, and a cold wind was blowing as Mayi parked her twelve-year-old Volkswagen in the employees' parking lot of the Robin Hood Club. After she got out of the car she stood for a moment staring at the Sierra Nevada, which loomed above the western side of the city. Leaden clouds lay low over the mountain range, hiding its peaks, and a flat, dank odor in the wind promised an unseasonably late snowfall before morning.

Mayi shivered and pulled the hood of her parka lower on her forehead against the bite of the wind before hurrying across the parking lot toward the three-story building that housed the Robin Hood Club. Business would be slow tonight, which meant tips would be few and far between. Mayi was a "tour skipper" and filled in for the other women on their nights off. She worked four nights a week, just enough to keep her afloat financially and still leave her time for a full load of classes and the homework it engendered.

She considered herself lucky to have found work hours that were so compatible with the rest of her busy schedule. Her job as a keno runner entailed placing bets for those gamblers who wanted to continue playing keno while they patronized the club's restaurants or bars. There were occupational hazards: aching feet from the hours of walking; an occasional sore loser who gave her a bad time; unwanted attention from men on the make. But the job paid more than similar work as a waitress or sales clerk, and Mayi got along well with her boss and co-workers and was popular with the keno players.

The time clock showed 5:00 when she punched in. Since she was running a little early, there was time to eat something before she changed for work. In the huge stainless-steel kitchen that serviced both the casino's posh dinner club and its equally popular coffee shop, she wheedled a cheese-and-sprouts sandwich from one of the cooks and carried it into the female employees' lounge.

She had the lounge to herself as she ate her sandwich, an English textbook propped up in front of her. Later, in the women's locker room, she changed into her costume—brief, hip-hugging suede shorts; a suede jerkin that laced tightly over her full breasts; calf-high, cuffed boots; and a green peaked hat that was some costume designer's idea of what Robin Hood's merry men might have worn. The hat was too large and had a way of slipping down her forehead when she tilted her head forward, but the boots fit well and were comfortably low heeled.

She was putting on pink lip gloss in front of the lounge mirror when the door swung open and one of the club's female blackjack dealers came in. She was a long-legged blond woman who had been a Las Vegas dancer until an automobile accident left her with a limp and ended her dancing career. Now she dealt blackjack to cowboys and tourists at the Robin Hood and supported herself and three children on her earnings.

"How's it going, Carol?" Mayi asked.

"Terrible. The tokes I've pulled in tonight wouldn't pay for that lipstick in your hand. The rent's gonna have to wait this month if things don't pick up soon."

"It's the weather. Things will get better as soon as it warms up again."

"Uh-huh. Always the optimist, aren't you? Well, you're doing the right thing, getting an education. This is no life for a reasonably sane person."

Most of the night-shift women—cashiers, blackjack dealers, change girls, cocktail waitresses, bookkeepers, the women who manned the casino's counting room—had straggled in by the time Mayi left the lounge and went into the main casino. For all its thick carpets and the acoustical tile on its high ceilings, the casino was very noisy. Slot machines buzzed; baccarat cages clattered; cards and dice slapped against felt; coins clanked into metal trays; and spinning roulette wheels added their own peculiar whirring sound to the general uproar.

Somewhere in the cluster of dollar slots a bell buzzed, sounding like an manic mosquito, and the carousel cashier announced over the loudspeaker that another lucky winner had just hit a hundred-dollar jackpot. Mayi jumped nervously as a woman gave a high-pitched scream. It was impossible to tell from the woman's glazed eyes if she had just lined up four 7's for the superjackpot or had lost the last of her "going-home money" to the slots.

At one time Mayi had been intimidated by the crowds, the gaudy neon lights, the constant clatter. Now the casino was so familiar that the continuous hubbub no longer registered. After all, this was just a stopping-over place. As soon as she found a teaching job she would quit—without regret. Her job as a keno runner was no worse, and certainly better paying, than the jobs she'd had as a waitress and clerk before she'd turned twenty-one and could work where there was gambling. Since she never gambled herself, she couldn't understand the lure of the tables or the slots, but if she'd learned one thing in her life, it was not to judge other people. But she would be glad when she could quit. In fact, it couldn't be soon enough to suit her.

The keno game was located in a quiet corner of the main floor, next to one of the casino's three bars. Like the rest of the club, the keno section affected an Old English motif, and murals of Sherwood Forest lined the wall. Players sat on green plastic chairs, and a glittering gold ball selector reflected tiny points of lights as it spun.

At the counter Mayi bantered with the keno writers while she waited for the runner on the day shift, a tall slender girl named Rita, to finish her rounds and report back for the next draw. When Rita came hurrying up, her tray loaded with tickets and money, Mayi helped her mark the official draw cards. After the draw, they walked back to the coffee shop together.

While Rita paid off a winner, Mayi ran a practiced eye over the booths and tables, noting that several of her regulars were there eating dinner: the retired navy captain from San Francisco, a talkative man who tipped generously whether or not he won; the sour-faced woman from Fresno who won often—and tipped very little; the middle-aged couple who played a single card between them and wrangled endlessly over the choice of numbers.

Mayi knew that most of the casino employees looked down on keno players, many of whom were elderly pensioners and tight with their tips, but she enjoyed talking to them. Most of them were lonely people, trying to substitute the excitement of gambling for the jobs or children or spouses that had gone out of their lives. Mayi understood loneliness, having lived with it so often in her twenty-three years, and didn't begrudge the time she spent exchanging a few words with the players, although the keno pit boss frowned on such fraternizing, because it delayed the frequency of the draws.

So what did it cost her to smile, laugh at her customers' jokes, show pleasure when they won or commiserate with them when they lost? It satisfied some need of her own for contact with older people, made the time go faster—and the amount of her tips would have surprised the other keno runners if she'd been foolish enough to brag about them.

Rita finished paying off her lucky customer and Mayi made the rest of the round with her, the shift transition going smoothly.

She was on her first break and was browsing through a women's magazine someone had left in the lounge when the door opened and Earl Jenkins, the keno pit boss, stuck his head in. "Someone here wants to talk to you," he said briskly. "You can use my office. I'll ask Christy to make the rounds for you until you're back on the floor."

Her boss was usually acerbic, and his mild tone alarmed Mayi. She was already braced for bad news even before she realized that the man waiting for her in Earl's office wore the uniform of a Nevada highway patrolman. Her heart thumped painfully as she acknowledged that yes, she was Mayi Jenners.

"Do you know a man named—" He consulted a piece of paper. "Pio Aquirre?"

Mayi swallowed hard before she managed a weak "Yes."

"Are you related to Mr. Aquirre?"

"I'm one of his students. Is something wrong?"

"I'm afraid I have some bad news, Miss Jenners. Mr. Aquirre had an accident. His car went off the road early this morning on Highway 80."

"An accident . . . how bad was it?"

"He was a DOA."

"What—what does that mean?"

"Dead on arrival. By the time the ambulance got there he was gone. But he was conscious long enough to ask the man who found him to notify you. He didn't give an address, but we got that off university records when we found out where he worked."

Mayi slumped down on a chair as her legs gave out on her. Pio . . . dead. It wasn't possible. It *couldn't* be true. Why, she'd just seen him two days ago.

"Was he speeding? He—he always went so fast when he was driving alone."

"The man who witnessed the accident reported it to the highway police by phone. He gave the location and said he stopped to see if he could help, that Mr. Aquirre had asked that you be notified before he passed out. Unfortunately the witness hung up before he gave us his own name, so we don't know any more details about the accident. That's a straight stretch of highway right along there, but— well, it's one of those freak things that happen, I suppose."

There was an evasiveness in his voice, in the way his eyes wouldn't meet hers. Mayi felt a stab of pure horror. Was it possible the officer was hinting at suicide? But Pio would never, never do that. He was a Catholic, and besides, he had no reason to commit suicide.

She took a deep breath to steady herself. "Have you notified his family yet? They live in Zubilibia, Spain—in Navarra Province."

"We're taking care of that. However, since Mr. Aquirre gave your name, we thought you should be notified in person. Not the sort of thing you'd want to hear over the radio or read in the papers."

"Thank you," Mayi said dully. "I appreciate that."

After he was gone she sat for a long while, staring down at her hands. How was it possible that Pio, so full of life, was dead? It must have been a freak accident, the way the officer had said. But the man had been so—so uncomfortable. Did he know more than he was telling? Maybe he had simply felt awkward at having to be the one to tell a stranger such bad news.

And even if he did suspect suicide, he was wrong. Pio had had his whole life before him. There was no reason for him to commit suicide— no reason at all. And the sadness she thought she'd seen in his eyes two nights ago—surely that had been her overactive imagination playing tricks on her.

Despite herself, the last conversation she'd had with Pio came back to her now, unreeling through her mind. She had rejected Pio's proposal, aware that it had been prompted by his desire to help out a friend. But he hadn't loved her. She was sure of that. Except for that one time in the car, they'd only exchanged a few good-night kisses. Her rejection couldn't possibly have meant so much to him that he would—no, she wouldn't even think such things. His death had been an accident, a tragic accident.

Pio's letter came the next day. Mayi had cut her classes, unable to face the inevitable gossip and speculation that must be running riot around campus, so she was home when the mail came. The first thing she saw was the envelope, addressed to her in Pio's angular handwriting. When she realized that he must have mailed it the afternoon before his death, a stab of pain went through her, so sharp that she gasped and stopped breathing for a moment. It was a while before she could bring herself to open the envelope. Even when she did, she sat turning it over and over in her hands before she finally unfolded the sheet of stationery inside.

Despite her fears the brief letter was cheerful, as casual as a couple of other notes he'd written her in the past few months. He thanked her for her friendship, told her that knowing her had brought him only pleasure, that he wished her great happiness and hoped that she reached all her goals—including the one of going to the Basque country for a year of study. At the end he told her that he'd see her in a couple of days. He was going into San Francisco to do some sightseeing, and he would call her when he got back so they could have dinner together again before he left for Spain. He ended the letter with the hope that someday she would get to visit Zubilibia.

She read the note again, trying to find answers to the questions haunting her. Was there a hidden message, something to explain what had happened? Despite its casual tone, was it a suicide note? And had it been her lack of perception, her insensitivity to Pio's agony of spirit, that had contributed to his death?

There were no answers. She put the letter away, and during the next few days she went through the motions of normalcy. She studied for an important French exam, attended classes, went to work, talked to people. No one she met would have suspected the sense of loss that made conversation, even the simple act of saying hello, a torment to her.

Somewhere along the way she came to terms with her fears that she'd failed a friend, but only after many restless nights of tossing in her narrow bed. During years of living in other people's homes, of being an outsider on the fringes of other people's lives, she had learned to hide her emotions and present a cheerful face to the world. But she found it almost impossible to smile during these gray days, and she lost so much weight that her clothes hung loosely on her already slender body.

A few days before graduation another letter came, this one on University of Nevada stationery, and Mayi was directed to drop by the business offices at her convenience.

She was already acquainted with Mrs. Gobel,

who had signed the letter, because she was the person who took care of students' fees. But when Mayi came into the office, she was sure she caught a question in the older woman's eyes.

"Did you want to see me, Mrs. Gobel?" she asked politely.

Mrs. Gobel shuffled a few papers on her desk. "As you may or may not know, the university carries life insurance on its faculty members," she said finally. "Professor Aquirre—well, he named you as beneficiary of his insurance, Miss Jenners."

"But—but why would he do that? We were only good friends. He has a family back in Navarra— or at least he has a brother. There must be some kind of mistake."

"No, there's no mistake. I filled out the change of beneficiary myself about—oh, a month ago, I think it was. I remember that I was rather curious and did—well, comment on it. He said something about—I believe his exact words were that his family was more than prosperous, and if anything happened to him, he would like to see the money go to someone who would put it to good use."

Numbly Mayi stared at the older woman, trying to assimilate this surprising information. Later, after she'd signed the papers that were laid in front of her, she listened as Mrs. Gobel told her that a check for ten thousand dollars would be coming to her from the insurance company after due process. She left the office and went to her next class, but when she got home she put away the copy of the paper she'd signed. She didn't want to be reminded of the insurance; it seemed wrong to benefit from a friend's death.

Later, when she was reading Pio's letter yet another time, still looking for answers that weren't there, her eyes fell on the final words. "And I hope that someday you will find a way to visit Zubilibia."

An idea came to her then, an idea that gave her the first comfort since Pio's tragic death. Was this—Pio's idle remark and the insurance he'd left her—some kind of mandate that she should go to Zubilibia to see his people and tell them what she knew about his last months of life? If they had any suspicions that his death hadn't been an accident, she could reassure them, and if she found that they were in need, despite what Pio had told Mrs. Gobel, then she would turn the insurance money over to them. Maybe then her conscience, her suspicion that somehow she had failed Pio, would be appeased.

CHAPTER THREE

THE INSURANCE PIO HAD LEFT MAYI was more than enough to finance a long stay in Spain, but as it turned out, it was fall before she finally made her pilgrimage to Zubilibia.

The week preceding graduation, she had been offered a job by the Reno school system to teach remedial reading throughout the summer. Professor Montaigne had recommended her for the position. Since she knew it would give her valuable experience to list on future résumés, the opportunity was too good to pass up. She had hoped it might lead to a full-time teaching job in the fall, especially since her efficiency evaluation at the end of the term was high, but the hoped-for position didn't materialize. In fact, two more Reno schools were closing because of a lack of students, and Mayi had been lucky to get even a summer job.

There was nothing to prevent her from taking the trip to Spain, and under any other circumstances she would have been delighted. For years she had dreamed of seeing the Basque provinces for herself. She had even hoped that somehow she might find the money to enroll in one of the University of

Nevada's Basque Country Study Programs and spend nine months in Spain. Now that one of her dreams was a reality and she was going to Navarra, she felt more apprehensive than happy about her plan to contact Pio's family.

To begin with, it had been surprisingly difficult to find Zubilibia on the maps of Navarra in the Basque Studies Program library. Only one map had shown the town at all. It was listed as having a population of 1030, which should have rated it an appearance on any map of the isolated region, where all the villages were so small. From its position on the map, above the upper tip of the Valle de Salazar, Zubilibia seemed to be located in the high Pyrenees. Mayi wondered if that meant transportation would be difficult to arrange.

It was with more than a few qualms that Mayi flew to Madrid in mid-September. Although she wanted to linger in the legendary city, to savor its baroque buildings, historical monuments and stylish shops, to wander among the Goya and El Greco masterpieces of the Prado and to explore the cathedrals and the Alcazar, she knew that she would enjoy it more on her return trip, when she would have less on her mind. The following morning, she flew on to Pamplona, where a friendly hotel clerk, intrigued by her perfect Spanish, convinced her that the best way to see Navarra province was to travel on one of the local buses. Since Mayi wasn't particularly eager to reach the end of her journey, she was happy to take his advice.

Although wheezing and obviously without shocks, the ancient bus took the Navarra foothills and the first range of mountains with surprising aplomb. From her first hour on the bus, Mayi was enchanted by the orderly beauty of the passing countryside—the graceful contours of the mountains and valleys, the incredibly blue sky and the deep valleys, now maize gold with autumn. The tiny villages delighted her. Each had its own handsome church, pelota court and clusters of whitewashed stone-and-timber houses decorated with chocolate-brown shutters. Mayi wished she could get off the bus and stay awhile in each of the villages they passed through.

At first, surrounded totally by local people, she felt uncomfortable, and as always her red hair was attracting too many speculative glances. Then her seatmate, an elderly woman dressed in rusty black, discovered Mayi could speak Spanish, which entitled her to a rather wary friendliness. In fact, Mayi was soon deluged with so many questions from other passengers, all of whom seemed to have relatives who had immigrated to the States, that she found it hard to watch the scenery outside her window.

When she reached Adiz, a tiny fairyland town that reminded her of the toy villages in a child's train set, she stayed in a small hotel for the night. The next evening, after another bumpy bus ride, she reached Ochagavia, a lovely town within sight of the high Pyrenees, and was lucky enough to find a room in a pension that catered to tourists.

Again she was tempted to stay there an extra day to explore the town and its ancient temple, the Basilica de Nuesta Señora de Musquilda, a thirteenth-century Romanesque building that perched on the summit of a mountain overlooking the city. But she knew it would be a mistake to delay her arrival in Zubilibia. Although talking to Pio's family and answering their questions would be painful, she had to do it. She owed it to Pio. What if his family had doubts about the accident? At least she could allay their fears, tell them in all truthfulness that Pio had shown no signs of mental disturbance during his final days.

Mayi winced, remembering their last visit together. Had it been desperation she'd seen in his dark eyes that evening? Well, she would keep her doubts to herself when she talked to—to whom? It seemed strange that she had no idea whether or not Pio had a family, other than a brother. During the six months she had known him, only once had he mentioned a relative—his older brother, who was *etcheko jauna* of the Aquirre family. She assumed that meant Pio's father was dead, but she had no idea if his mother was still living, or if he had any other brothers or sisters.

The truth was, during the months they had been friends, Pio had seldom talked about himself. He'd described excursions he'd taken as a boy into the mountains surrounding Zubilibia, talked about the shepherds he'd met there and the local legends that had been passed down for hundreds of years. Without self-consciousness, as if singing was as natural to him as talking, he'd sung the old songs of his region to her in his fine baritone voice. He had also tried to explain his people's character to her. This alone, he'd told her ruefully, set him apart from his countrymen, who seldom worried about such intangible things as their national character.

But he'd said nothing about his own life as an adult, though once he'd mentioned that his ambition was to be a writer, and only now did she realize how unusual that had been. Well, the Basques were a reticent people; she'd heard that a dozen times during her studies. Still, it was strange how little she really knew about Pio.

That evening after an excellent meal of lamb cutlets cooked over coals, which her landlady called *costillas a la brasa*, Mayi asked about transportation to Zubilibia. On the map it seemed only a few miles to the north of Ochagavia, but to her dismay her landlady, a middle-aged woman with snapping black eyes, shrugged her shoulders and informed her that there was no public transportation into the Valle de la Añara, where Zubilibia was located.

"Not enough people go there to make such a line profitable." She eyed Mayi with thinly veiled curiosity. "It is a very isolated place. Perhaps you have relatives there who might come and get you."

"I'm afraid I don't know anyone there. But I've heard such good reports about the beauty of the region that I wanted to do some sketching," Mayi told her, thankful that she had brought along her sketch pad in hopes that she would have the opportunity to do some preliminary work for future paintings.

"Well, I've heard that it's beautiful, though I have never been there, but I'm sure it can't compare with our own Ochagavia. And the people of Zubilibia are—I believe the English word is insular. They will not make you welcome, Señorita Jenners."

Since there was more than a hint of acerbity in her voice, Mayi thought it prudent to soothe the woman's partisan feathers. "I have a special reason for wanting to sketch Zubilibia. A friend of mine who can no longer travel has a deep, personal attachment to the town."

"Ah, one of the American Basques. Always they come back to the old country, looking for relatives, searching out their past. It is very touching. But seldom does anyone from Zubilibia migrate elsewhere. Yes, that is very rare indeed. It may make a difference in the way you are received, especially since you speak Spanish so fluently. Of course, the people of Zubilibia mainly speak Basque, but most of them also speak some Spanish, too. True, your accent is Castilian, but that will not be held against you when they realize you are an American."

Mayi hid her amusement at this latest bit of partisanship and said, "I speak Basque with the Navarrese dialect, as well as two of the French dialects."

The woman's eyes widened and her mouth rounded in surprise. She called to her husband to come quickly and witness this wonder—a foreigner, an American at that, who spoke Eskuara, the language of the Basques. Mayi felt like a butterfly pinned to a specimen board as she found herself with a mug of tea at her elbow and the rapt attention of both her hosts focused on her. In the next few minutes, their not-so-oblique questions forced her to tell them about her Basque grandmother, who spoke only the Basque language, and about her language studies at the University of Nevada. By the time the tea was gone, she found that she had gained respectability—as much, she suspected, as any foreigner who didn't have local family connections could. It was a long time before she got a chance to return to the subject of transportation to Zubilibia.

"Do you think I could rent a car?" she asked.

"It would be very expensive, and there are complications about special licenses and insurance and such," her landlady said. "But I do have a possible solution. Perhaps you could make arrangements with the Spaniard, Señor Roche, who sometimes delivers supplies to Zubilibia in his pickup truck. It is possible that he would drive you there—for a fee, of course."

Her husband nodded agreement. "The tourists,

they are a strange lot, with their foreign ways and their foreign speech, but what can we do? We need the tourist money. And of course we welcome the American Basques when they return to visit the land of their ancestors. The people of Zubilibia have no such tolerance—or so I have heard. They are a private people, as you will discover. But perhaps, since you are a very lovely young woman, you will not find it so difficult, eh, wife?'' He winked at his wife, who gave him a sour smile.

Prudently Mayi changed the subject, and an hour later she was making arrangements to leave the following morning with Señor Roche, a tall bony man, whose hair seemed to have slipped off his head and settled in a thick fringe around his chin. Although he warned her that his vehicle was not intended for passengers, she assured him that it didn't matter, she was grateful to have any transportation.

Early the next morning, after breakfast of coffee, croissants and cherry jam that her now-friendly landlady provided, they were on their way. As Señor Roche had warned, his truck was even more ancient than the bus that had brought her from Adiz, but soon the red roofs of Ochagavia were behind them and they were passing through the narrow upper tip of the Valle de Salazar, which was almost totally surrounded by a low range of mountains.

Señor Roche, she soon discovered, liked to talk. He told her he was from Madrid and he had married a woman from Ochagavia. He obviously took a gloomy pride in relating tales about the difficulties of being an outsider in a Basque world.

A few minutes later, as they traveled through a gorge where the mountains rose around them like the walls of some ancient fortress, Mayi felt a deep chill, as if those cold walls of granite were falling toward her. On the floor of the gorge a mist still lingered, though it was almost noon, but when the road rounded a promontory of rock, they came out into full sunlight. It flooded the valley around them with gold, and Mayi's breath caught sharply at the wild beauty spread before her eyes.

"You are impressed by what you see, *señorita*?" Señor Roche asked. "The Valle de la Añara is really two valleys, one higher than the other. It is a wonderland for artists or photographers, and yet so few of them come here. They go to see the Casas del Rey, where the kings of Navarra once reigned, or to the woods that surround Irabia Dam with its hanging ivy and its close-packed trees, or they photograph the Artola and Anzola gorges, but they ignore the wonders of the Valle de la Añara because the people are so inhospitable. Once I approached the municipal council of Zubilibia and offered to provide bus service into the area during tourist season and solicited a small sum to help me purchase a bus. But no, they were not interested. They are such provincials. They seem unaware that there is such a thing as progress."

He shook his head at this sad state of affairs, then asked, "You are an artist, *señorita*?"

"It's only a hobby," Mayi said truthfully. Although she'd always been interested in art, her practical nature told her there was little chance of earning a living at it. She'd sandwiched in a few art classes when she could, chalking them up to recreation, even though she'd been encouraged by a few of her teachers to continue with her studies.

"Well, you will find many things to sketch in Valle de la Añara. You must try to see the famous grotto that is the source of the Rio de la Añara, which flows into the Rio Uberuaga. It is said that the water of the falls is warm, not cold, though it is the runoff from the snows that lie thick on the high Pyrenees until well into the summer. The water is heated by internal hot springs and the grotto is noted for its beauty—and, unfortunately, its inaccessibility. Since it is located on private land, you would need permission from the owners to view it, of course."

"I'm surprised it hasn't been turned into a tourist attraction," Mayi said.

He shrugged. "The people of the Valley don't encourage outsiders, which is probably why there are no public inns in Zubilibia."

"Not even a pension?" she said with dismay, wondering if she had misunderstood the concierge in Ochagavia.

"One—but the proprietors are very particular. I

shall wait to make sure you have a place to stay. You may be returning to Ochagavia with me.''

He paused to give her a sly smile, but she didn't find his words amusing. ''If you pass the sharp inspection of Señora Bilbao, you are in luck, because she is a very fine cook. Well, I will introduce you and tell her of your need. She will make up her mind quickly. Who understands the Basques? Not I—and I have dealt with them for thirty years now.''

He went on to regale her with examples of the perversities of Basque character, and though she had heard most of it before, this time she listened with growing disquiet. It was one thing to be told by an American college professor that the Basques had maintained their racial purity for thousands of years because they were so adept at closing ranks against foreigners. It was quite another thing to hear it from a man who, after thirty years of marriage to a Basque, was still an outsider.

At length she said, ''I do speak Eskuara. Surely that will be an advantage.''

Señor Roche took his eyes off the road long enough to give her an astonished look, as if, she thought with amusement, she'd said she had wings and could fly. ''You understand that miserable language? How is that possible? Only a Basque who has heard it from the cradle can speak it.''

''My grandmother was Basque. I learned it from her.''

''So that explains it. Of course, it is true that my

friend, Jose Martinez, who married an inn-keeper's widow in Artajona and who now runs the inn, did learn the language in a matter of some ten years. But you do not look Basque, *señorita*! You look very American. Of course I have heard that there are fair-skinned people in the mountainous regions of Pays Basque. Perhaps your grand-parents came from there?"

"My grandmother was from Navarra. And some Americans are now studying Eskuara. There are many Basque in Idaho, where I was born, and in—"

"Ah, Idaho! I have heard of this place. It is in the province of Boise, no? So you are from the American West! Do you know any cowboys?"

"I do," she said, and saw that she had just scored a hit. For the next few minutes Señor Roche plied her with questions about cowboys and then about Indians, who, he was convinced, still roamed the west attacking settlers.

The grinding of gears sounded as the truck started up a long, slow grade. The road was very narrow, filled with potholes and deep ruts, and conversation ceased as Señor Roche focused all his attention on driving. The battered truck, which she was sure must be of World War II vintage, wheezed and rattled, sometimes giving out an alarming bang. Mayi clutched the handle on the door, and her teeth chattered from the vibrations that shook the front seat as they climbed higher, leaving the lower valley behind them.

Below, on her side of the truck, a deep gorge cut into the sides of the mountains. Only a few inches separated the truck from the awesome drop, and she wasn't at all surprised that few people came there. Who in his right mind would risk his life on such a road unless it were absolutely necessary? Was the condition of the road deliberate, she wondered, to keep strangers out?

They reached the second valley, dotted with farmhouses, and she stared around eagerly, wishing she hadn't left her sketchbook in her suitcase. There were so many things she wanted to get down on paper, such as the fawn-colored oxen browsing in a field across the valley. The air was so sparkling and clear she was sure that if she reached out her hand she could touch them. Then there was the farmer, his shoulders as straight and proud as the black beret that rested squarely across his broad forehead. He stopped the swing of his scythe to wipe the sweat from his brow and stare at them as they passed. Her fingers itched to capture on paper the rough-hewn man jogging along in the middle of the road on his tiny donkey, his stocky legs stretched straight out in front of him, and the blue-smocked boy who strode by swinging a book on a belt.

Everything she had ever imagined about her grandmother's native land was before her. The farmhouses were scattered throughout the valley, white against the browning fields, each crouched under the weight of its broad, sloping roofs, one end open for the housing of cattle during the winter months. She felt as if she had come home after a long absence, and yet she had never seen this place before, not even in photographs.

A few lines from one of her grandmother's songs slipped into her mind.

> *Ikusten duzuk goizean*
> *Argia basten denean—*

"Do you see, in the morning, at the first light of dawn, on a small hill, a small house, white fronted? It is there that I dwell in peace...."

Unexpectedly Mayi was swept by a deep longing. She found herself wondering what it would be like to have been born in one of those stone-and-timber farm houses, to know exactly who she was, her place in life, what was expected of her. Would she have been happy, or were there other stresses, other problems, as difficult as her own had been?

The valley narrowed, and terraces of vineyards filled the slopes that faced the afternoon sun. At the far end, a gap in the hills showed another narrow valley, set higher than the other two, and she caught a glimpse of a great stone house, surrounded by trees and what looked to be formal gardens.

Then they were passing between two long rows of tall poplars, whose leaves were yellow with fall color, and when they reached the end of the lane, a village burst into view. It was nestled into the slow, lovely curves of a narrow stream, and she didn't need Señor Roche to tell her that the town was Zubilibia, the river, the Rio de la Añara.

The houses were clustered in groups of ten or twelve and spread out in all directions from a large grassy square, at one end of which a massive stone church rose to an impressive height. The square was bordered on three sides by narrow shops and other buildings, including a small sidewalk café, the inevitable pelota court and a large, ivy-covered stone building, which she guessed to be the local seat of government. As they drove past the café, she saw that most of the customers seated at the small round tables were men, though she did see one couple and two elderly women sitting together.

Señor Roche waved a greeting, and though it was returned by a couple of the men, the delay and lackluster of their response confirmed what he had told her. The people of the village would be polite but not friendly to a Spaniard. And what would they think of an American, especially a woman traveling alone?

Soon after they left the square they passed a cluster of handsome houses, all surrounded by neat lawns, each large enough to be called villas. Mayi studied them with interest, noting the swastikalike decorations that had been carved into the brown shutters and the strings of red peppers hung out to dry on the wood balconies that surrounded the upper floors. A few of the shutters and corner support beams were blue, but most were a rich reddish brown called *granat*, and Mayi wondered if they had been painted, in the old way, with ox blood.

As they drove along a winding, twisting road, which had obviously started out as a cattle path, she had the eerie feeling of being watched, even though there were no people in sight. A few minutes later the truck came to a shuddering halt in front of a large three-story house. Like the others they'd passed, it was built of timber and stone, and its wide wooden balconies were painted the deep blue she'd been told the Basques favor. The engine died with one final wheeze, and she breathed a sigh of relief that this part of the journey was over. Her body seemed to have developed a multitude of aches and pains, and she was eager to get out and stretch her muscles.

"Well, this is the pension. I'll tell Señora Bilbao that you'd like a room. Perhaps you'd better wait here while I prepare the way for you."

Mayi felt deserted as the Spaniard disappeared around the corner of the house. At the house across the street, the starched blue curtains of an upstairs window twitched, and she knew she was being watched. Would Señora Bilbao permit her to stay, or would she be forced to leave before she got the chance to talk to Pio's family?

If that happened, she didn't intend to give up. Next time she'd rent a car, even if she had to post a bond and get a special license. That way, if it became necessary, she would have a place to sleep overnight. But maybe such measures wouldn't be necessary. After all, the Basques were a practical people, and she was willing to pay extra for a room.

"Señora Bilbao will talk to you," Señor Roche said at her elbow. At her involuntary sigh of relief he smiled, showing a mouthful of too-perfect teeth. "She claims they have no room at present, but she also wonders why a young woman from America would come to Zubilibia so late in the season. Since I had no answer to that, she must speak to you in order to satisfy her curiosity." He gave her a roguish wink, and she realized he was enjoying himself. "It is up to you now, *señorita*."

Hiding her misgivings, Mayi preceded him through a wide doorway, which opened into a dark entrance hall that smelled of wax. She looked around with interest, taking in the polished wood floors, the white walls hung with religious pictures, a staircase that climbed upward at square angles to the upper floors of the house.

There was a sound behind her, and she turned to see a woman who could only be described as elderly standing there. She wore the sober black that Mayi had come to expect for elderly women in Spain, who seemed to be in perpetual mourning, and her face, inlaid with hairline wrinkles, was wary. But her lively eyes took in every detail of Mayi's appearance, and Mayi was glad she'd worn a simple cotton suit and sensible walking shoes.

"Yes, *señorita*? You have business with me?" was the woman's discouraging greeting.

Mayi summoned her friendliest smile. "I would like very much to rent a room for a few days," she said in Basque.

For a long moment the woman stared at her, and then she disappeared so quickly from the doorway that Mayi gave a startled gasp. Señor Roche smiled, obviously unconcerned, and she tried to contain her own impatience. A few minutes later Señora Bilbao reappeared, this time with an elderly man in tow. It seemed that history was repeating itself. Like the concierge of the pension in Ochagavia, Señora Bilbao wanted her husband to see this phenomenon, an American who spoke their language. Not for the first time Mayi was glad that her grandmother's dialect had been the same as Pio's.

Ten minutes later she was sitting on a stiff, springless sofa in a room she knew must be the parlor reserved for company. She had been provided with tea, served in a fragile cup, which could only be an heirloom, and from the expectancy on the Bilbao couple's faces, she knew they were hopeful she'd have an interesting story for them. Deciding to temper the truth a little, she told them that she'd heard about Zubilibia from a friend. He had spoken of it so highly that she had decided to make some sketches of the village and the valley to present to him as a gift.

"He has spoken of this area's beauty many

times," she concluded. "Unfortunately he can no longer travel, and I have come in his place."

"So your friend is elderly—and an artist, too?" Señora Bilbao said. "Well, artists sometimes come here to paint the gorge and the mountains and, if they can get permission, the Grotto de la Añara."

"And how is it you speak our language? Surely you are not Basque," her husband said. He was a spry-looking man with a long lean face and a large wedge-shaped nose. Although he must have been in his seventies, he carried himself like a much younger man, and his eyes were bright with curiosity beneath heavy brows and a shock of salt-and-pepper hair.

"But I *am* Basque—at least I'm half-Basque."

"And you learned to speak the language from your grandparents? This is very unusual. Even in our own Navarra there are many who only know a few words of Eskuara."

"My grandmother spoke only Basque and a little Spanish. She died when I was nine, but later, in college, I took language courses—" As she went on to explain that there had been a revival of interest in ethnic roots in her country, she knew she would be making these same explanations many times in the future—if she stayed in Zubilibia.

"This is all very interesting." Her landlady got to her feet. "Well, you will find few frills here, Señorita Jenners, but we eat well. And there are many places of interest that you will want to sketch, I am sure."

It was a moment before Mayi realized that she'd just been offered a room in the Bilbaos' pension. Señor Roche had been remarkably silent, and from the expression on his face, she knew that he was just as surprised as she. A few minutes later, after he'd carried her suitcase inside, he wished her good luck, then told her that when she was ready to leave, she should use the village wireless a day in advance to make arrangements for him to pick her up.

"But don't wait until after the snows fall," he warned. "The road is impassable much of the winter. Once you are snowed in, you will have to arrange with the air-service company in Pamplona to send a helicopter or plane to pick you up, and that is very expensive."

It was with some misgiving that Mayi watched Señor Roche drive off in his ancient truck. Had she made a mistake coming here? Had her decision to be discreet and not rush in with questions about the Aquirre family been wise? She had heard so many times how difficult it was to get information from a Basque, that one should use indirection and a subtle manipulation of the conversation instead of direct questions, but perhaps simple directness would have been best after all. Well, she would try to be reasonably patient, but if that didn't work, she would do it the American way.

She insisted on carrying her suitcase up the stairs, followed closely by Señora Bilbao. Surprisingly chatty now that Mayi had passed muster, the elderly woman deluged her with information about Zubilibia and the Valle de la Añara.

"The history books will tell you that our church was erected in the times of Louis XI, but they are wrong, of course. We in Zubilibia know that the church was built long before that, and even then, it replaced an even older church from Visigothic times that was burned by one of the ancient invaders of our land. There is much history here in Zubilibia, and much to see and do, too. Tomorrow afternoon, for instance, there is a tournament that you may want to attend."

"What kind of tournament, Señora Bilbao?"

"Why—pelota, of course. Many fine pelota players have come from Zubilibia. Some of our men have competed in Pamplona and even in Madrid and have carried off many prizes. Also, next week we honor our patron saint, Saint Michael the Archangel, with a festival. After the religious ceremonies there will be dancing in the square, and you must join in. My husband is a fine dancer. It was exciting to see him do the *jota* when he was a young man! Even now he can dance with the best of them. Not as long, perhaps, but certainly his feet have not lost their skill."

Mayi smiled at the pride in Señora Bilbao's voice. "Will the festival draw many tourists?" she asked idly, wondering how they would get there and where they would stay.

A veil dropped over Señora Bilbao's eyes. "Our festival is not for tourists."

Mayi, guessing that she had intruded upon a sore subject, asked, "When is market day? I would love to go to your local market."

"Each Monday the farmers of the valley bring their produce to the square to sell." Señora Bilbao hesitated briefly, then added, "Perhaps you would like to go with me when I do my marketing."

They had reached the top of the stairs now. Señora Bilbao opened a door and motioned Mayi inside. "This is your room. It overlooks the vegetable garden. When the window is open, the odor of fresh herbs fills the room."

A few minutes later Mayi was unpacking her clothes and hanging them in a large sweet-smelling armoire. As Señora Bilbao had said, the room had few frills, but the walls had been washed in pale blue, the curtains at the windows were freshly starched, and the bed, which had a high old-fashioned back, was covered with a blue comforter. Her landlady must have seen her glance toward the bed, because she rose from the armchair where she'd been watching Mayi unpack, saying that if Mayi wanted to take a nap, she would call her in plenty of time for dinner.

Mayi took a long nap, and that night, after a meal of *calderillo*, a rabbit dish with vegetables, which, Señor Bilbao told her proudly, his wife was famous for, she slept like a baby. For the first time in months she didn't dream about Pio.

In the morning she set about trying to locate Pio's family. She had made the decision to be cautious with her questions and was glad when Señor Bilbao gave her the opening she needed by asking her about the Basques who had immigrated to Idaho.

"There is quite a Basque community in Boise and also in the states of Nevada and California. In fact, one of our United States senators comes from French Basque stock," she said, then added, "I went to school with a boy named Aquirre, who told me his father was from Navarra. I wonder if he could have come from Zubilibia?"

"Aquirre?" Señor Bilbao turned the name over on his tongue as if he were tasting it. "There is no family of that name in Zubilibia, nor in the Valle de la Añara, either."

"Then I guess I was mistaken," Mayi said, hiding her disappointment. She wondered if she had spoken too quickly. Did this come under the heading of one of the direct questions that Basques found offensive?

"Navarra is very large." Señor Bilbao's gesture was so expansive that he could have been describing the globe. Mayi hid a smile, wondering what he would say about the vast stretches of unpopulated areas in her own native Idaho. "Even here in Zubilibia, a few of our younger sons have been forced to migrate to other places, including America. We follow the old ways of inheritance, with family properties going to the oldest son or daughter. That is how we keep our property from falling into the hands of foreigners."

His wife made a small clucking sound, and he changed the subject and began describing a meadow that afforded a panoramic view of the upper valley and would be a good place for her to start her sketching.

"Of course, some say that the meadow is haunted, that at times you can hear the shouts of children who are long dead—not that I myself believe such things," he added. "However, the village children stay away from there, so you will have privacy if you want to make sketches of the village for your friend."

After breakfast Mayi followed her landlord's directions and took the road that bisected the village and ended in a path leading up the side of a bracken-covered hill. Although she saw no one except a couple of children playing kickball in a yard, again she had the feeling of being watched.

At the edge of the village she passed two men, stocky men with heavy shoulders and straight, tight mouths who were squatting by the side of the road, smoking their pipes and talking together. Their clothes were rough, and from the thick *makhila*, the walking stick that was lying beside each man, she knew they were *etcholak*, shepherds come down from the high pastures for supplies, a little companionship and a few drinks of Pernod at the village café. She wished she could stop to talk to them, to ask them how it felt to live alone so much of the time in the far reaches of the Pyrenees, but even though both inclined their heads and one murmured a polite "*Gabon Jainkoak dizula*"—God give you good-morning—she only smiled, returned their greeting and went on without stopping.

Later, as she was following the stone path Señor Bilbao had described, she met a young boy. He gave her an oblique glance from his dark eyes, and again she only nodded and exchanged a polite greeting with him as they passed. She was the outsider there; she must wait for overtures—if any— from the local people.

As it turned out, the first overture she received was not from a child but from an adult. She was climbing the hill, still following the stone path, when a middle-aged man with a thin, fleshless face came striding along, swinging his arms, so preoccupied with his own thoughts that he almost ran into her. He skidded to a halt just in time to prevent a collision, and his smile was so friendly that she was nonplussed for a moment.

"Ah, the American artist," he said in thickly accented English. "I have plan to call upon you when I have finished my morning—uh, constitution."

So the whole village already knew about her. Well, that wasn't so surprising.

"I'm Mayi Jenners," she said, smiling back.

"Mayi—a good Basque name," he said approvingly. "Please to pardon my English. It is not so good. For long, I have try to perfect it, but I get small practice. So few Britishers or Americans come to Zubilibia. Someday, when my English is improve, I shall convince our municipal council to allow me to teach it to the children.''

"You are a teacher?"

"Permit me to introduce myself," he said, switching to Spanish. "I am Francisco Idiart, schoolmaster for the children of Zubilibia."

"And you want to teach them English? For what purpose?"

"Ah, things do not stand still, not even in Zubilibia. Someday we must cater to the tourists, and when that happens, we must speak English. But the people here—they do not like changes."

"Then you are not a native of Zubilibia?"

"Oh, I was born here. But unlike others I could name, I look outward—" He made a wide circular gesture. "I see the future approaching. We must have a steady source of income. Now that the old way is no longer practical and is in fact very dangerous because we are watched so closely by the authorities, we must look to the tourists to bring money into the valley."

Mayi started to ask him what he meant by the "old way," but a sudden memory stopped her.

Smuggling—he's talking about smuggling, she thought. Pio had told her that, although smuggling was not a particularly honored profession among his people, it was also not considered a criminal one. The mountainous region and a language that shut out outsiders made it difficult for the French and Spanish governments to prevent the passage of contraband over the Pyrenees, especially since the Basques knew every inch of their mountains.

"Some of the most famous smugglers in history have come from Zubilibia," he said matter-of-factly. "We're an ancient people with an ancient sense of what is right and what is wrong. We don't care for laws that are forced upon us by outsiders. Even today the village gets a trickle of income from the illicit traffic of horses and cattle, silk and Spanish shawls and sometimes liquor. But our area seems to have been singled out lately as a special target by government agents, and the penalties if caught make it very dangerous. I wouldn't be surprised if the practice doesn't eventually die out, although never entirely."

Realizing that Señor Idiart was waiting for her to speak, Mayi decided this was a good time to make an inquiry about the Aquirres. "I once had a school friend whose parents came from this area," she said casually. "His name was Aquirre."

"Aquirre? That is not a local family name." He spoke with such certainty that her spirits plummeted. How was it possible that Pio's family was unknown to the local schoolteacher—*and* to her landlady, who must know everybody in the valley? Was it possible that Pio had lied to her for some reason? But why would he do such a thing? No, there had to be some other explanation. He had stated so clearly in his last letter that he hoped that someday she could visit Zubilibia.

"This is important to you, Señorita Jenners?"

His expression was so sympathetic that she was tempted to tell Señor Idiart the whole story, but she sensed that he was too free with his tongue. There were so many factors she still didn't know about Pio's relationship with his family. In the end she gave the schoolmaster the same explanation she'd given her landlady.

"Well, it's possible you are under a misapprehension," he said, absently slipping into Basque. "The word *zubilibia* means two bridges. You can still see the old stone bridges, one of them now in ruins, that gave the village its name. Place is everything to our people. If a man married a woman who is *etcheko jauna* of her house, he is expected to go to her house to live. In such cases he takes the name of her house. And on the rare occasions when a family dies out and a stranger purchases their holdings, then from then on, he, too, is known by the name of his new house. Which is why most family names are derived from places. For instance, *Etcheberri* means 'new house' and *Dargainerotz* means 'rising rocks.' Since most villages are named from landmarks, it is very likely that there are more than one with the name of Zubilibia. I suspect your friend was using the local name for another settlement in Navarra, perhaps one that is too small to get on the maps."

Mayi started to shake her head, then changed her mind. This was an explanation that fit all the facts. Pio's description of the village could suit any of a hundred similar villages in Navarra.

Hiding her disappointment, she said, "Señor Bilbao tells me that there will be a tournament this afternoon. I have never seen a pelota game. Are the rules difficult to understand?"

"It is a simple—and very arduous—game. You will enjoy it. Perhaps you would permit me to escort you this afternoon?" He bowed with old-fashioned courtesy. "I am perfectly respectable, and besides, I am sure the Bilbaos will accompany us, too."

"That would be lovely," she said, smiling at him.

After a few more minutes of conversation, while Señor Idiart tried out some of his English on her, Mayi went on. As she followed the path around the base of a pile of boulders, she wondered idly how many years ago its stones had been laid. Were they creek stones, eroded by the rush of water, or had they been worn smooth by human feet over countless decades?

At the edge of a large meadow bordered with outcrops of rock, she clambered over a stone fence and walked through waving grass, which had already turned golden in the autumn sun. She was in a small world all its own—the sky, a flawless blue overhead; the soft sigh of the wind as it rippled the tips of the dried grass and intermingled with the cry of a bird; the odor of woodsmoke from some far-off chimney in the valley.

The knowledge that the meadow must have looked the same for countless centuries gave her the illusion of being suspended in time, as if she had slipped through a portal into another age. She stopped to listen, and for a few seconds she was sure she heard the voices of children, until she realized it was only the wind whistling around the rock-strewed hill that overlooked the meadow. Even so, she felt an urge to tiptoe, and impulsively she slipped off her tennis shoes, tied the strings together and flung them over one shoulder. The tangle of grass was like a spongy rug underfoot as she went on, her head flung back so she could breathe in the aromatic air.

In a nearby clump of tall grass she caught a flash of golden brown, and a moment later a dog, a retriever, broke from cover. He was a large male, and when he spotted her, he stopped to stare at her with aloof, golden eyes. When she didn't move, he approached her cautiously and sniffed at her bare toes.

"You're a handsome fellow—and very much aware of it, I suspect," she said softly.

At the sound of her voice, the dog's plumed tail began to sway back and forth. She knelt and extended her hand, and he tilted his head to one side. Gently she scratched the fur beneath his chin, and when he accepted this gesture of friendship, she rubbed the small indentations behind his ears. His eyes closed and he gave a low groan of pleasure. She knew she'd just made a new friend.

She gave him a final scratch and rose to her feet. "Come, dog, I'll race you to that stone building over there," she said. She began to run, and when she looked back, the dog was scampering after her, his canine dignity forgotten. The air was soft, summer warm but autumn sweet with the odor of recently cut hay. From the valley below she heard cowbells, or perhaps it was the tiny bells that hung around the necks of sheep. It might even be the laughter of the Laminak, the little people of Basque legends, she thought.

Mayi laughed aloud at her own fanciful thoughts and flung her arms out wide, whirling around and around, and suddenly there was magic in the serenity of the meadow, the golden sunlight, the whole perfect day. As if agreeing that it was indeed a wonderful day to be alive, the dog gave a deep-throated bark. Mayi laughed again and pulled off her scarf to let her hair stream down her back as she ran, liking the feel of the wind against her face, the odor of dried grass in her nostrils.

Putting on a burst of speed as if showing off, the dog passed her, and because she knew from the gray of his muzzle that he must be very old, she came to a halt, not wanting to be responsible for overtaxing his strength.

Now that they were close to the building, she saw that it was a relic, a burned-out shell. Only its gray stone walls were still standing. The fire must have happened a long time ago. Waist-high grass grew inside the building, and vines, now brown and withered, completely enveloped the holes that had once been windows. She started to step through a gaping doorway to explore, but when she saw the fire-blackened cradle lying near the doorway she stopped, fighting a desire to cry.

"Come on, dog," she called to the old retriever. "We aren't wanted here." She turned away, rubbing her eyes with the back of her hand.

Squinting against the sun, she headed for the hill that rose behind the meadow, intending to climb to the top to look at the view. But when she spotted a large table-flat rock near the base of the hill, it looked so inviting that she paused to touch it with her fingertips. The rock was warm from the sun, and she flung herself down upon it to rest, her hands supporting her head. The old dog, his claws making scrabbling sounds on the rock, joined her and collapsed nearby with a sigh. When he laid his head on her stomach she felt privileged, as if she had just been given a rare gift.

"I never had a dog—or any other kind of pet," she told him. "So I don't really know the rules of behavior between one of your kind and one of mine. But I've always wanted a dog just like you. Unfortunately the timing is all wrong, isn't it? Besides, it's obvious someone has taken very good care of you, dog."

The dog made a snorting sound, and she laughed again. "You don't like being called 'dog,' do you? Maybe I'd better give you a proper name...how about Argus? That's a very honorable name for a dog. The original Argus lived long after his prime, waiting for Ulysses to return from the wars. He died happy because he got to lick his master's hand one more time before he died. So—Argus it is. Do you like that name?''

The dog opened his eyes, looked at her, then closed them again and went to sleep.

Mayi pushed the hair back from her forehead and tilted her face into the warmth of the sun, yawning. For a while she watched a white dovelike bird winging its way toward the south, and then, feeling more relaxed and content than she had in months, she put her arm over her eyes to shield them from the light. She was soon asleep.

Because the sun had been in her eyes for the past few minutes, she hadn't noticed the tall dark-haired man who was sitting with his back against a gray slab of granite a few feet above the rock where she slept—and who had been watching her with intent eyes as she ran in the sun with his dog.

CHAPTER FOUR

EVER SINCE HE WAS A BOY, Laurens Pelente had come to the haunted meadow when he was deeply troubled, or simply when he needed solitude to work out some knotty problems. Although the Basques had fewer superstitions than other old races, and the stone farmhouse in the meadow had burned down so many years ago that few people remembered the name of the family who had once lived there, most of the local people, including the children, thought it only prudent to avoid it—just in case.

This time he was escaping the tedium of trying to decipher the new government wine-tax regulations, which were so complicated they had taken up most of his waking hours for the past two days. On the third morning, when he found himself being short-tempered with his aunt and sister at the breakfast table, he knew it was time for an hour or two at his own private sanctuary. He whistled for Topet, his aging golden retriever, who was sleeping in the courtyard, and took off at a brisk pace, heading for the meadow.

Topet, who at fifteen was well past his prime,

had been more than willing to go along on the excursion. He moved sedately, though, as if his old bones were stiff, and Laurens wondered, not for the first time, how much longer the old dog would be with him. The thought made him wince; it brought with it a host of painful memories. Since he didn't want to be reminded of other losses, one of them so recent, he put everything else out of his mind except the pure physical enjoyment of stretching out his long legs and feeling the sun-warmed wind moving his hair across his forehead, and the freedom of knowing that for an hour or so nothing would disturb him or intrude upon his thoughts.

When he reached the meadow, he skirted the edge and then started up one of the small finger-hills that radiated out from the thickly forested mountain range behind the villa. A quarter of the way up, he stopped and settled himself in his favorite spot, a natural chair formed by several large rocks. From this vantage point he could look down at the red-tiled roofs of the village and the winding curves of the Rio de la Añara, which sprang from the bowels of the mountain behind the villa.

Zubilibia...the hub of his life and yet, in so many ways, also his prison. He was not only head of the Pelente household, but, by tradition, the patron of the village. So many problems and so few easy solutions. Sometimes he felt as if he was walking on the edge of an abyss. If too many outside elements were allowed to intrude, then the village, its uniqueness and serenity, would be destroyed. Yet how much longer could they survive with only the vineyards and the winery, the cottage crafts of the women, which the newly organized co-op was marketing in the cities, and the dwindling profits from the sale of wool and sheep?

He realized he was allowing his problems to intrude again, and he put them out of his mind and looked around for Topet, realizing it had been a while since he'd seen the dog's golden head bobbing up and down among the high stands of dried grass. To his right he caught a flash of color, but when he turned his head to look in that direction, he saw that it was a girl—a slender girl with hair so red in the full sunlight that her head seemed to be on fire. Behind her he saw Topet, and both of them were running.

Laurens stood up and started to call out that his dog was so gentle he wouldn't hurt a fly. Then the girl threw back her head to laugh, and he realized that she was simply running for the joy of it. As for Topet—could this scampering animal possibly be his dignified and aloof friend, who never made up to strangers?

"Shame on you, you old fool," Laurens muttered. "Losing your head over a redhead."

More amused than annoyed that the privacy of the meadow had been invaded, he watched as the girl stopped in front of the burned-out farmhouse. When she stooped to peer in through the gaping hole where the door had once been, he expected her to go inside to explore. But she turned away, brushing the back of her hand across her eyes, and he realized that she'd been touched, as he always was, by the poignancy of that fire-blackened cradle, still sitting there as mute evidence of a long-ago tragedy.

"Come, dog, we aren't wanted here," she called out to Topet in English, and began to run again.

Since she was heading toward the hill where he sat on this throne of stone, Laurens expected her to look up any minute and spot him. But the sun was in her eyes, blinding her, and when she reached the stone slab at the base of the hill and flung herself down, her arms up over her head, he knew that she hadn't seen him.

Topet scrambled up on the rock and rested his head on her stomach, and Laurens found himself envying the old dog his soft—and undeniably seductive—pillow. For a while the girl talked to the dog, so unselfconsciously that Laurens knew she believed herself to be alone.

He smiled when she told the old dog that she'd never had a pet and didn't know the rules for dog-human relationships. And Topet, who was usually as aloof with strangers as any Basque sheepherder, was thumping his tail and looking so silly that Laurens shook his head in disbelief. Was this girl a witch, or simply one of those rare people who have a natural rapport with animals?

Maybe the old boy is getting senile, he thought, smiling. *Argus indeed.*

After a while the girl fell asleep. Her arm fell away from her face, and for a long time Laurens stared down at her from his rocky perch, watching the strong pulse at the base of her throat, noting how her dark lashes, which fanned across her cheeks, contrasted so strikingly with her red hair and the cream-pale skin that was innocent of make-up. He studied her hands. Her long, slender fingers were entangled in the ruff of fur around Topet's neck as if, even in her sleep, she felt a need to touch something alive to give her comfort.

What would it be like to kiss those full, seductively parted lips, to caress the ivory smoothness of that throat, to cup those full breasts in his hands and sink into the softness of that sweetly curved body...?

With a shock of self-disgust, Laurens realized the direction of his thoughts and was ashamed. Even his eyes were an invasion of the girl's privacy as she lay sleeping, looking so defenseless and vulnerable not only to his intruding stare but to the sun. That milk-white skin looked as if it would burn easily, and he knew that the cool wind and the high altitude were deceiving to newcomers.

Laurens waited another few minutes, and when the girl still didn't stir, he rose and gave the sharp, two-toned whistle that was Topet's signal to follow him. When the retriever lifted his head, then rose stiffly and shook himself, the girl opened her eyes and sat up, yawning and stretching. A brief image of taut fabric outlining full, rounded breasts was etched into Laurens's brain as he slipped away behind the rocks, knowing Topet would follow him home.

When he returned to the villa, the first thing he did was seek out his housekeeper, Constancio Arana, who knew village gossip almost before it happened. He asked her what she knew about a girl, an outsider, who spoke English and who had flame-red hair.

MAYI ATTENDED THE PELOTA MATCH that afternoon, accompanied by her hosts, the Bilbaos, and the schoolmaster, Francisco Idiart.

The pelota court was located off the square, next to the village's café. As Señor Bilbao pointed out just before he took himself off to join his friends inside the café, "Pelota is a convivial game and calls for a cognac or a glass of Pernod to make the hours shine." Since this didn't seem to include women— or schoolmasters—Mayi and Señora Bilbao were left in Señor Idiart's care to watch the preparations for the match.

They seated themselves on benches of rough wood planks in an upper gallery that overlooked a large court. The court was enclosed on three sides by whitewashed stone walls and on the fourth by tiered galleries, which were covered by a pointed roof and supported by solid oak beams. The beams were silvery gray with age, and Mayi knew the court had been there a long time, even as time was measured by the Basques.

Vitality seemed to fill the court as the players and their backers arrived, laughing and joking and jostling one another like a gang of playful schoolboys. Señor Idiart pointed out the two contestants, who were dressed in white shirts and trousers with red sashes which gave them a Moorish look. Like the other men at the event, they both wore the flat, broad beret of the Basques.

"It is what you call—I think the American expression is a grudge match," the schoolteacher explained. Mayi had already noticed that he seemed happiest whenever he was imparting information. "Everybody agrees that Laurens Pelente is the best of our town's younger players, everybody but Juan Goiz, who believes that *he* is best. Which is why he has challenged Laurens to a match today." The scorn in his voice showed on which side his loyalties lay. "Soon we shall see who is right."

He went on to explain that pelota was more than a game, it was a way of life to Basque men, not only a part of their heritage but a method of proving their manhood.

"We Basques are very competitive," he said proudly. "We have always sought occupations that require much courage and strength, such as whalers and soldiers and sailors. Did you know, Señorita Jenners, that it was a Basque who navigated the ship of the Italian, Columbus, when he discovered your New World? So you can see why our games are not intended to end in a draw. Pelota is dangerous and fast, requiring great strength and courage. It is not for the fainthearted, even though these days they use the basket, the *cesta*, instead of their bare hands to throw the ball. The ball is very hard, and it travels at such speed that it can easily cause a concussion or break an arm—"

Although she was aware that the schoolmaster was still expounding on the finer points of pelota, Mayi stopped listening. Below on the court, one of the two competitors had turned and was facing the gallery now. As if a wall of silence had suddenly dropped around her, the crowd noises faded, and she was only aware of this man. He stood out from the group of boisterous men, not only because of his height, but because of something indefinable, an aloofness, that set him apart.

At first she thought he was unusually tall, several inches over six feet, and then she realized it was an illusion, because he towered over the stocky, much shorter men around him. He was also extremely attractive and had a rugged face, thick, glossy hair as black as the wings of a raven, and luminous amber-colored eyes. Even though he was lounging against the wall, he seemed to radiate energy, and when he threw back his head to laugh at someone's joke, she found herself leaning forward, as if drawn to him.

Then his head turned, and he looked up into the galleries, directly at her. As their eyes met, the silence seemed to settle in around her again, and she felt dizzy and disoriented, as if she'd jumped up too quickly from a nap. Although she tried to blame the sensation on belated jet lag, on too much sun or fatigue or even the excitement of being in a strange place, she knew that it was something else, something overwhelming.

A moment later someone called out to the man, and she realized his name was Laurens Pelente, the player Señor Idiart had called the best of the local pelota players. He turned away and Mayi took a long breath, chiding herself for her own too-vivid imagination. And yet, for a moment, she had been so sure that he had been expecting to see her in the stands, that this wasn't the first time they had met.

She smiled at such a foolish and romantic idea. She wasn't impressed by a man simply because he was so incredibly attractive.

Señor Bilbao returned, his eyes suspiciously bright, only to wander off again a few minutes later to join a long row of older men who sat in the uppermost gallery. The men all wore black berets and *chamarras*, the workingmen's smocklike shirts, and with their beaked noses and dark eyes, Mayi thought they looked like a row of crows sitting on a telephone wire, passing judgment on lesser birds. She wasn't surprised when Señor Idiart told her that it was the collective opinion of these elderly men rather than the official score that would determine the real winner of the match.

The game began to the accompaniment of shouts and cheers from the spectators. As Señor Idiart went on to explain the rules of the game, Mayi found it impossible to tear her eyes away from Laurens Pelente. Although he had the powerful arms and the well-developed shoulders she had come to associate with Basque men, his lithe body moved around the court with the grace of a matador as again and again he caught the ball in the banana-shaped wicker basket strapped to his arm, then flung it fiercely against the wall.

The ball moved so fast that it was hard to follow, and every time it struck the wall it cracked like a rifle. Even to Mayi's inexperienced eyes it was obvious that the second contestant, a chunky man with a dour expression, was outclassed. She wasn't surprised when, half an hour later, Laurens Pelente was declared the winner.

"It's a very exciting game," she said in answer to a question from Señor Bilbao, who had rejoined them.

"Laurens Pelente could be a master if he were so inclined," he said. "He has great natural talent, and he has more energy than most men, too."

"Then he isn't a professional pelota player?" she said.

"Indeed not." The idea seemed to amuse him. "He has other responsibilities. Well, it was a good match, but of course it can't compare with the old days, when the bare hand was used instead of the *cesta*."

"When was the basket introduced, Señor Bilbao?"

"In the late fifties," he said, shaking his head dolefully. "It was a mistake, allowing it."

"Come now, Arnauld," Señor Idiart said. "The

game is just as fast as it's ever been, and the toll in swollen and broken hands made the change necessary. Even a traditionalist like you has to admit that after a hundred and twenty-odd years, the new way has had a fair trial.''

Mayi bit her lip to keep from smiling. She'd assumed that Señor Bilbao had meant the *cesta* had been introduced in 1950. And wasn't her landlord's stare at the schoolmaster just a little too baleful? Although they were polite to each other, she sensed there was friction between Señor Idiart and her landlord. She wondered if it was a matter of temperament, or one of the old Basque feuds she had heard so much about.

As she was leaving the galley she looked back—straight into Laurens Pelente's eyes. Although he didn't nod or smile, and in fact looked very grim, she had the feeling once again that they had met before.

After dinner that evening she excused herself early and went to her room, saying she'd had too much sun that day. That night she dreamed again, but this time it wasn't a nightmare about Pio, trapped in his wrecked car and calling for help. No, this time she dreamed of a tall lithe man with square shoulders and raven-dark hair who moved like lightning around a pelota court, and who looked at her with luminous amber-colored eyes that seemed to be asking a question, a question to which she desperately wanted to answer *yes*.

CHAPTER FIVE

PIO HAD ONCE TOLD MAYI that a Basque is offended by a direct question and so will seldom answer it directly.

"In his own good time and only if he trusts you will he part with the information you want," he had said. "When two Basques meet, unless they are related or lifelong friends, the first subject of conversation is always the weather. Then gradually they may move on to other things, provided neither has reason to draw back. To rush into conversation recklessly is considered gauche, and discretion is always practiced. For instance, it is not proper to ask a question outright. There are no secrets in the village, not for long, but things are revealed slowly, a morsel here, a morsel there. Only someone who understands this and is willing to play the game can hope to be accepted. Which doesn't mean an outsider is always given the same courtesy. He is fair game for questions, because of course his opinions don't really have much value."

Mayi often thought of that conversation in the days following her arrival in Zubilibia. As she accompanied Señora Bilbao while she purchased vine shoots and vegetable marrow at the market stalls in the square or bought long loaves of bread at the bakery, or whenever they stopped at the café for cups of coffee laced with chocolate and cinnamon, Mayi was careful to allow the people to whom she was introduced to set the pace of the conversation. Mostly they talked of impersonal things, though the Basques seemed to be inordinately interested in the American West, as they called it. Only when the opportunity arose naturally did she drop a casual remark into the conversation about a schoolmate named Aquirre whose family had once lived in a village that had the same name as this one.

But her inquiries, careful as they were, met with blank stares and the characteristic Basque shrug, which could mean so many things, and she was eventually forced to accept the truth. Either Pio, for some reason of his own, had given her the wrong information, or she had come to the wrong Zubilibia.

Of course there *were* other possibilities. Pio's reminiscences had always been of himself as a boy, never as a young man. Perhaps his family had once lived in Zubilibia and had moved away later. But time had a different weight in these remote mountain villages. The Bilbaos spoke of events that had taken place decades ago as if they had happened only yesterday. Surely the villagers would remember the Aquirres, even if they had only lived here for a short time.

A fourth possibility came to Mayi when she

heard someone speak of the "old way" one day in the marketplace, only to be quickly hushed by a friend. It occurred to her that the whole village might be in some kind of conspiracy to keep the truth from her. Did they suspect her motives for asking about the Aquirres? She wondered if Pio's family could be tied in with smuggling. If so, no one, not even the loquacious schoolmaster or the village priest, Father Ignatius, a plump man with a tonsure of reddish hair, was likely to acknowledge their existence to an outsider.

Eventually she became convinced that her search was at a dead end. The only thing open to her was to seek out another Zubilibia—if it existed. But still she lingered on, finding some new excuse every day to postpone sending a wireless message to Señor Roche, and each day she fell a little more in love with the village and with the mountains, covered with thick growths of elm and walnut, oak and chestnut.

She blamed her reluctance to leave on her fondness for the Bilbaos, who had so quickly accepted her into their lives. She even told herself that she was staying on because of the old dog she called Argus, who met her every morning when she climbed to the meadow and ran with her in the sunlight.

But the real reason she stayed was her growing admiration for the people of Zubilibia, even though they still treated her with wariness. She, who had maintained her own independence against such odds, was impressed by their rugged independence and innate dignity. Even the roughest shepherd who came to the village in his lamb's wool jerkin and woolen cloak demanded and received respectful treatment from the people he encountered, no matter how high on the local social ladder they might be.

She was also touched by the beauty of their voices and their songs, which somehow seemed at odds with their pragmatic natures. Once when she was sitting quietly in the meadow, the retriever's golden head in her lap, she heard a boy's voice lifting a love song into the wind, and the sweetness of it pierced her heart and made her think of her grandmother, and of Pio.

In the slow acceptance of the villagers she found something that had been lacking in her life, a sense of her own worth as a person. She had always been able to win the casual friendship of others because of her unusual appearance, which people found so intriguing, or her cheerfulness, which sometimes hid a deep melancholy, or her willingness to listen to other people's troubles.

Now she was exerting no special effort to win friends, and still she succeeded in gaining a certain cautious approval from the clannish and reserved villagers. She treasured the slightest sign of a thaw, the smallest gesture of friendship, knowing that it stemmed from their appraisal of her as a person.

She was aware that there was much curiosity about her, but she also knew that the people accepted her story of being an amateur artist on a holiday. Even a village as remote as Zubilibia attracted the attention of a few artists, photographers, writers and poets as well as a trickle of American Basques, seeking their own roots. Mayi's familiarity with the local dialect was an immense help in winning them over, and the fact that she was from the American West was a constant source of interest. But in the end it was Mayi herself who won acceptance—at least the degree of acceptance possible to an outsider who had no family ties in the village.

The first to become her friends were the Bilbaos. Since she was not accustomed to idleness and had learned very young that the best way to win approval from new foster parents was to shoulder a good share of the household chores, she was soon helping her landlady around the pension. She took over the care of her own room and made herself generally useful elsewhere with cleaning and polishing and with the laundry and cooking.

Within a week the Bilbaos were calling her Mayi and treating her as if she was their daughter. It was only natural that when the village's saint's day festival arrived, she was invited to be their guest.

At first when Señora Bilbao suggested that Mayi wear the traditional costume of the village, she declined. She was convinced that if she did wear it, she would appear to be trying to push her way into village life. Even though her ancestry was Basque, her grandmother had come from another valley, and she had no right to the traditional costume of Valle de la Añara.

Señora Bilbao scoffed at her feelings. "I myself am from Guipúzcoa. I came here on a holiday and snatched my Arnauld from under the noses of the local girls. They were a long time forgiving me for that, you can be sure. But I wore the costume of the village proudly at my very first festival and right up until I put on so much weight. The old hens of the village thought it disgraceful for a married woman no longer young to wear anything but black, and they whispered about me behind their fingers. But since I wasn't in mourning, I saw no reason why I should dress in black—not until I had to. The costume has been packed away for many years and it needs a good airing. You will look charming in it, my dear."

In the end Mayi gave in, though not without reservations. When she saw herself in the costume, she had to agree with Señora Bilbao that it was becoming. The full skirt was blue and banded with white. Red lacings crisscrossed her slender calves to the knee, a perky white cap sat atop her red hair, and the tight lacing of the black jerkin emphasized her slender waist and her high, round breasts. Because of her landlady's good food she had gained a bit of weight; her skin glowed and her eyes had regained their old sparkle.

"You look a true daughter of Navarra," Arnauld Bilbao told her approvingly when she presented herself that evening. He looked handsome in his white shirt and trousers, a contrast to his wife's subdued black, and his eyes were as eager as a young man's. He was wearing a red beret, set squarely across his forehead in the Basque manner, and Mayi wasn't surprised that his wife was eyeing him with what could only be described as a gleam in her eye as he added, "And I will teach you the *jota*. It is a lively dance. You will learn it quickly."

"But I already know it—or at least I remember some of the steps my grandmother taught me," Mayi told him.

"Then I will claim the first *jota* with you. I'm sure to be the envy of all the young men of the village," he said, his black eyes snapping.

His wife shook her head. "He's such a ladies' man, this Arnauld of mine." But she sounded more proud than jealous.

Even before they reached the square, they heard the sound of drums and the *txistu*, a three-holed flute that had a high, sweet wail. A man's rich baritone was raised in song.

"That is Nicanor Carrera," Arnauld told her. "He has been compared to Iparraguirre, and everybody knows that Iparraguirre was the finest *bertsolari* of them all."

"That's a troubadour, isn't it? I would love to witness a *bertsolari* contest someday."

"And so you shall if you stay here long enough. One Georges Ugari, who lives in Ochagavia, fancies himself as the reincarnation of Iparraguirre." Señor Bilbao's upper lip quivered with disdain.

"He has challenged Nicky Carrera to a contest. Someday, when God wills it, Nicky will accept the challenge. There will be much at stake as it will be our duty to back him with our money, of course."

The singer, a square-set young man with handsome dark eyes, was just starting a new song when they reached the square. His head was thrown back as he sang, and he seemed oblivious to the crowd listening to him. Mayi's heart throbbed with excitement when she recognized his song; it had been her grandmother's favorite.

"White snow dove, whither are you flying?
All the passes into Spain are full of snow.
Tonight you will take refuge in our house."

Unexpectedly her eyes filled with tears. Señora Bilbao saw them and gave them her own interpretation. "It is a sad song, yes, but also a very beautiful one. Soon it will be time for the migration of the snow doves. It is appropriate that this song be sung now to show our respect, just as we say a special mass for the doves after the hunting season is over."

Mayi didn't tell her that the song had aroused a more personal sorrow than sadness for the fate of the snow doves. Instead she asked, "What will be next?"

Señor Bilbao answered her question. "It is time for the *aurresku*. Now you will see some very fine dancing."

Mayi watched the dance floor with keen interest. The *aurresku* was such a sensual dance, she'd read, that the priests had tried to ban it. At one end of a roped-off space in the middle of the square, a group of young women, each wearing the traditional costume of the valley, had gathered. In their midst, one girl was silent, her eyes downcast, while the others chatted and laughed around her. At the opposite end of the dance area, a similar group of young men, handsome in their red sashes and white shirts, also gathered. A noisy group, they shouted good-natured insults at one another, and now and then one would give out a wild *irrintzina* yell, the war cry of the Basques that had struck such terror in the hearts of their enemies in earlier times. It started out as a wolf yowling and ended, after several ear-piercing seconds, in an unearthly howl.

"Is something wrong?" she asked Señora Bilbao, noting the grave expression on her face.

"That is Luis Hiribarren." She pointed to a stocky young man who seemed to be the center of an argument. From his folded arms and sullen expression, she could tell he was being stubborn about whatever his friends' gesturing meant. "It is said that tonight he will declare his intentions toward Engrace. And I fear—" She broke off with an expressive shrug.

"I don't understand."

"The *aurresku* is a courting dance. Luis has arranged with his friends to approach Engrace, the girl he intends to court. More likely he has already been courting her on the sly. Only a fool, which Luis is not, would approach a woman who has not already shown that she will accept his attentions. So I am afraid this night will end in trouble."

"Is that why his friends are arguing with him?"

"They realize it is not fitting that he court Engrace and they are trying to dissuade him."

"Why don't they simply refuse to approach her?"

"It is not their choice. They are his friends and must do as he asks."

A roll of drums came from the small raised stand where the musicians stood. Across the field, the four young men who had surrounded Luis Hiribarren ran into the center of the dance area. The bells on the ties that bound their trouser legs tinkled wildly as they broke into an energetic display of dance steps. When they stopped, Luis joined them. His head high, he advanced across the square, coming to a stop in front of the group of girls. He exploded into a burst of intricate steps with an abruptness that made Mayi gasp, then came to a sudden stop, his arms folded across his chest, his chin tilted at an arrogant angle.

As his friends approached the group of young girls, he seemed aloof, as if he had no interest in their actions. The girls parted before the onslaught, allowing the men to surround the small dark-haired girl who had been so silent among the others. With just the right amount of reluctance, she allowed them to coax her into the center of the dance area, then stood there, her eyes fixed on the ground.

Luis, his face strained, approached her as the music swelled. His back was so arched that he seemed in danger of losing his balance. He extended his hand, not to the girl but to one of his friends, and led him around the dance floor in a giant circle. When he was standing in front of Engrace again, he began a series of wonderfully graceful and complicated steps, posturing and preening himself like a young rooster. Engrace seemed to ignore him, but her cheeks were flushed, and Mayi was sure she was watching from under her eyelashes as he burst into a shower of leaps and turns, each more difficult than the last. His hunched shoulders, his strained face and his eyes burning with passion made him look both threatening and seductive. Mayi felt her own pulse keeping time with the beat of the drums, and she wasn't at all surprised that the priests had put restrictions on the dance.

When he was finished, his face streaming, Luis gave three abrupt bows, to his right, to his left and then to Engrace, who seemed only then to notice him. He presented her, his chosen one, with the end of a large white handkerchief. Holding the other end tightly in his hand, he led her from the floor to the exuberant shouts of his friends, who seemed to have forgotten their misgivings about his choice of sweetheart.

Mayi guessed that the handkerchief was one of the innovations the priests had insisted upon.

Perhaps they had reasoned it was best to keep the couple from touching while their blood was still leaping from the dance. She was surprised that they had allowed the dance at all; it was obvious it must have evolved from some pagan fertility rite that predated Christianity.

A lively fandango started and the floor was soon crowded with couples, some old and some young, all having a rousing good time. Children of all ages ran between the dancers, and the square was filled with the wild beat of the drums and the high, sweet soaring of the *txistu*.

Señora Bilbao's dour voice was a shock. "Nothing good can come of this. There has been bad blood between their families for many decades now."

"Maybe this will mend things," Mayi said hopefully.

"It will only make things worse. We Basques don't forget insults easily. Luis's grandfather was an injudicious man. He said many things of insult about Engrace's grandfather, who was the patron of our village. There has been no communication between the two families since."

She gave a quick look around the crowd. "Luckily Engrace's brother has not yet made an appearance, or perhaps some of Luis's friends are keeping him occupied. This whole business was very foolish, but then Luis is an impetuous young man. Well, nothing good will come of it," she repeated.

The musicians began a *jota*, and Señor Bilbao, bowing with a grace that belied his years, claimed Mayi for a dance. As he escorted her onto the dance floor, she exchanged smiles and nods with others she knew—the schoolmaster and his wife, the shoemaker who had replaced a heel on a shoe for her, the greengrocer and a rosy-cheeked girl who looked so much like him she had to be his daughter. Even Father Ignatius, whom she had met when she'd attended church with the Bilbaos, was dancing sedately with one of the older matrons.

Señor Bilbao began the first bowing and head-tossing movements of the *jota*, and as she aped his steps, Mayi was delighted to find that she could follow him easily. As the beat of the music seized her, she was caught up in the excitement, and an exuberance that seemed to be as much a part of the *jota* as the music took her over. She forgot everything else as she whirled and bowed, whirled again, her full skirts billowing. As she tossed her head, her white cap fell off and released the hair that she had pinned up so carefully, but she hardly noticed. All that mattered at the moment was the beat of the drums and the wild keening of the pipes, and the sheer joy of the dance.

LAURENS KNEW that the American girl was still in the village because of Topet's daily desertion. Every morning when the sun had risen halfway up the sky, as if summoned by some distant command, the old dog would stir from his mat in a sunny place on the terrace outside the library doors and stretch his stiff legs before he trotted off toward the meadow.

It took all of Laurens's willpower not to follow him. On the day of the tournament he'd found himself thinking more of Mayi than of the game, and he had made the decision to avoid her. She was an outsider and would be there such a short time. What he hadn't realized was that staying away from her would be so difficult. Even though he knew there was real danger in the powerful attraction he felt for her, he found it hard to keep away from the village—and from the meadow.

There was a family legend that the Pelente men loved only once, and if that one love failed them, they never loved again. Although he didn't believe in legends, particularly romantic ones, he did know that he had never before felt so strongly about a woman, especially one he'd only seen twice.

Not that he was celibate. There had been women in his life, more than a few. But they had never meant anything to him beyond the usual youthful sowing of wild oats. He'd always been careful not to show any interest in the women in his own village, because he realized that a casual affair was not possible. But when he went to Pamplona or Madrid or Paris on business, there were plenty of women he could call for a dinner out, or for a warmer relationship if it was agreeable to both of them.

But no woman, not even during his years as a college student in Madrid and then at the Sorbonne, had gotten under his skin as this American had with her vivid hair, her white skin and brown velvet eyes. And because he knew there could be no future in a relationship with a foreigner, one who would eventually leave Zubilibia, he had avoided the village, waiting for her to go.

He was even tempted to ignore the festival this year, but his aunt was suffering from a flare-up of an allergy and had to stay out of the night air, so he had no choice but to escort his sister, who loved to dance, to the festivities. But he made a vow to avoid the American girl—if indeed she was still in town.

Early that afternoon he dropped his sister off at a friend's house and then went to have a quiet dinner with Father Ignatius at the rectory. Later, on his way to the square, he stopped at the café to watch the older men at their endless *mus* game and to banter with two of the men he'd gone to the village school with. When he finally left the café and strolled toward the square, the first person he saw was the American girl.

She was dancing with Arnauld Bilbao, and as he watched her, a knot formed in the pit of his stomach. Her feet moved swiftly, surely, through the intricate steps of the dance, and her eyes flashed fire. Her vivid hair swirled around her head, and she looked like a dryad who had stepped out of the forest to join a human celebration. He knew then that he had to dance with her, if only once.

Not waiting for the dance to end, he threaded his

way through the dancers toward the oddly matched couple. Arnauld saw him coming and with a twinkling smile yielded up the girl. She showed no outward surprise as Laurens placed his hand on her waist and whirled her away. If the idea hadn't been so ridiculous, he would have imagined that she was expecting him. The thought slipped away as he was caught up in the madcap bowings and facings, the head tossings and leaping steps of the *jota*.

EVER SINCE SHE HAD STARTED DANCING, a strange excitement had possessed Mayi, a feeling of déjà vu, as if she had danced the *jota* in this square with its lanterns and its lively, colorful dancers and noisy spectators many times before. So when Laurens Pelente appeared in the middle of the dance, she felt no surprise, not even when he put his hand on her waist and, without a word of explanation to Señor Bilbao, whirled her away.

In some part of her mind she noted that he looked very handsome in his white linen suit with the red beret and sash, and that his step was light and sure as he led her through the steps of the *jota*. She followed his lead without any trouble, feeling tireless and incredibly buoyant in his arms.

And then the dance was over, and Laurens was still holding her hand, staring down at her as if they were the only two on the dance floor.

"My name is Laurens Pelente," he said in perfect, slightly accented English.

"And mine is Mayi Jenners," she replied. She

hoped he would attribute the breathlessness in her voice to the strenuous dance.

"Will you walk with me?" he asked.

"Walk with you?"

"Accompany me to the café for a Pernod and water, or perhaps you'd prefer wine?"

Although she felt no need for alcohol, not when her head was already spinning, Mayi nodded, trying not to show her eagerness. He took her arm and lead her from the floor, and it was only later that she realized she had left without one word of explanation to the Bilbaos.

The small round tables in front of the café were all taken, mostly by older people. But when Mayi and Laurens approached, another table and two chairs appeared as if by magic, and a minute later the proprietor himself brought them Pernod and water with his own hands. From his beaming smile, Mayi suspected that Laurens Pelente's skill as a pelota player made him some kind of local celebrity.

It was impossible to pretend that everything was perfectly normal. For one thing, Mayi was aware of the covert glances and the whispers of the people around them. She wanted to stare at Laurens, to see if his eyes really were luminous, but she was afraid of what her own eyes might reveal. Instead she watched the passing throngs, the uninhibited shoving and pushing of the children she'd thought were so quiet and reserved, the bursts of rowdy singing from a passing group of youths, the loud arguing of two middle-aged men who obviously had different views on politics.

In the square the dancers, all women now, were doing a traditional folk dance, the *makel*. They looked like tulips in their billowing skirts. "How well they dance," she said aloud. "Does every Basque dance that well?"

"We are born knowing how to dance," Laurens said. "And we all sing at the drop of a hat." He hesitated, staring at her. "You do the *jota* beautifully, and yet you are not Basque."

"My grandmother came from Roncal Valley. She taught me to dance the *jota* and the fandango. I wasn't sure if I still remembered them. A few times there, as you probably noticed, I was making up my own steps."

He threw back his head, laughing, and she stared with fascination at the strong lines of his throat. His cheekbones were high, his mouth firm, his nose strong and well-shaped, and his eyes.... Now that she was so close she could see that they weren't really amber; tiny gold streaks in his brown irises gave that illusion. His dark hair was rumpled from the dance, and when she found herself wanting to reach out and brush a strand back from his wide forehead, she turned her eyes away and pretended an interest in a line of children who were doing a wild serpentine dance, threading in and out of the crowd.

"We have a friend in common," Laurens said suddenly.

"A friend?"

"His name is Topet, but I understand you call him Argus."

She gaped at him. "Argus is *your* dog?"

"So I believed until a couple of weeks ago. Now I'm not so sure."

"Oh, dear. I knew he must belong to someone but—I hope you don't mind. It's just that—well, he's really such a gentlemanly dog."

He smiled at her choice of words. "He's also a dog who walks alone. He does damned well what he pleases, especially now that he's become a senior citizen. And since he had the good taste to be enchanted by someone like you, how can I object?"

Mayi felt herself blushing at the compliment. "How do you know that I call him Argus?" she said quickly.

"He told me so."

She studied his smile with suspicious eyes. "Uh-huh. How did you know—really?"

"Really? I think I'll keep that a secret."

She shook her head. "I hate secrets."

"Then I'm *sure* I'll keep it a secret. That way you won't be so eager to get rid of me."

The teasing in his voice made her smile, and his own face sobered. He looked at her so strangely that she asked, "What is it?"

"Did anyone ever tell you what happens to your face when you smile?"

"No," she said.

"Well, they must be blind in the United States. That *is* where you're from, isn't it?"

"Yes. I was born in Idaho."

"So my housekeeper tells me. She was very impressed that you knew some real cowboys. How many times since you came to Zubilibia have you been asked if you knew a distant nephew or cousin who immigrated to America?"

"Often. Unfortunately I can't help them, because I wasn't really a part of the Basque community. After my grandmother died I was raised in foster homes."

"You had no other relatives to take you in?"

"My grandmother had broken off with her family when she left for America to marry a man they didn't approve of. He died in a ranch accident before I was born. My mother was their only child. I don't remember her. She was killed in a hotel fire when I was three."

"And yet I am told that you speak our language like a native."

Mayi started to tell him about the Basque Studies Program and about Pio, who had helped her perfect the Navarra dialect, but the subject was still too painful, so instead she said, "My grandmother spoke only Basque and a little Spanish. We lived in the boarding house where she worked as a cook, so I heard very little English spoken until I started school. Since my grandmother was from a border village in the Roncal Valley, that's the dialect I learned. After I went to live in foster homes I—

well, I refused to allow myself to forget her language. Later on I took a few Basque language courses. It was my way of holding on to her memory.''

Laurens was so silent that she wondered what he was thinking. Was he wondering what had happened to her father, and why none of his people had stepped forward when she was orphaned? She met his eyes and knew that she didn't have to explain, that he had sensed what lay beneath her dry, brief words. How strange, she thought, to meet someone, a stranger, and immediately feel as if she had known him all her life.

''Come,'' he said, rising and holding out his hand. ''They're playing a fandango.''

Willingly she put her hand in his. The strength of his hand started a tingle in her own, warming her. As he led her back to the dance area, she found it difficult to breathe normally. He whirled her into the dance, and as the music rose around them, the insistent beat of the drums seemed to vibrate through her bones, making her part of the music. She forgot everything else except the pressure of Laurens's hand on her waist and the intensity of his gaze, which never left her face. She felt a pure physical pleasure following his lead through the graceful steps of the fandango.

Afterward, when they had danced several more times, oblivious to the other dancers or the spectators, they returned to the café for glasses of red wine. As they sipped the sweet cool liquid, they looked at each other, saying little, and Mayi was sure the image of Laurens's eyes would never leave her, no matter how long she lived.

When she finally remembered the Bilbaos they returned to the dance and discovered that the elderly couple had left for home. Laurens, sounding very formal now, asked if he could escort her back to the pension before he went to find his sister. When she nodded, excitement rising in her throat, he took her hand and she went off with him without a thought for the oblique looks and the whispers that followed them.

They were silent as they walked along the quiet road. When they reached the Bilbaos' house, Laurens took her in his arms, just as if he had been doing so for years. Mayi felt a wild turmoil in her chest and realized it was her heart, beating in unison with his. His touch was so gentle that she felt no embarrassment as he smoothed back her wind-ruffled hair, doing the very thing she had been wanting to do to him all evening. His hand dropped to her shoulder and then to the small of her back, and every place he touched felt sensitized, as if his hand had the power to set her skin to tingling.

"Lovely Mayi," he murmured against her ear.

His lips brushed hers, tentatively at first, as if he was afraid she might rebuff him, but when she didn't pull away, the kiss deepened. His mouth was firm and surprisingly warm, and as the pressure increased, her lips opened so willingly under his that a small tinge of danger brushed her mind.

But the excitement building inside her was too strong to be denied, and she slid her arms around his neck, locking her fingers together, wanting to feel his hard body against her softer one, wanting the kiss to go on forever.

He groaned as if he was in pain, and then his arms tightened around her, pulling her so close that she felt the hardening of his body and knew that he was aroused. Her pulse throbbed painfully, and she felt as if only his touch could quench the flame that had sprung to life inside her. But the hunger that surged through her as his tongue took possession of her mouth was so strong that it frightened her, and her body stiffened in his arms.

He pulled away immediately, and in the faint light she saw that there were beads of sweat on his forehead and a taut line around his mouth. He ran his hand over his hair, looking so troubled that she wanted to comfort him and assure him that she wasn't offended. Only her inexperience kept her silent, and when he bent his head again, this time for a chaste kiss that left her dissatisfied and wanting more, she was sure that her lack of experience and gaucheness had disappointed him.

It came as a complete surprise when he asked her, his voice formal again, if she would have dinner with his family the next evening.

"I want you to meet my aunt and sister," he said.

CHAPTER SIX

LAURENS WOULDN'T ALLOW himself to think of consequences or of any of the things that had seemed so important during the days when he had forced himself to stay away from Mayi. After he left Mayi at the Bilbaos' pension, he drove his Mercedes toward the villa with his sister by his side, and all that mattered was the incredibly strong sense of well-being he'd felt at the sight, the touch of Mayi Jenners. After all, there were no real obstacles between them. She had no close ties, no relatives to make her want to return to her own country, and she was Basque. More important than all the rest, it was obvious that she loved being in this small corner of the world.

God, I want her to stay, to marry me, have my children and live with me for the rest of my life.

A small cynical part of his mind intruded, telling him that he was moving too fast and that he still had no idea what she felt for him. Yes, she had responded to his kiss with a passion that had almost made him lose control, but what if that was simply the novelty of being among strangers, the excitement of dancing the fandango and the *jota*—the newness of it all?

One thing he couldn't be mistaken about. Her response hadn't been triggered by experience. There was an innocence about her, a shyness in the way her eyes had widened when he'd kissed her, as if she was experiencing an emotion totally new to her. Then she had lost her inhibitions and her shyness, and her mouth, so incredibly soft, had moved under his, and she'd pressed her warm, supple body against his, arousing him until he had almost taken her, right there in the Bilbaos' doorway.

Laurens discovered his mouth was dry and his hands had tightened on the wheel. To change the direction of his thoughts he spoke quickly to his sister, realizing that she had been unusually quiet. "Did you enjoy yourself tonight, Engrace?"

She took so long answering that for a moment he thought she hadn't heard. "Yes, I enjoyed myself." Her face was turned toward the window, and her words had a muffled sound.

"I'm afraid I wasn't much of a chaperon," he said teasingly. "Maybe we'd better not tell Tia Petra how little we saw of each other this evening. Well, festivals are for enjoyment and letting go. You probably enjoyed a little freedom from Tia Petra's rigid supervision. After all, you are almost a woman now."

"I *am* a woman," she said, so sharply that he gave her a surprised glance. "*You* certainly seemed to be having fun. I saw you dancing with that American girl. Do you find her interesting?"

Interesting? What a strange word to describe what he felt for Mayi. "I find her enchanting," he said, surprising himself. "Which is why I invited her for dinner tomorrow night."

"Tomorrow night? But the Carreras are coming tomorrow night."

"I'm aware of that. Since when haven't our *lehen aizoa* dined with us on the third Friday of the month?" he said lightly. As the neighbors closest to the villa, the Carreras were the Pelentes' *lehen aizoa*, their "first neighbors." In the old days the first neighbors were closer than those with blood ties and were consulted on major decisions during times of trouble. Although some of the old customs were dying out, the first-neighbor relationship still remained, taking the form of a monthly exchange of dinners between the Carreras and the Pelentes. To invite Mayi, an outsider, on this day was tantamount to declaring the seriousness of his intentions toward her.

"They will be just as impressed with Mayi as I am, and as you will be when you meet her. She's part Basque. Her grandparents came from the Roncal valley."

"Then we'll make her feel welcome," Engrace said listlessly.

He glanced at her curiously. She seemed depressed, not at all the way she usually was after a dance. "Did you dance often tonight?"

"As often as I liked," she said shortly, the tone of her voice telling him that she wanted to end the conversation.

Laurens shrugged mentally. For all her gentleness, Engrace had a strong stubborn streak, and an even stronger sense of privacy. If something had happened tonight to upset her, she would tell him in her own good time, or not at all. Either way, he would respect her need for privacy. It was not his place or his habit to pry, not unless it involved family honor.

As Laurens prepared for bed that night he had so many things to think about that he knew he would have a hard time sleeping. Images of Mayi haunted him—the curve of her wrist when she pushed her heavy hair back from her face; the supple feel of her skin under his hands; the radiant smile that came so unexpectedly to her usually grave face. He wanted to bury his face in that marvelous hair, to feel her lips giving under the pressure of his mouth, to touch the soft swell of her breasts. . . .

He realized what he was doing to himself and swore out loud. Tossing back the covers, he got up, put on his robe and left the villa for a walk in the moonlight. When he heard a padding sound behind him, he knew that Topet had left his doghouse to join him. At one time the golden retriever would have made a dozen side trips into the dark, tracing down enticing odors and sounds that no mere human could detect. It was a sign of his age that he seemed content tonight to stay close to Laurens's heels.

Later, as Laurens leaned against the stone wall that bordered the estate and stared down into the valley, he thought of some of the problems that beset the village—and beset him, since he had inherited the responsibility of helping to make decisions for the general welfare of the Valle de la Añara. So many problems, such as how much to encourage tourist trade in the village, and so few sure answers. If the village actively courted tourism—and the villagers were equally divided on the issue—then a better road and reliable transportation were a must. Since the township couldn't possibly afford this kind of expense, it would mean a compromise with the provincial government.

As recently as the past month there had been inquiries about the possibility of building a new dam to supply water to the farmlands of other valleys in the area. If the township didn't present any obstacles and the dam was built in return for the government building a decent road into the valley, they would have to face other considerations. How would the dam affect fishing in the Rio de la Añara and other streams, and how much would the water reservoir encroach upon precious farmland?

Then there was the Valle de la Añara Co-op, the source of so much dissent in the village. The bookkeeping alone was a headache, and Laurens always seemed to be in the middle of the infighting between the two different factions. One group wanted things to continue as they were, the other was eager to expand and employ modern production and marketing methods to what was, at present, a cottage industry. He also had his own private concerns, one of them the marketing of the Rioja wine that the Pelente Winery was noted for. Worldwide competition was increasing from countries that had never before produced their own wines, a situation he couldn't ignore.

There were so many problems to consider, yet all he could think of was Mayi, and the things about her that enchanted him. There was the impact of her smile, and the way she played with a strand of hair when she was lost in thought, and the grace of her body when she was dancing. How he had wanted to crush her against him, to lift her in his arms and carry her away into the darkness and make love to her in some secluded place.

Was it possible that Mayi felt the same way about him so quickly? With her in his life he knew the sadness of the past months would change. God knew he didn't want to forget his brother or the tragic circumstances of Pio's death. His brother had loved too unwisely, so unwisely in fact that after he'd been betrayed, he had lost his zest for life.

Had Pio committed suicide? The question haunted him, haunted the whole family. Whatever the truth, and eventually he hoped to ferret it out, the woman Pio had called ''my lady'' had been the cause of Pio's deeply depressive state at the time of his death. Unfortunately—or maybe not so unfortunately, Laurens thought grimly—the woman was beyond the reach of his justice. She lived six thousand miles from Navarra, and he didn't even know her name.

Pio had always kept his personal life a secret. The wall between them, created by the eight years' difference in their ages and their different natures, had never been breached, not even in Pio's final letter, the one Laurens had been so careful not to show Engrace or his aunt. But Pio's agony of spirit had been apparent in his words, those strange wild words about the woman he loved. He couldn't get her out of his mind, even though she'd betrayed him and had turned out to be not the angel he had believed but a devil in woman's form. She had destroyed him, either by malice or through callousness, and his death, whether an accident or suicide, could be laid at her door.

Laurens shook his head to clear his thoughts. No matter how hard he tried to find answers to questions surrounding Pio's death, it couldn't bring back the brother he'd loved. But maybe he should take warning himself from what had happened. He had always been so practical and careful in his emotions, but he had been just as hasty as Pio to fall in love. He had allowed an achingly lovely girl to invade the deepest reaches of his heart, and yet the only intimacy between them so far had been one kiss.

Well, tomorrow evening Mayi would be in the midst of his family and also with the Carreras. Laurens gave a rather sour smile. His first neighbors would not be happy about her presence. But he would have the chance to see Mayi under different circumstances, in a much less romantic light, and maybe he would find out then that it had all been some kind of illusion, the result of an admittedly romantic first encounter.

ALL MORNING Mayi had hugged her secret to her chest, not even wanting to share it with the Bilbaos. Although they had said nothing about the way Laurens had monopolized her at the festival the evening before, she sensed a change in their attitude toward her, a return of their initial formality. Perhaps she had been too bold, walking and dancing with Laurens to the exclusion of others. She hoped they weren't offended that she'd allowed Laurens to walk her home, but the temptation had been too great for her to resist. Her lips still burned when she thought of his kiss. Had it meant something special to him, or was it just the normal interest of a man toward a new girl in town?

She thought of the evening ahead and discovered that she was apprehensive. Tonight she would be meeting Laurens's family. She wondered what they would be like. Would they accept her or snub her? She was sure they would be very curious about her. What if they treated her with the cold Basque reserve that could be so devastating to an outsider?

And what kind of people would they be? She already knew that Laurens came from a farming family, because he'd mentioned sheep, so he must live on one of the farms scattered in the valley. He had been away to school, though, and had had an American roommate who spoke Spanish with such an atrocious accent that Laurens had learned to speak English in self-defense. The story had amused her, as he'd intended, but it also pointed out that he was not a simple farmer. He had talked knowingly about places such as Paris and London and Rome, saying he went there often on business trips, and though he seemed to be well-thought-of by the men of the village, she'd sensed that he wasn't really one of them. Was that because of his skill as a pelota player, or because of his wider experience in the world outside the valley?

Well, her questions would be answered soon, she thought as she slipped out of the house. As soon as she returned from her morning run in the meadow, she'd have to tell the Bilbaos that she wouldn't be having dinner with them tonight. When she reached the meadow, Argus—no, she must remember to call him Topet now—was waiting for her. Although the retriever was never exuberant in his greeting, his plumed tail waved in a rhythm of welcome when he saw her, and after they'd had their run, he rested his head on her outstretched legs while she sat dreaming in the sun on the rock at the foot of the hill.

"I'll see your master again tonight," she told the old dog, speaking her fears aloud. "But what if his family doesn't like me—or if Laurens is sorry he asked me for dinner?"

At the sound of Laurens's name, Topet lifted

his head and fixed his eyes on her face. There was a glaze over his eyes, like a silver veil. Were those cataracts—was the old dog going blind? But the thought was too hurtful, and she put it out of her mind. She didn't want to think of anything sad to-day; she only wanted to think of Laurens, of the whiteness of his teeth against his dark skin when he smiled, of the luminescence of his eyes, of the warmth of his lips when he'd kissed her.

When she returned from her walk, she told the Bilbaos that she would be having dinner with the Pelente family that evening, and from their un-concealed surprise, she knew they found it hard to believe. Was it all that rare to dine with the Pe-lentes at their farmhouse? Were they inhospitable people, or was it something else? She had once read that meals were usually family affairs among the Basques, that they guarded the sanctity of their home to the extent that sometimes lifelong friends had never eaten at each other's tables.

That evening Mayi dressed carefully in her one really expensive dress, the one she'd worn on the few occasions that she went out to dinner. Some impulse, perhaps the hope that just such an occa-sion would arise, had made her pack it along with her skirts and jeans. It was a deceptively simple dress of crepe de chine; the silky material touched her curves lightly but was far more suggestive than a tighter fit would have been, and the mist-green color brought out the vividness of her hair. She had to settle for her sole pair of high-heeled pumps, which were black, and the few inches of height they added gave her a bit more confidence.

She brushed her hair until it fell in deep waves to her shoulders, then pinned the front strands back from her face with a tortoiseshell comb that she'd treated herself to in Madrid. She applied makeup sparingly, as always, but the deep pink of her lip gloss emphasized the slight golden tan her mornings in the sun had given her, and her eyes seemed very bright, as if, she thought, she really did have stars in her eyes. As she whirled in front of the mirror, giving herself a final inspection, she smiled with satisfaction.

Laurens arrived on time—to the minute. She had to smother a laugh as she acknowledged his formalized compliments, knowing from the twinkle in his eye that they were for her hosts' benefit. For a few minutes he exchanged polite conversation with the Bilbaos, who treated him with surprising deference, before he finally escorted Mayi to a small sports car, a dark-maroon Maserati.

As he handed her in, she was aware that they had an audience, though not an overt one. One neighbor was scything a nonexistent patch of weeds in the corner of his lawn, while another was busily cultivating a bed of autumn-weary mums, already going to seed, and two women, both appearing to ignore the car, were talking together near the fence that separated their yards. Mayi, who had had little experience with small-town nosiness, felt a moment's annoyance, until she reminded herself that in a town as isolated as Zubilibia, even an event as small as a man taking a young woman home for dinner must be of interest.

"Do you have the feeling of being in a fishbowl?" Laurens said, and she knew he'd been reading her mind again.

"Yes," she said dryly, "and I'm sure I'm receiving a few glares from the younger women of the neighborhood and their matchmaking mothers."

He gave her a sidelong grin. "What did they expect? You're the prettiest girl to come to the village in years."

For some reason the compliment chilled her. Was that all she was to him—a pretty girl, a novelty, someone new? She met his eyes and was reassured. His invitation to have dinner with his family didn't stem from any shallow reason. As for his motive in inviting her so soon after they'd first met—well, she would just have to wait to find that out.

Both of them seemed disinclined to talk as Laurens steered the car along a narrow country road that was little more than a lane, heading not toward the valley as she'd expected, but upward, toward the mountains. They passed several farmhouses and a couple of handsome villas, but there were no more houses once the road began a zigzag course up the side of the mountain. On one side of the road, terraced vineyards climbed upward, and she looked in vain for another farmhouse.

"Where is your farm?" she asked finally.

He gave her a puzzled look. "Farm?"

"Didn't you say we were dining with your family?"

He smiled and shook his head. "I see the Bilbaos have been discreet."

"I don't understand."

"No farm." The car rounded a long curve, and he pointed ahead to the large stone villa she'd noticed the day she'd come to Zubilibia. "That's the Pelente house. It's a monstrosity in many ways, but still—what can you do? It's been in the family since the fifteenth century."

"Good Lord," she said in dismay. At his laugh, she flushed scarlet. "I didn't mean to sound— well, it took me by surprise. I thought you were a farmer. You did say something about raising sheep."

"The sheep keep down the grass, which is more practical than mowing. And the vineyards we passed provide grapes for the Pelente Winery, which is a good source of income not only for our family but also for the village."

Mayi looked at him with troubled eyes. "Then your family is—" She broke off, not knowing how to continue.

"If you're asking if we're prosperous, the answer is yes, reasonably so. But I'm afraid the responsibilities outweigh the privileges of being *etcheko jauna* of my house."

Etcheko jauna. So he was head of his family.

"Then your father is dead?"

"Both my parents are." He glanced at her briefly before he returned his attention to the steep, sharply curving road. "We have a lot in common, since both of us are orphans. Luckily I had Tia Petra, my father's sister, as a surrogate mother. You'll meet her shortly. She's a bit of a grande dame but really very warm-hearted underneath. And you'll meet my sister, too. Somehow our paths never crossed last night, or I would have introduced you two. I guess Engrace was too busy having a good time with her friends."

"Engrace.... Is she a dark-haired girl with gray eyes, very pretty?"

"Yes. You've already met my sister?"

"No, I didn't meet her, but I saw her dancing the—"

Her voice faltered as a bit of gossip came back to her. So Laurens's sister was being courted by the son of a family hostile to the Pelentes. Hadn't anyone told Laurens yet that Engrace had permitted Luis Hiribarren to show his intentions of courting her? If not, then it wasn't her place to tell him.

In an effort to change the subject, she said quickly, "Tell me about the villa. It looks even older than the village church."

"It is, but only by a few years. Early fifteenth century, in fact—or at least the original building is. Since it was built, of course, it's been added to several times. My grandfather had indoor plumbing and heating and electricity installed, and we've done a bit more modernizing since then. The founder of the family was Francisco Pelente. He enriched himself at the expense of one of the kings of Castile, then retired to a place where he would be out of reach of the king's revenge—or so the story goes. After that, the village grew up in the valley, and since the villa has never suffered any fires or other disasters, it's remained pretty much intact through the years.''

''It must be difficult to keep in repairs,'' she said.

''And expensive. Luckily the winery, started by my grandfather, helped restore the family's solvency.''

''He was the patron of the village, wasn't he?'' she said, remembering more of what Señora Bilbao had told her about the feud between the Pelentes and the Hiribarrens. ''Does that mean you now have the same responsibility?''

He hesitated briefly, then said, ''We still live by many of the old edicts here—and yes, some of the responsibilities are hereditary.''

Mayi was silent as the car followed a long half circle and then pulled up in front of the villa. She wondered, suddenly depressed, if one of the edicts Laurens lived by was the impossibility of getting serious about an outsider, especially one whose parentage was so doubtful.

At close hand the villa was even more intimidating. Its great stone walls rose so high they looked like battlements. The tile roof was of varicolored browns, and narrow iron balconies encased the tall windows. Heavy stone escutcheons made the Romanesque doorway appear rather forbidding, but once Laurens had escorted her through the massive copper-trimmed door, she discovered that the hall inside, for all its grandeur, had an unexpected warmth. From the center hall a divided staircase rose in two long graceful curves to the upper level. The black-and-white mosaic floor, though obviously very old, had a freshly buffed look, and the rugs that covered it were Oriental, so rich with color that they negated the chill of the tiles.

Laurens ushered her into a sitting room, and though she had an impression of old, obviously well cared for furnishings, it was the paintings on the walls that took her breath away.

"That *is* an original Monet, isn't it?" she said, staring at the gilt-framed painting above a white marble fireplace.

"It is. My grandfather was an art collector. He bought most of the paintings in the house. My own interest leans toward books. I'm afraid they're my biggest extravagance."

"Which makes my nephew something rare among Basques," a voice said in a dry tone from the doorway. The speaker was a tall regal-looking woman with a handsome nose that dominated her face, and sharp eyes the color of walnuts. She was dressed in black, but not the rusty black that the older village women wore. In fact, Mayi decided, the woman's dinner gown had Paris written all over it. "We Basques are not noted for our scholarship, Miss—it's Jenners, isn't it?"

"Yes, Señora Pelente. I'm Mayi Jenners. You do have your poets, though. What about Etchahoun of Barcus?"

"Oh, there are exceptions—and since I'm not a señora, having never married, do call me Tia Petra." She seated herself on a curved-backed sofa. "So your Christian name is Mayi. Very unusual for an American."

As she repeated the explanations she'd made so many times since she'd come to Navarra, Mayi was aware that the woman was studying her closely. She seemed so relieved, behind her polite smile, that Mayi wondered if Laurens's aunt had been expecting a cowgirl in a ten-gallon hat.

A few minutes later she met Engrace and decided immediately that she would like to be friends with this dark-haired girl with the shy smile and quiet voice. Señor and Señora Carrera, however, were a different matter. Unyielding and unsmiling, they looked like two mourners at a funeral in their unrelieved black clothes as they sat side by side on a damask-covered sofa, acknowledging Laurens's introduction with stiff nods.

Engrace had joined Mayi on another sofa. She waited until a conversation about the weather, which had been unusually dry, had started, then she leaned closer and said in a low voice, "Don't be offended by the Carreras' formality. They're our *lehen aizoa*, which is like saying they are our traditional best friends. It's the custom to exchange hospitality with them, but—well, they are very formal with everybody, even us.''

Mayi hid her surprise and her sudden elation. To be invited to dine with the Pelentes on the same evening that they entertained their first neighbors was so unusual that she couldn't help feeling optimistic. Or was she reading more into it than was intended? As Arnauld Bilbao had told her, the old ways were changing. Surely the old relationships were changing, too. It was even possible that when Laurens had invited her he'd forgotten there would be other guests. As for why the Carreras were regarding her with such hostility was it because she was an outsider, a foreigner?

The answer came when Engrace offered to show her the house. For a while, as Engrace pointed out paintings of her ancestors, most of them fierce-looking strong-featured men who looked more like pirates than the landowners they'd been, the conversation was polite and impersonal.

The house, which Engrace told her contained more than thirty rooms, most of them unused at present, seemed to go on forever. The bedrooms were furnished with heavy bureaus and beds that seemed to grow out of the highly waxed floors, which were of the same dark wood. Although the house had been modernized by bathrooms and closets, and wooden floors now covered the original stone of the downstairs floors, little had been done to change the nature of the house. Mayi admired the arched doorways, the carved doors, the library and its walls of books and stone fireplace. Obviously pleased by her interest, Engrace showed her the inscription over the fireplace.

"To friends first of all, to the poor when they come, to enemies, for who is without them, to all I am open wide," Mayi translated aloud.

"You speak Basque so well, and Laurens tells us that your Spanish is almost without accent," Engrace said, smiling at her.

"Languages come easy to me, but I can't add two and two without making a mistake," Mayi confessed.

Engrace giggled, her formality slipping. "Neither can I. It's a good thing I don't have to take care of the family finances, that at least one of my—" She broke off, her face sobering.

Mayi waited for her to go on; when she didn't, she said diplomatically, "It must be very exciting to live in this old house, like living with part of history."

Engrace shrugged listlessly. "Sometimes I hate it. Living here, being a Pelente, sets one apart from—from other people. I think I'd prefer to live in one of the farmhouses."

Mayi hesitated, then ventured cautiously, "I saw you last night at the festival. The *aurresku* is a very exciting dance. Too bad only the men dance it."

To her dismay, a wave of red swept Engrace's face. "That was so foolish of Luis! I should have stayed home with Tia Petra last night," she burst out. "Someone is sure to tell Laurens and then he'll be angry and storm around and—and probably have me chaperoned every time I leave the villa."

"Is that why the Carreras seem so—so strained tonight?"

Engrace gave her a startled look. "Oh, no. As I told you, that's their usual manner. Of course—" a dimple showed in her cheek "—they are not too happy that you have been invited."

"Do they have some prejudice against Americans?"

"It isn't that. It's because they hope that Laurens will choose their daughter Chartal for the great honor of becoming a Pelente just as they hope that I will marry their son, Nicky, and become the daughter of *their* house in exchange." Again bitterness tinged her voice.

"I don't understand. Why would the fact that your brother invited me to dinner have anything to do with—with his relationship with Chartal Carrera?"

"Because Laurens never does anything without purpose. Inviting you here tonight was his way of—well, declaring that his interest in you is more than—" She broke off, blushing again.

"I'm sure it was simple courtesy," Mayi said quickly.

"Oh, no—and I do hope it means more than that to you, Mayi. Laurens—well, he is a very strong person and does his duty as most of the Pelentes do, but he is also a man. He has never shown so much interest in a woman before. The Pelente men are very particular about the women they love. There's a legend that they love only once.''

"Surely that can't be true.''

"But it is. And if they love someone who betrays them, it can be very tragic.'' Briefly the sadness was back in her dark eyes. "But this shouldn't give you concern. Surely Laurens has touched your heart, too. How could any woman resist him? For all his faults, he is a man all women would like to win.''

"His faults?'' Mayi said.

"Oh, he is so stubborn—pigheaded is a better word! Once he gets an idea in his head, nothing can change him. And he treats me like a child. You would think I was ten instead of almost nineteen!''

"Just be careful you don't marry someone just like him,'' Mayi said, hiding her amusement.

"Luis is very different. He is—well, he is the only man I've ever wanted. Unfortunately—''

She broke off again, as if afraid that she'd already said too much. Wisely Mayi changed the subject and asked her about the fretted work on a richly carved chest that held a copper bowl filled with nasturtiums. Engrace told her the chest was called a *kutchak* and was very old, and the conversation once more was on impersonal things.

When they finally returned to the drawing room, dinner had just been announced. Mayi looked around with delighted eyes as she and Engrace followed the others into a large formal dining room. The massive table and open-backed chairs were carved in the Spanish style, the wood so dark that it looked more like ebony than the walnut Mayi guessed it to be. The walls of the room were covered with blue wallpaper, delicately patterned, and the buffet, which displayed a collection of antique blue-and-white china, was so large that it took up most of one wall.

Dinner was served by a buxom, rosy-faced young woman who stared at Mayi with open curiosity as she set a tureen of soup in the center of the table.

Mayi had expected excellent food, but the meal exceeded her expectations. The soup was rich with crayfish and vegetables, and the fish course was mountain trout, broiled to a crusty brown and so tender it almost melted on the tongue. The meat was mutton, delicately seasoned with herbs and served with a capsicum-and-tomato sauce. For dessert the cook had provided *mistela de guindas*, cherries preserved in liquor. The wine, Laurens told Mayi, was Rioja, made in their own winery from the Pedro Ximenez grape.

Most of the dinner conversation centered around the winery, which Señor Carrera obviously had some business interest in. Señora Carrera made a point of apologizing stiffly for the absence of their son and daughter, claiming that both had been afflicted with illness at the last moment.

It was later, after the Carreras, still unbendingly formal and disapproving, had left for home, that Laurens took Mayi back to the village. As the night wind whipped through the open window, he asked her solicitously if she was cold.

"My sweater keeps me warm, and anyway, the wind feels good," she said. "I'm afraid the food was so wonderful that I overate."

He laughed. "Oh, you'll work it off tomorrow morning when you run in the meadow with Topet."

She gave him a startled look. "So you've been spying on me," she said, not sure whether to be angry or not.

"Only once—and by accident. I was sitting on the hill above the table rock where you and Topet were resting after a run. I didn't want to startle you, so I stole away quietly when you fell asleep." He was silent for a moment. "You cried when you saw the cradle inside the old burned-out farmhouse. I wanted to come down and comfort you, an impulse that scared me so badly I deliberately stayed away from the meadow after that, even though I knew Topet was going off every morning to have a run with you."

"But you didn't stay away from the festival," she said, her heart pounding. "And you asked me to dance, too."

"You know why, Mayi. My resistance is only so

strong, and this attraction between us is very powerful. It isn't just sexual, although—'' he gave her a lopsided smile ''—I've been losing a lot of sleep lately.''

She was quiet for a long moment. "I haven't been sleeping well, either, not since the pelota match," she said softly.

Laurens's hands tightened on the steering wheel. Abruptly he steered the car into the shadows beneath an oak tree at the side of the road and turned off the engine and the headlights. He got out of the car and came around to open the door on Mayi's side. When he lifted her into his arms and carried her to a mound of soft dried grass in a patch of moonlight, she didn't protest, though something inside her warned her of danger. Suddenly all her defenses, her reasons for not getting involved with this man, her knowledge that it couldn't last because she must eventually return to her own country, deserted her. All that mattered was the pressure of Laurens's arm under her knees and behind her back, and the rapid beat of his heart near her ear.

"I won't get a chance to kiss you good-night properly when we reach the pension," he said huskily. "I have to guard your reputation, you know."

His lips claimed hers, and as the pressure of his mouth deepened, the kiss stirred her, cut off her breathing and accelerated her heartbeat.

She felt the velvet touch of his tongue probing

the soft depths of her mouth, and she welcomed the invasion and returned it in kind. As the kiss went on, her body seemed to catch fire. Her skin tingled as if she'd touched a live electric wire, yet at the same time a deep languor filled her limbs. She wanted desperately for him to do more, to caress her further, and when he finally did, when his lips drifted down to the pulse that throbbed in her throat, she trembled under a surge of desire.

Laurens gave a low laugh; he lowered her to the grass and then knelt beside her. In the moonlight his eyes took on a silver cast as he stared down at her, and his face was so taut that she knew he was fighting a battle with himself. When he gave a groan and reached forward to cup her breasts in his hands, it was with such tenderness that she felt no threat, not even when he buried his face in the hollow between them, inhaling deeply as if he wanted to possess even the fragrance of her body.

"Your scent reminds me of the haunted meadow in April when all the field flowers are in bloom," he said thickly.

His hands moved to the sensitive peaks of her breasts, and as he caressed them, they throbbed with a painful intensity, and she arched her back to give him better access. He pulled her closer, and there was no mistaking his ardor as his hard body pressed into the softness of her thigh. Wanting more, she slid her arms around his neck. Gently he pushed her backward until she lay on the sweet-smelling grass, and as he began a slow searching out of places that she'd never guessed could be so sensitive, it was her turn to moan with pleasure.

As if she was caught in a trance, she allowed him liberties she'd never permitted any other man, and as his slow exploration continued, the excitement built inside her until she was trembling, aching with need.

He must have realized that she wouldn't stop him, because his caresses grew bolder. He unbuttoned the front of her dress and pushed it off her shoulders, then unhooked her bra so he could touch her naked breasts. As his lips enveloped her nipples and his tongue moved against them, a burning sensation, an intermingling of agony and intense, mindless pleasure started in her loins.

Then he was touching the soft flesh of her inner thighs, inflaming her further, and suddenly the world around her, the soft night wind against her exposed skin and the odor of the dried grass beneath her faded, and all that mattered was the pulsating need to be possessed.

He murmured something, a question, but the words he whispered had no meaning. Frantically she tugged at his shirt, wanting to feel his naked flesh against hers.

"My God, Mayi, you're driving me out of my mind," he said, his voice so hoarse it sounded like a stranger's. His hands stroked her with even more intimacy, and as they caressed her and explored the warm, moist secrets of her body, a wave, incredibly sweet and all-encompassing, engulfed her and sent her soaring out of control. The sweetness intensified, ebbed slightly and then built even higher until at last it exploded deep inside her and sent wave after wave of pure delight through her body.

She gasped and lost her breath, and for a moment, she seemed to lose consciousness. When she came back to earth, Laurens was bending over her, and in the moonlight his face looked worried. When she said his name, he let out a deep breath and buried his face in the softness of her throat, his breathing uneven. As she lay there, bewildered and confused, a question came to her. Why hadn't he taken her, satisfied his own desire as he had satisfied hers? She knew from his tortuous breathing and the shudders that shook his body that he must be fighting frustration. Had her easy surrender repulsed him?

He rolled away from her and rose to his feet. She stared up at his strong, masculine body silhouetted against the moonlight. "Why didn't you . . . ?" She was unable to put the question into words.

"Because it wouldn't be fair to you, Mayi," he said. "I only meant to kiss you good-night, but it got out of hand. I had no right to make love to you like that, Mayi, but once it had gone so far I couldn't leave you—unsatisfied. This is so new to you, isn't it? You've never allowed a man to touch you that way before, have you?"

"I've been kissed before, but it was never anything like this," she said. "But it just isn't fair. You must be—" Again she broke off, blushing.

"Let me worry about that."

She stared up at him. In the moonlight his face seemed tight, as if he was holding himself in check only by the greatest effort. "I—if you want to make love to me, I—I won't stop you," she blurted.

"I'm not going to take advantage of you, Mayi," he said quietly. He helped her to her feet, then waited while she buttoned her dress. "And I think I'd better take you home before I forget my noble intentions and ravish you on the spot," he said. "Right now I don't even dare kiss you again."

Mayi laughed at the wryness in his voice. Now that her passion was appeased she felt strange, buoyant and relaxed, yet dissatisfied, too. Some instinct told her that what she'd just experienced was only a small sample of what love between a man and a woman could be. Until tonight she had never known the strength of her own slumbering sexuality, how it could awaken so quickly at a man's touch and soar out of control, sweeping a lifelong abstinence before it.

Was *this* what had warned her off so many times before, the reason why she hadn't indulged in casual affairs, even though she had never condemned others for their own life-styles? Had something, some innate self-knowledge, told her that sex could never be casual for her, and that when the right man came along she would lose all her inhibitions so quickly, so totally, even without any commitments on his part? And Laurens had seemed to know this about her instinctively.

"Did you know that I might lose control like that?" she said slowly.

He smiled at her. "No, or I wouldn't have started anything here tonight. But I did know that cool manner of yours hides a very warm heart. Remember, I heard you talking to my turncoat dog when you didn't know anyone else was around. I found out a lot about you that day."

No, not everything, she thought. *You don't know that I came here to find the family of a man whose death I may be responsible for.*

But her quest seemed very far away now. She pushed it to the back of her mind as they returned to the car. Laurens opened the door for her, then bent and kissed her on the forehead. "Now you know why I was afraid to kiss you good-night at the Bilbaos' front door," he said. "Can you imagine the scandal if I'd pulled you down on their freshly scrubbed cobblestones and made passionate love to you? So it's home to a cold shower for me, my lovely Mayi, and off to your virginal bed for you."

"Right now, I don't feel like a virgin," she said honestly. "I feel very much a woman."

"Oh, that was only a hint of what's to come. Wait until you experience the real thing."

"Will that be soon?" she whispered, her face flaming.

"Soon. Very soon," he promised, and he motioned for her to get into the car, so careful not to touch her that she had to smile.

He didn't speak until they reached the pension,

and at the door he kissed her cheek formally, as if she was a mere acquaintance. But the words he murmured in her ear were so outrageous that she was blushing as he turned to leave.

A few feet away he turned back to ask her, "Would you like to go on a picnic tomorrow?"

"To the meadow?"

"Not this time. There's another place I want to show you. You haven't been into the woods yet, have you?"

"I've been warned so many times how easy it is to get lost there that I've hesitated to do any exploring."

"It can be dangerous if you wander off the paths, but you'll be safe with me. I'll have my housekeeper, Constancio, pack up a lunch, and I'll pick you up at ten o'clock."

Then he was gone, leaving her standing alone in the empty courtyard.

CHAPTER SEVEN

THE MORNING HELD A GOLDEN QUALITY for Mayi as she sat beside Laurens in his small sports car. She knew it was one of those rare days she would remember over and over again in coming years, like the day she'd enrolled at the university and had walked across the campus for the first time, knowing that at last she could turn her back on her years of dependence on others.

Now, suddenly, she was no longer totally free and yet she didn't care. It was enough for the moment to be with Laurens, to meet his smile, to have a whole, lovely day with him ahead of her. And if there was danger there, if she ended up with a broken heart.... Well, she couldn't live in an emotional cocoon forever. Eventually she had to open her locked-up heart to someone.

Suddenly she found herself thinking of Pio and his disappointment when she'd rejected his proposal. There had been an almost desperate look in his eyes. Was it possible that she'd been wrong and he had felt something like this for her? If so, why couldn't she have returned his love? Why had this feeling of excitement, of rightness, come so unexpectedly and unbidden with Laurens, a stranger? If she had to fall in love, why couldn't it have been with Pio? If she had accepted his proposal, maybe it might have changed things, and Pio would still be alive.

As if he sensed some of the turmoil inside her, Laurens turned his head and smiled at her. "Getting hungry?"

She took a deep breath and pushed the image of Pio to the back of her mind. "Not really. Señora Bilbao insisted I have a couple of her wonderful croissants for breakfast."

"Well, it will be a while before we eat."

"And of course you aren't going to tell me where we're going," she said reproachfully. "Even though I told you how I hate mysteries?"

"I am not. And why do you hate mysteries so? They add spice to life."

"You really want to know?"

"I really want to know. I want to know everything about you."

She was silent for a moment. "It might affect your opinion of me," she said finally.

"Nothing could do that, Mayi. Don't you know that?"

Her heart leaped convulsively. "I—I know that," she lied.

"So explain. Why do you hate mysteries?"

"I think it's secrets that I hate. There were so many secrets when I was growing up, things my grandmother would never talk about. The Basque family who owned the boarding house where she worked allowed us to live there so Grammy could be there very early to start breakfast preparations. But we were never really part of their family, although they were kind people. And things were said, little remarks and comments that I'm sure they thought went over my head. I heard them the way a child does, not understanding but knowing they had something to do with my father. It was only when I was older that I realized my parents hadn't been married. My father had deserted my mother when he'd found out she was pregnant, and I really had no right to the name on my birth certificate. So you see, both of us lost our mothers young, but my background is quite different from yours.''

"If you thought it could make any difference in the way I feel about you, why did you tell me this?''

"For the very reason that I don't like secrets. They have a way of—of festering and ruining things.''

"Then there'll be no secrets between us. Maybe this is time to tell you that I have a lot of faults— quite a lot, according to my aunt and sister. I can be overbearing when I think I'm right. I want my own way too much—and usually get it. It's even possible that I snore.''

She saw that he was smiling, and in her relief, she laughed. "I believe you, I believe you,'' she said. "Do you want to hear about my faults?''

"No. I want to discover them, one by one, on my own.''

She suddenly found it difficult to breathe. There had been a promise in Laurens's words, a promise that there would be time enough for them to get to know each other's faults. Maybe he was only teasing, but she wouldn't worry about that now. She would enjoy this day, this gift that life had given her, and she wouldn't think of the past or the future, only the present.

She sighed from pure pleasure, and Laurens reached for her hand and held it tightly as the car purred up the zigzagging road to the villa.

Although she knew there were several people on the Pelentes' household staff, no one was in sight when they got out of the car and passed through the villa to the rear wing that housed the kitchen.

She stopped, looking around with pleasure as they came into the kitchen. It was an enormous room, and windows on two sides opened to a wide patio and the thickly wooded mountain that rose directly behind the villa.

Although the appliances were modern, the kitchen still retained more than a flavor of an earlier era, so different from the formality of the rest of the house. A huge fireplace dominated one wall of the room. Its tiles were so white that it was obviously no longer used, but it was open on three sides so that the hearth seemed to be part of the room. The massive mantelpiece was covered with a fringe of white linen embroidered with blue and red threads, and pewter and brass candlesticks and red copper trays held places of honor on the mantel itself. A heavy chain from which pots had once been suspended still hung from the fireplace's tiled wall.

Mayi sniffed appreciatively, staring at the strings of red pepper and wreaths of garlic that filled the kitchen with their aroma. She discovered that she was hungry after all.

Laurens introduced her to his housekeeper, Constancio Arana, a plump middle-aged woman, to her daughter, Maria, the girl who had served dinner the evening before, and then to Manuel, the estate's head gardener and handyman, a sturdy-looking man who stared at Mayi with undisguised curiosity. Constancio, who had the innate dignity of someone who knows her own worth, greeted Mayi with a reserved smile and produced a small knapsack, which Laurens slung over his shoulder.

"I hope you enjoy yourself, Señorita Jenners," she said, and her words seemed sincere.

Laurens was silent as he led the way through the extensive gardens behind the villa. A few minutes later they plunged into a thick growth of chestnut and oak. Delicate ferns had encroached upon the path in many places, and Mayi suspected the route was seldom used. The branches of the trees, full of fall color, were so thick overhead that they filtered out the sun, and the undergrowth was mostly ferns. But in a few sunny places where the trees were younger and not as thick, Laurens had to stop to hold aside the branches of shoulder-high scrub to protect Mayi's face.

She was struck by his protectiveness, and though

she was perfectly capable of fending for herself, she prudently held her tongue.

At one point he stopped to help her over a fallen tree that had collapsed across the path, and the touch of his fingers stirred up memories of the night before. As if he sensed the direction of her thoughts, he bent and kissed her lingeringly. The cool darkness under the trees seemed to catch fire from the brilliance of the fall color overhead and sent a warm glow through her whole body.

It was about half an hour after they'd left the villa that they reached a break in the trees. Mayi stopped at the edge of the clearing, her breath catching as she stared around, and in her delight she clasped her hands in front of her chest.

The clearing was obviously a natural one, created by a crescent-shaped rock formation at the base of a granite cliff that loomed several hundred feet in the air. From the summit of the cliff, a silvery waterfall splashed downward to a crystal-clear pool. On the three remaining sides, trees so tall they must have been ancient formed a natural barrier around the moss-covered rock and kept the forest from overwhelming this serene spot.

A brook, narrow and shining with pebbles, flowed from one end of the pool. In the silence it bubbled and chuckled as it rushed away to be lost in the forest. Because of the stark grandeur of the cliff, it could have been a gloomy place, but tiny ferns, multicolored lichen and other moisture-loving plants had found a home in the crevices of the cliff, and a thick carpet of moss softened the contours of the rocky grotto below.

"It's lovely," Mayi said, her voice catching on the words. "It's like a cathedral."

"There's a legend that the grotto was once the gathering place for the old religion. Even today the woodsmen and shepherds stay away from here, especially at night."

She shook her head. "But this is a happy place," she protested.

"I know, but I'm glad it has a bad reputation. That's probably what has saved it from destruction. It's on Pelente land, and we seldom give permission for outsiders to come here. The environment is too fragile to handle too many intruders."

He dropped the knapsack on the rock and pointed toward another path, barely distinguishable among the ferns at the edge of the clearing. "The family lodge is further along the path, about a five-minute walk from here. I'll show it to you another day."

She turned to look into his eyes. "Are you so sure there'll be another day, Laurens?" she asked.

"There'll be many more days for us," he said simply.

The amount of relief that surged through Mayi alarmed her; again the old caution stirred. She looked away, and then smiled as a tiny squirrel scampered over to sniff at the knapsack, his tail jerking and his bright eyes curious. "It's a good thing for you," she told it, "that Argus isn't with us today, or you wouldn't be so bold."

"Topet," Laurens reminded her. "You're going to give that dog a complex."

"I doubt that. He's much too sensible."

"A true Basque," he said complacently.

She laughed and then began exploring the grotto. When she dipped her fingers in the pool of water at the foot of the waterfall, she was surprised to find that it was warm. It was then she realized that this must be the Grotto de la Añara. *Grotto of the warm waters,* she thought dreamily.

"The waterfall is the snow runoff from the high Pyrenees, but the internal heat of the mountain warms it—something to do with rock slippage inside the mountain, the geologists tell us. Taste it, Mayi."

She cupped a handful of the sparkling water and lifted it to her lips. It had a strong mineral taste, not at all unpleasant.

"The old people of the valley use it for any number of ailments, though I'm afraid the cure is mostly in their heads."

"This is where the Rio de la Añara is born, isn't it?" Mayi asked, suddenly remembering more of what Señor Roche had said about the grotto. "How wonderful to stand at the birthplace of a river!"

"So you're a romantic, are you?" he said.

"Yes, and even romantics get hungry," she said lightly, wondering if he were laughing at her. "The next thing I'd like to explore is that knapsack. If it's anything like the dinner last night, it must be a feast.''

And a feast it was. There was half a loaf of crusty bread, slices of delicately pink ham and spicy sausage, a cheese, which Laurens told her was made from goat's milk, and a small container of red wine. After they had finished off most of the food, Mayi groaned and stretched out on her back on a mossy mound. "I'm stuffed—like a toad.''

"You do look rather like a toad," he agreed, his eyes teasing. "Or maybe a plump snow dove.''

"What does a snow dove look like?''

"They're white with black markings. They spend their summers in the northern countries and migrate south to North Africa in October and November. They fly low through the passes of the Pyrenees. There are many Basque songs about them.'' He hesitated, then added, "Have you ever heard of the towers of death?''

Mayi shivered, suddenly cold. "Yes, I've heard of the Basque practice of netting birds as they fly through the mountain passes. It seems so cruel.''

"Don't judge us so quickly.'' There was a sober look in Laurens's eyes. "Life is very hard in these mountains, Mayi. It's not from any sadistic trait that the Basques trap the birds. They are a source of much-needed protein in the diets of some of our people, and only one bird in many thousands is netted.''

"I'm sure you're right, but it's hard to picture

civilized people taking part in such—such a slaughter.''

''I'm not so sure civilized is the proper way to describe the Basque,'' he said, and his words sounded like a warning to her sensitized ears. ''There are two sides to our nature. There's the dancing, singing people you saw at the festival, but there's also a part of us that is pragmatic and does what must be done. And we don't suffer insults. An insult to our honor is never forgiven. It's a part of us that must be accepted if you want to understand us.''

''Like the feud the Pelentes have with the Hiribarren family?'' she said without thinking.

His face darkened. ''I see that the Bilbaos haven't been so discreet after all.''

''They've never discussed your private business with me. I overheard a conversation at the festival,'' she said quickly.

''And you're wondering if it's true, if there's still bad blood after so long a time? Well, it's true that the Pelentes and the Hiribarrens don't associate with each other. It may seem stupid to you, but we live by our own codes. We have to. These provinces hold a strategic position between France and Spain, and there have been numerous invaders during the centuries, invasions we've managed to survive as a people.'' Some strong emotion deepened his voice as he added, ''The last invaders were the Germans during World War Two. Did you know that they occupied Zubilibia, Mayi?''

When Mayi shook her head he went on, "The German commandant and his senior officers were quartered at our villa, and his junior officers in other villas and manor houses. The troops were quartered in the town hall, the winery and some of the smaller houses in the village. The villagers used their own tactics to defeat them. No one spoke to the Germans. No one would trade with them—not voluntarily. When they went to the marketplace, the farmers covered their stalls and turned their backs, and when they came into the square, the shopkeepers closed and locked their doors. In the end the Germans took what they wanted, leaving the money behind, but no one picked it up. It lay there, untouched, until finally the commandant ordered it to be retrieved and carried away. When the Germans wanted information about the secret passes through the mountains, no one would admit that they knew of such ways. When they tried to force the information out of three of the older shepherds, the men made sure that nothing helpful could be tortured out of them."

"You mean—they killed themselves?"

"We're devout Catholics, Mayi. To commit suicide would be to shut ourselves off from heaven. There were bars on the windows of the room where the shepherds were imprisoned, but they weren't narrow enough to stop a knife, not if the victim stood close against them."

"They allowed themselves to be killed by their own people? But who would do such a terrible thing?"

"Terrible? It was an honorable thing. Each man was killed by his own son or a close relative."

He must have seen her horror, because he added, "It's our way, Mayi. You must accept us as we are, even if you can't understand it."

Mayi stared at him, feeling bewildered and chilled. This man, with his cool eyes, his deadly serious voice, was not the same man who had shown her such tenderness the night before. His face softened and he took her into his arms, kissing her forehead gently.

"You will stay, won't you, Mayi? This could be your home, the place you've been searching for."

"Why do you say that?"

"Because you have the look of someone who has been hurt but who is looking for happiness. I recognize it because I've had my own recent—disappointments. But I don't want to talk about that now. Later on, when it's the proper time, I'll tell you about it. Right now, say that you'll marry me, Mayi, that you'll bear my children and live here with me for the rest of your life."

She clung to him, weak with relief. "I will, I will, I will," she said, her voice trembling.

With an exuberant shout, he lifted her in his arms and whirled her around and around. When he kissed her, it was a deep, possessive kiss, as if he couldn't believe his own good fortune. For a brief moment she wondered what had happened to her own hard-earned independence, and then she forgot everything but the searing quality of his kiss and the erotic movement of his tongue against hers.

They sank down upon the spongy moss, and his kiss moved to her throat and the pulse that throbbed so erratically there. As he touched it with his tongue he moved his hands over her breasts, then laughed softly when her pulse quickened.

"You'll never be able to keep any secrets from me," he teased. "Your pulse is a barometer to how you feel."

"You have your own barometer," she retorted, giddy with happiness. Boldly she ran her hand over his chest and flat stomach, then touched the hardness that revealed all too plainly the effect she was having on him. He groaned and pulled her over on top of him, ravishing her mouth. When he slid his hands under the waistband of her jeans and cupped the soft mounds of her hips, an ache came to life deep inside her. Wanting to be even closer, she fitted her body around his hardness, then gasped at the sensation that swept through her.

He said her name as if it was a talisman, then rolled over, taking her with him. When he raised himself up so he could look down at her, she stared into his eyes, unable to look away. The taut lines around his mouth, as if he was holding himself in check only by sheer willpower, stirred her, and a slow, sweet languor started to fill her limbs.

Slowly he pulled at the knot that tied the ends of her blouse together over her midriff. It parted easily, exposing her breasts to the golden sunlight and to his ardent gaze. "Your breasts are like ivory," he whispered. He touched each nipple with the tip of his tongue. "And they taste like honey warmed by the sun."

With a quick movement, he slid her jeans down over her hips and legs, taking her shoes with them. His gaze moved over her, and when the pupils of his eyes dilated with excitement, she felt a rush of pleasure.

"And this—" he touched the downy triangle between her thighs "—is like a mound of ripe wheat." He bent his head and pressed his face against her, and she was sure that she would die from the rush of voluptuous longing that came to life within her.

Eager to see him as he saw her, without the encumbrance of clothes, she began unbuttoning his shirt, but her hands were trembling so that in the end he had to finish undressing without her help. As he knelt beside her, the sight of his strong, fully aroused body was so beautiful that it brought tears to her eyes.

Laurens saw the tears and misunderstood. "Are you afraid of me, Mayi?" he said. "Don't you know that I'll never hurt you? That's why I won't take you today, although you're driving me out of my mind. God knows, I'm tempted, but I want you to come to me untouched on our wedding night. I've waited all my life for you, and I can wait a little longer."

He smiled then, a wry smile, as if he were laughing at himself. "But not too long. The first banns can be spoken next Sunday, but the wedding will be in a week. If I don't have you soon, I'll really go out of my mind.''

He lowered himself beside her, and his lips came down upon hers. She felt the warmth of his flesh against hers, his hardness against her own softness, and she pressed her body closer, wanting the sweet agony never to end. Laurens gave a convulsive groan. When he kissed her breasts, the intensity of her hunger was so strong that her whole body trembled.

''I know it's dangerous, but I had to see all of you, touch you, feel you against me,'' he said, his voice full of torment. ''If I do any more, I won't be able to stop, and I have to be strong, because this is all so new to you that you don't have any defenses. But I promise that our wedding night will be beautiful, I'll keep you safe, protect you all the days of your life—''

His words should have reassured her, but instead Mayi felt a strange coldness. Living in a cocoon. Wasn't that the way Engrace had described her life as a Pelente? But she wasn't Laurens's sister, to be kept under wraps until she was ready to be turned over to a husband. She had managed her own life since she was seventeen, asking and accepting no help. She had worked in a gambling casino, where it was impossible to remain ignorant of the more sordid side of life, and yet she had come out unscathed.

Didn't Laurens realize any of this? He couldn't believe she was a complete innocent, could he? Of course she hadn't told him anything at all about her later life, only about her childhood. There was so much about her he didn't know—and how little she really knew about this man she had fallen in love with so deeply, so quickly, the man she'd just promised to marry....

Laurens kissed her, a long, lingering kiss that set her pulse racing again, and then he sat up and smiled down at her.

"I think it's time we went back," he said firmly. "There is so much to do to get ready for the wedding. Tia Petra will have all sorts of plans, and I think we should let her have her own way—except about the shortness of our engagement. I hope you agree that we can't wait until the banns are posted three times. This is going to be a very short engagement, but we do have to conform to some of the traditions. Tomorrow we'll go to see Father Ignatius, and then I'll take you and Tia Petra and Engrace to Pamplona so you can shop for whatever women need at such a time. I'm going to give Tia Petra orders to see that you have a whole new wardrobe, since you couldn't have brought much with you in your suitcase."

She started to speak but he shook his hand, stopping her. "Before you start making noises about being able to buy your own clothes, I want you to accept this as my wedding gift, Mayi. From now on, I'm going to take care of all your expenses. After all, you've just made me the happiest man in the world."

"And I'm the happiest woman in the world," she said. "But until we're married—well, I'd like to pay my own way. I've been on my own since I was eighteen. I hope you can understand."

For a moment she thought he would argue with her, but instead he gave her a rueful smile. "My funny American. I have a hunch we're going to learn a lot about each other in the next fifty years."

Fifty years.... She must have smiled again, because his eyes darkened and then he was kissing her again, and suddenly nothing else seemed to matter except the flame that came to life when he touched her.

TEN DAYS LATER, on another sunny autumn day, Mayi was standing in front of an ornately carved mirror in the spacious bedroom she would be sharing with Laurens after they returned to the villa.

As she stared into the mirror, she had a feeling that the woman she saw there was a stranger, someone completely alien to the person who had come to Zubilibia a month earlier. The chatter of the young women around her seemed unreal, too. Most of the women were Engrace's friends, who had come to help her take off her wedding gown. Although she knew that most of the covert glances in her direction held goodwill, she was aware that others were still resentful that she, a stranger from America, had won the heart of the most eligible man in the valley.

A slender girl with a mischievous look in her eyes

hummed a few notes of a song that made the other
girls laugh, including Engrace. Mayi smiled to herself. She recognized the tune and knew the words
that went with it.

> In the month of May, the cuckoo sings
> In the garden of the bride;
> Ten angels have entered
> Into the bride's heart.

Ten angels. . . at the moment she felt as if a hundred angels had entered into her heart. Her own
soaring happiness, the knowledge that this was her
wedding day, that soon she would be alone with
Laurens, were all that really mattered to her now.

The ceremony that had joined Laurens and her in
the sight of God had been solemn and deeply moving. They had knelt before the altar of the ancient
church in view of most of the villagers to take their
vows.

Afterward, as was the custom, she and Laurens
had gone alone to the cemetery where his family
was buried. It seemed so poignant to Mayi that she
and Laurens, both in the bloom of their youth,
should walk among the common graves of his ancestors, knowing that someday they, too, would be
buried there.

Laurens saw the sadness in her eyes and held her
hand tightly. "This isn't a time for sadness, Mayi,"
he said softly. "It's only fitting that on the happiest
day of their lives a bride and groom should pay

homage to their ancestors, those who have gone before and made such happiness possible.'' What should have seemed morbid to Mayi, raised in a different culture, suddenly seemed natural and right.

Life and death, she'd thought as they stood among the discoidal tombs with the Pelente name inscribed across the death stone at the top. *How closely they're connected in the minds of the Basque.*

After they left the cemetery, they returned to the villa for the traditional wedding feast the village expected, a celebration that would last far into the night. There was dancing—the fandango, the *jota*, and more modern dances like the fox-trot and waltz. And the singing. Mayi knew she would never forget the singing at her wedding, especially that of Nicky Carrera, whose voice dominated all others.

Later, after numerous toasts, the feasting began, and the great quantities of food Constancio and her kitchen helpers had been preparing all week were consumed. After another round of toasts, the musicians struck up a lively fandango, and Laurens gave Mayi the signal they'd arranged beforehand. Quietly she had stolen away to the bedroom they would share as man and wife, only to find that her bridesmaids were already there, waiting to help her change her clothes.

Her wedding gown was very old. It had been worn by both Laurens's grandmother and his mother on their wedding days. Fragile and delicate, it would be put away carefully for the next Pelente bride, possibly Engrace, or, if it survived the ravages of time, perhaps Mayi's own daughter would be the next one to stand before the altar and take her marriage vows in it.

Mayi touched the exquisite lace, creamy with age, that fell in graceful folds to her white satin slippers. How beautiful it was, and how natural she looked in it, as if time had slipped a cog and the valley had returned to an earlier age. Was this why Lauren's had restrained their lovemaking? Was he old-fashioned enough to want to make sure that his bride would wear his grandmother's wedding gown with honor?

She smiled dreamily. If she'd had her way, it wouldn't have been a virgin who'd stood beside him at the altar. She had wanted him so badly that she would gladly have come to him any time he'd asked. It was only his own strength that had kept them apart. Briefly she wondered at herself, at her shamelessness, and then felt a second wonder at her own surprise. Hadn't she always known in her deepest heart that if the right man came along she would feel like this? From the first time she'd seen Laurens, so virile and strong on the pelota court, she had wanted him—so badly that at this very moment she was trembling, just thinking of spending her wedding night in his arms.

"Stop daydreaming about Laurens and remove your gown so I can hang it up," Engrace said, her voice amused, and Mayi realized with a start that the two of them were alone. "I chased the others out of here so you could have privacy. I know you're not used to being surrounded by giggling girls. I wouldn't hurry you, but any moment now Tia Petra is going to descend upon us and start barking orders. She thinks it's disgraceful that you and Laurens aren't going on a long wedding trip.''

"We are, but not for a few days," Mayi said, smiling at the dark-haired girl. "We've decided to spend the first part of our honeymoon at the lodge, so we can be completely alone."

"Uh-huh. That sounds like Laurens's idea. Well, I can't blame him. He's lost at least ten pounds since he met you."

She laughed at Mayi's blush. "He's waiting at the bottom of the service stairs to carry you off to the lodge, but I'd be surprised if you made it that far before—" She stopped, and now she was the one who blushed.

"I would, too," Mayi confessed. Impulsively she hugged her sister-in-law. "I didn't know it was possible to be so happy, Engrace! And I'm so pleased that I have a sister now."

Engrace kissed her cheek, looking shy. "I've always wanted one, too. Being the only girl in the family with two—" She broke off, and a shadow passed over her face. "And you'd better get dressed or Laurens will carry you out of here in your slip."

Mayi helped her hang up the wedding gown, then changed quickly into jeans and a coral sweater. Feeling like a conspirator, she crept down the back stairs. Sounds of revelry filtered in from the side terrace, and it was obvious everybody had come prepared to spend the night celebrating, even though the bride and groom were expected to steal away to start their honeymoon.

Right now the older women, gathered in a central place where they could keep a sharp eye on the children and the goings-on of the younger people, were undoubtedly swapping reminiscences of earlier weddings, some of them decades in the past. The younger people would be dancing, and some of the older men, too.

Señor Bilbao, for one, would be whirling the prettiest girl he could find around the terrace flagstones, his feet flashing like swords, his dapper figure as proud and taut as a young man's. Mayi had asked him to give her away, but he had declined in horror, telling her that Señor Carrera, the Pelentes' *lehen aizoa*, must have the honor. But he'd been pleased at the request and had assumed a proprietary air toward Mayi, treating her as if she was his favorite granddaughter. And Señora Bilbao, just as proud, had sat in the front row in a place of honor during the wedding ceremonies, nodding with dignity to all who crowded into the church.

So the wedding had been a success, one that would be talked about for years, if not decades, to come, and soon she and Laurens would begin their married life together. Eager to see the man she'd just promised to love and cherish for the rest of her life, Mayi hurried her step. When she saw Laurens, dressed in jeans and a light jacket, smiling up at her from the bottom of the service stairs, she laughed aloud and ran down the final steps to fling herself into his arms.

He swung her off her feet, then held her tightly against his chest. "Hello, wife," he said.

"Hello, husband."

"If you don't stop looking at me like that, I'm going to lose my head and make love to you right here on the stairs," he said. He carried her through the kitchen, and she clung to him tightly, feeling safe in his arms. No matter what else happened to them, illness or disappointments or even tragedy, this closeness and love and feeling of rightness would never pass.

When they were in sight of the woods behind the villa they began to run, holding hands like two children. As they paused among the trees a few minutes later to catch their breath, Laurens told her he had seen that the lodge was well stocked with food.

"And I pity any jokester who guesses where we've headed and decides to give us a midnight serenade," he said darkly. "I laid all sorts of false trails, even putting our suitcases in the back of the Mercedes and giving it out that we were going to San Sebastián for our honeymoon. I'm sure my friends are busy right now tying shoes and tin cans on the car bumper. As soon as it gets dark, Nicky Carrera is going to drive the car to his house to throw them off the trail."

"Very sneaky. And I thought Basques were such honest and forthright people," she teased.

"Devious and complicated are the words to describe the Basques," he said, looking smug.

As she preceded him up the path, Mayi was aware that Laurens was watching her every movement and she felt a breathlessness that couldn't be explained by the exertion of the walk. During the past few days they had seldom been alone, and then only for a few minutes at a time. But the ache, the wanting hadn't abated, and she'd had a hard time sleeping.

Although Laurens had wanted her to move into the villa, she had decided for propriety's sake to stay on at the pension. After a little argument he had given in and admitted ruefully that perhaps it was a good idea, after all. But there had been nights when she had wished that she hadn't been so sensible and concerned about her reputation. If Laurens's bedroom had been just down the hall, she could have crept into his room and into his bed. Her body had ached with strange urgings, and her thoughts had been filled with images so erotic that she might have been ashamed, except that the images were of Laurens.

When they reached the grotto they stopped to rest. Mayi stretched out on a patch of moss, and because she'd been too excited to sleep much the night before, her eyes were soon heavy. She put her arm over her eyes to shield them from the sun, and the last thing she remembered was thinking how good the warmth felt against her face and throat.

She must have slept for a long time, because when she awoke she felt disoriented for a moment. Laurens was bending over her, tickling her chin with a piece of twig.

"Wake up, sleeping beauty," he said. "Your prince is feeling neglected."

She sat up, hugging her knees and smiling at him. "How long have I been sleeping?"

"For about an hour. I didn't have the heart to awaken you, so I went to the lodge and got some food together."

"Oh, that sounds wonderful! I was too excited to eat anything earlier."

"So I noticed. How about shepherds' fare? Complete with red wine from a *chahakoa*?"

"From a goat-hide wine bag?" she said, intrigued.

"Since I'm going to transform you into a true Basque wife, you may as well start by learning how to drink your wine as the shepherds do."

"Oh, that shouldn't be too difficult," she said airily. "I'm really good at flipping popcorn into my mouth. It's one of my many talents."

"We shall see about that." With a flourish, Laurens produced a small wicker basket. Mayi explored it quickly and discovered cheese, a round loaf of bread and a long sausage in a net holder. They both ate hungrily, and she was sure that nothing had ever tasted quite as good as the shepherds' simple food.

"You like it?"

"I like it," she said, licking a crumb of bread off her lips.

"And I like you." Laurens stroked her hair. "I love your hair, Mayi. It looks as if it could burn my fingers. In fact, I love everything about you. Your straight little nose—" he touched the tip of her nose "—which you must have inherited from your father, because it's so different from the strong noses of our Basque women. I love your eyes." He kissed her eyelids, one by one. "And your breasts." He buried his face in the hollow between them.

Mayi felt a deep stirring in her body, and her skin seemed so sensitive that even the slight breeze against her face felt like tiny fingers caressing her. She wanted Laurens to continue, to touch her more intimately, and when he didn't, she stood up and stretched, knowing what the fabric of her sweater, pulled taught by her gesture, was doing to her breasts.

In the pool of sunlight she began to undress, deliberately prolonging every movement as she exposed her pale body to his ardent gaze. As if mesmerized, Laurens sat motionlessly, watching her, but the flame in his eyes told her that he would wait no longer, that their love would be consummated in this peaceful and beautiful place in the forest.

At last she stood naked before him, glorying in the knowledge that he found her nude body beautiful and exciting. He groaned, as if waking from a trance, and began to undress.

Mayi stopped him. "Let me do it," she said.

Slowly she untied the scarf at his neck, then unbuttoned his shirt. When she slid it over his arms, she was standing so close that she could feel his warm breath on her cheek, and she caught the heady male scent of his body, mingling with the woodsy odors of the forest. More quickly now she finished undressing him, and she knew that he was ready for love. But now that there were no more obstacles between them, she felt a playful desire to prolong the sweet anticipation for a little while longer.

"I'm thirsty," she said, moving out of his reach. "I'd like to have some wine."

"What a tease you are, wife! Very well, you can have your wine—provided you can drink it from the *chahakoa*. But I'm warning you, it's not easy."

She sank down on the moss, hugging her knees. Now that the conversation had returned to something mundane, such as drinking wine, she felt shy about her nudity. Laurens obviously didn't share her embarrassment. As unselfconscious as if he was fully dressed, he got the leather *chahakoa* and held it up at arm's length, demonstrating how to press it just so to direct the stream of red liquid into the mouth.

"That looks easy," she said confidently.

"You think so, do you?"

He handed the small leather-bound bag to her, placed her fingers on the stem and then stepped back. Confidently she lifted the wine container and pushed it gently. She gasped with shock as a thin stream of wine soared past her ear. A few drops splashed over her breasts, her stomach and onto her thighs. Laurens flung himself backward on the moss, roaring with laughter, but she set her chin and tried again, this time managing to get most of the stream of red liquid into her mouth.

"I'll have to take a dip in the pool now," she said ruefully as she laid the goat-hide bag aside.

"I have a better idea," Laurens said, his eyes gleaming. He picked her up, carried her to a large sunny patch of moss. He bent over her then and touched his tongue to the liquid that stained her mouth, licking it off with obvious enjoyment. But what had started out as a joke became something else as his breath quickened and his hands tightened on her shoulders. She felt a sharp thrill, a warmth in her loins when he touched his tongue to the drops of wine on her breasts. He pushed her backward, his hands gentle, and she settled against the cool moss, stretching her arms over her head, a mute invitation for him to go on.

He followed the line of wine down her body, applying his tongue effectively and driving her out of her mind. When his lips and tongue took other liberties, she was sure she would die from the voluptuous ache in her body, and she wanted to pull him down on top of her and open her thighs to him. But she seemed powerless, incapable of movement as gently, relentlessly, he licked the wine from her breasts, her soft stomach and her thighs. Not that she wanted him to stop what he was doing. She wanted the sweet sensations to go on forever, yet at the same time she also wanted to pleasure him, too.

She lifted her head and blindly pushed her face against the hardness of his body, her own lips searching.

"Not yet, Mayi." His voice was so rough that his words were almost incoherent. "I want the first time we make love to be good for you. Lie back and let me make love to you. Later I'll teach you the ways to add to both our pleasure."

She stared into his eyes, and the tiny amber streaks there seemed to glow like molten gold. With a sigh of trust she lay back again, her hands touching his square shoulders.

He caressed her, using his strong hands, his warm moist mouth, his supple, knowing tongue, and just when she was sure that she could no longer bear the waiting, when her body was ready, frantic to receive him, he finally entered her. There was a white-hot moment of pain, and then a rolling wave of delight as they became part of each other, and she knew what he'd meant when he'd told her that their lovemaking until now had been a mere sample of the real thing.

Instinctively she moved in perfect unison with Laurens, welcoming the stroking, throbbing penetration of her body as they consummated their marriage. Without reservation she yielded herself up to Laurens, glorying in her own femininity and in his rampant maleness.

As if the world around them had disappeared, she was conscious only of their union, of something that transcended the physical and added a new dimension to the act of love. There was a sweetness, like molten honey, in her veins and as her body trembled on the brim of the ultimate ecstasy, she gave a keening cry. An explosion deep inside her sent her senses reeling until she lost all concept of time and place. . . .

Later, as they lay exhausted in each other's arms, Laurens stroked the damp hair back from her face and murmured words of love in her ear.

After a while he reached for his jacket, which was lying in a heap nearby. He produced a small velvet-covered box from a pocket. "A present for you—to remind you of our wedding day, should the time ever come when you doubt my love."

She shook her head, denying the possibility of such a time. She opened the box and gave a small cry when she saw a tiny gold bell winking up at her. Exquisitely engraved with her name, it had its own gold chain set with tiny emeralds.

"It's beautiful, but why a bell?" she asked.

"Because every time I look at you, I think of a few lines of poetry that Cyrano de Bergerac wrote for his lady."

"Poem—about a bell? What are they, Laurens?"

" 'Your name is like a golden bell in my heart, and when I think of you, I tremble, and the bell swings and rings,' " he quoted softly.

Her eyes filled with tears. "That's beautiful, Laurens, and I'll always treasure your gift."

"Shake it, Mayi."

She held it near her ear, and when she heard a tiny tinkling sound, so enchanting that it could have been fairy bells ringing, she examined the bell more closely and saw that the clapper was a perfect pearl-shaped emerald. She kissed Laurens and then bent her head so he could put the chain around her neck.

"I have a gift for you, too," she told him. "It's in the suitcase you had your gardener take to the lodge."

"*Our* gardener. Manuel works for you, too, now. And my curiosity just might give me the incentive to dress and go to the lodge. If I stay here one minute longer looking at you, I'm going to make love to you again, and it's getting more than a little chilly."

"I hadn't noticed," she said truthfully.

He laughed and pulled her to her feet. "Which is why you need someone to take care of you," he said fondly.

After they'd dressed, they walked up the path, arm and arm, and again she felt a golden happiness, but this time she knew that it wasn't because of the perfect weather, but a reflection of her own inner contentment.

Ten angels have entered into my heart today, she thought as she looked at Laurens, her husband and her lover.

CHAPTER EIGHT

MAYI AWOKE SLOWLY, becoming aware of her surroundings in degrees—the trilling cry of a bird outside the window, the odor of coffee titillating her
nose, a soft light against her closed eyelids. She
became aware of her body next, and of a delicious
languor in her limbs, a sense of well-being. A flush
warmed her cheeks as memories of the night before
flooded in. After she had given Laurens his gift, a
gold signet ring, he had initiated her to more of the
wonders of lovemaking, evoking a wildness, an
abandon in her that she hadn't known was there.
She had spent the rest of the night in his arms, her
head cradled on his warm shoulder.

During the night she had awakened once and had
tried to edge away, afraid that she might be cutting
off the circulation in his arms. But in his sleep
Laurens had reached out to pull her close again,
and she had fallen asleep with her face buried in the
crisp hair of his chest, feeling safe and wonderfully
happy.

A cheery whistle intruded on her thoughts and
her eyes flew open, only to discover she was alone
in bed. She felt a moment's panic until she realized

that Laurens was already up, and it was his whistle that must have awakened her. The tune was familiar, and she puzzled over it a moment, finally recognizing it as the snow-dove song Nicky Carrera had sung at the festival.

She stretched contentedly, then snuggled back under the warm covers, thinking that in a minute or two she would get up. Her thoughts drifted, and she must have fallen back to sleep. This time it was a warm breath stirring the loose hair on her forehead that awakened her. Even before she opened her eyes, she knew that Laurens was bending over her.

"Time for breakfast, sleepyhead," he said.

"The honeymoon must be over. Already you want your wife out of bed and in the kitchen," she grumbled.

"Breakfast preparations have already been done by your bridegroom—all except the finishing touches. As soon as you get out of bed, I'll take care of that, too."

Mayi gave him a skeptical smile. "Are you telling me that *you* know how to cook?"

"I'm full of surprises, as you'll find out the next fifty years or so."

"I'm sure I will," she said, bemused by the thought of spending fifty years with Laurens.

He bent to kiss her. Her mouth softened under his and her arms crept up around his neck. "Hmm. A little more of that and I'll crawl back in bed with you," he murmured.

"Why don't you?" she said, giving him a sultry look.

He groaned. "You're a wanton woman—and very tempting to a hot-blooded man."

"I'm full of surprises, too. In fact, I surprised myself—" She stopped, embarrassed to admit that she had initiated some of their lovemaking during the night.

"Don't be ashamed of what's natural and good, Mayi." He brushed her hair back from her face. "You're all woman—warm and sensual and loving."

"Then come back to bed," she coaxed.

He kissed her again, this time on her throat, his lips lingering. She was so confident he would join her that when he gave her derriere a playful swat, she yelped indignantly. "Up, woman! And put on jeans and walking shoes because we're going to take a hike after breakfast."

"A hike? Where to?"

"To France. I'm going to show you one of the old ways across the border. It's not much traveled now, but it's still passable and goes through one of the most beautiful passes in the high Pyrenees."

"By the 'old way,' are you talking about a smugglers' trail?"

"Smugglers? We Basques don't smuggle. We just carry on a little trade with our compatriots in France."

"Uh-huh. Is that how the Pelentes built their fortune?"

"Could be. We're a—"

"Practical people. I've heard that before somewhere."

"We're also romantic as hell, too—on occasion."

"I'll drink to that," she said, laughing. "And tell me more about this excursion into France. I didn't realize we were that close to the border."

"Well, it does zigzag back and forth, you know, through these mountains. The path that leads to Basse Navarre starts just behind the lodge in some of the most beautiful virgin forest you'll ever see. Few people except hunters go there these days."

She sat up, intending to ask him more. The covers fell away, revealing her nude body, and Laurens's eyes darkened and took on a hungry look. He touched the pink areolas of her breasts with his fingertips, and then kissed them, one by one. She slipped her hand inside his robe, stroking him, arousing him, and he groaned and sank down into her arms; it was a long time before they finally got around to breakfast.

After she had showered and dressed in jeans and a crocheted top, Mayi sat sipping coffee from a mug, watching Laurens as he moved around the kitchen. The night before she'd been too occupied to notice her surroundings, but now she saw that the lodge's rustic appearance was deceptive. The living room was furnished with several comfortable chairs and a sofa grouped around a stone fireplace, and the kitchen, despite its unfinished plank walls, possessed most of the modern amenities, including a brass-trimmed wood-burning stove and a small propane refrigerator.

She realized that Laurens was whistling again, the same plaintive song as before. "My grandmother used to sing that song when she was working in the boarding-house kitchen. I remembered it when I heard Nicky Carrera singing it at the festival, but I've forgotten most of the words now."

" 'White snow dove, whither are you flying?' " Laurens said softly. " 'All the passes into Spain are full of snow. Tonight you will take refuge in our house.' " He stopped to give her a quizzical smile. "Do you remember the rest of it?"

Mayi thought a moment. "I think it goes: 'I am not afraid of the snow or of the darkness, my beloved. For you I would pass through night and day, through night and day and through deserted forests.' " Her voice faltered, and unexpectedly her eyes filled with tears.

Silently Laurens put his arms around her while she wiped her eyes. She gave him a tremulous smile, and the warm happiness welled up inside her, so deep and strong that she felt a stab of fear. Maybe it was dangerous to be so happy, only how could she help it when the sight of Laurens, his touch, made her heart pound faster?

"I get nervous when you look at me like that," Laurens said. "What if I can't measure up to what you expect of me? I'm only human, you know.

I'm not perfect, and I'm not always kind or patient or fair. But I can promise to love you till the day I die, and I've never said that to another woman."

"That's all I want—for you to love me," she told him.

He gave her another hug, then moved back to the stove to finish cooking breakfast while she set the table with a blue cloth and the blue-and-white dishes she found in a cupboard.

The meal, as promised, was superb. "How did you learn to cook like this?" she said around a mouthful of peppers-and-mushroom omelet.

"From the shepherds. When I was a boy I ran off to the mountains to stay with the shepherds every chance I got. They taught me how to cook. Unfortunately, all I can manage is shepherds' fare." He cocked a hopeful eyebrow at her. "How about you? Any skills along those lines?"

"Oh, I can boil water if I put my mind to it," she lied cheerfully. After all, she had her own secrets. Let him find out in all good time that she loved to cook and was good at it.

He groaned. "How did it happen that this subject never came up before the wedding? I suppose this means that when we stay at the lodge I'll have to do the cooking, or else eat American hamburgers and hot dogs."

Mayi smiled at his rueful words, but something about them troubled her. "There's a lot of things that haven't come up, Laurens. You don't really know much about me, do you?"

"Nor you about me. Luckily we have a whole lifetime to get acquainted."

"A whole lifetime—oh, Laurens, I want so much to spend a whole lifetime with you!"

He reached across the table for her hand. He tucked it in the breast pocket of his knit shirt, telling her that he intended to keep her in his pocket for the rest of her life, and because she liked this playful side of Laurens, she began tickling him, an uneven match that ended up with her begging for mercy and promising him the most outrageous things if he'd only stop tickling her.

Later they packed cheese and bread and fruit in a knapsack and started up the mountain behind the lodge. The leaves of oak and beech trees formed a scarlet-and-yellow canopy overhead, and their feet sank into spongy layers of dry leaves, stirring up the pungent odor of moist earth. As they went deeper into the forest, a feeling that she had entered into an alien world crept over Mayi. The stillness was so complete that even the sound of their footsteps was an intrusion, and unconsciously they lowered their voices when they spoke.

A little later, when the path grew even steeper, Mayi was fervently glad that her job as a keno runner had kept her in good physical shape; even so, she was sure she'd have more than a few aches and pains the next day.

At the top of the first ridge they stopped to rest and look out over the valley below. From this height the village looked like a toy, and the air was so clear that she felt as if she could bend down and touch the tile roof of the church. The barking of a dog drifted up from the valley, and she wondered if it was Topet, lonely for his master and his new mistress.

They ate their lunch under a wide-spreading oak that stood alone at the edge of a growth of beech. Mayi was glad for the rest, but when Laurens asked if she wanted to turn back, she shook her head stubbornly.

A few minutes later they heard the sound of a horn, and Laurens stopped, frowning. "Dammit. I forgot that this was the season for—" He broke off.

"The season for what?"

"Never mind. I think we'd better turn back. No, on second thought, we might as well go on. It's best that you see it and get it over with."

She started to question him, but he was already moving away, and she had to hurry to catch up. As soon as they reached the summit of the next ridge, Laurens stopped her by putting out his arm. Ahead, in a small clearing at the edge of a deep drop-off, was a cabin. It was so ancient that its lichen-covered stone walls seemed to have grown from the roots of the oak trees that surrounded it.

Smoke rose from a blackened hole in the roof, but at first she didn't see any life. Then her eyes adjusted to the sunlight and she saw that several men, dressed in rough clothing, were standing in the deep shadows behind a crude wooden barricade. The barricade was covered with ivy, which had been trained up over the top; one man stood beside a great wooden lever, staring through a narrow eye slit that had been carved into the barricade.

"This is the *palombiere*, the place of doves," Laurens said, his voice low.

The wind gusted, and from the corner of her eyes Mayi caught a shimmer, like a giant cobweb. A series of nets, fine as lace, hung from slender poles, blocking the lower reaches of the mountain pass. She realized what it was then, even before Laurens pointed to a wooden structure perched high in the branches of the largest oak and added, his voice low, "The tower of death."

"Who are those men?" she whispered, trying not to shiver.

"House sharers—each has a house share in the hunt. It's hereditary, handed down through the centuries."

Mayi was silent. She recognized some of the men now—a shopkeeper from the village, two farmers she'd seen at the marketplace, the local postman, who delivered mail twice a week on his rusty bicycle. To her surprise, Señor Carrera, wearing work clothes, was among the men.

The horn sounded again, and when she looked upward she saw a flight of white birds coming through the pass. From the perch in the oak, a long wooden projectile rose, aping the flight of a hawk. The birds veered from their path and dived downward, en masse, toward the ground.

For an instant she heard the throbbing sound of wings drumming the air and caught the wild beauty of the white doves etched against the azure sky, and then the man at the lever was pulling on it frantically and the nets fell, smothering the birds in their web.

Methodically, as if it was as routine as plucking corn from husks, the men walked among the nets, extracting the birds and killing them with quick, economical twisting movements, then tossing them into a pile.

Sickened, Mayi turned away. "I've seen enough—I want to go back to the lodge."

Laurens pulled her against his chest. "You're angry, and you think that killing the snow doves is barbarous." His voice was soft, sympathetic, but she sensed that it was very important to him that she understand and accept what she had just seen. "But you can't escape it by walking away. It's part of what we are. It's been going on for hundreds of years and it's really a humane form of hunting. It isn't done for sport, Mayi, but from a need for food. I hope you can learn to accept it, just as you've already accepted a lot of our customs that are strange to you. Perhaps our ways will seem cruel sometimes, but this is our way. You can't sit in judgment, not if you want to be happy here."

She looked up at him with searching eyes. "And if some of *my* ways are different from yours, will you be understanding, too, Laurens?"

"I'll try to be," he said simply. "I can only promise that I will always try to be, Mayi."

Mayi stood there, frozen into place, watching as the men finished their job, then threw themselves down on the ground to rest. Although she realized that by now they all knew they had an audience no one looked in her direction. One of the hunters, a fresh-faced man not long out of his teens, threw back his head and began to sing, and the others joined in, one by one.

"Snow dove, snow dove,
Tell me if you please
Where are you traveling
Your route so straight, your heart at ease?

"From my country
I departed with the thought of seeing Spain
I flew as far as the Pyrenees
There lost my pleasure
And found pain."

Mayi knew that she'd had enough. Silently she turned and moved down the trail. Although she realized that what she'd seen was no worse than the slaughter of domestic animals for food, she knew it would be a long time before she could watch the snow doves flying overhead without remembering the tower of death and the cruel nets of the Basques.

The words of the song Laurens had been whistling that morning came to her, and suddenly they had a deeper meaning. In the song, the woodsman had offered the snow dove shelter from the cold, and the dove had replied that she was not afraid of the snow or of the darkness, that for love of the woodsman she would pass through night and day, through night and day and through deserted forests.

That song seemed to have a special meaning for her, a bride from a foreign land. Was it telling her that she must accept Laurens's people and his way of life? And if she did, would that guarantee her his lifelong love and devotion?

And what of the other song, the one the hunters had sung? Did it, too, hold significance for her? Would she find pain as well as pleasure in her marriage, in giving her heart to a man who, until just a couple of weeks ago, had been a stranger to her?

When they returned to the lodge, they found that someone had been there in their absence. A freshly baked loaf of bread lay on the scrubbed oak worktable. A note from Constancio told them that there was cold roast and salad in the refrigerator and that she'd taken the opportunity of sending food with Manuel when she'd learned that he would be delivering an important message from Señor Echeberri, the winery manager.

Laurens opened the second note; his jaw tightened as he scanned it quickly.

"Dammit—I have to leave you for a few hours, Mayi. It seems the tax-revenue men have arrived to inspect the winery accounts. Sabino Echeberri could handle it, but someone let it slip that I was at the lodge, so now they're demanding my presence. Well, it won't take long. Do you want to go back to the villa with me or wait for me here?''

''I'll stay here,'' she answered without hesitation. ''I'll unpack my suitcase and maybe take a nap.''

After Laurens had kissed her, a thorough kiss that promised more of the same later, he left, and the lodge seemed very empty. Mayi wondered if it would always be this way. Would Laurens fill her life to the point that when he was away from her, she would feel bereft?

She picked up his robe and held it against her face, inhaling his clean male scent. Sighing, she hung it on a hook in the bathroom, then went to unpack.

Since she'd packed only a minimum of clothes, it didn't take her long to empty the suitcase. As she searched a side pocket, looking for any stray toiletries that she might have missed, she heard the crackle of paper. Smiling, she took out their marriage license, an ornate document that proclaimed their marital intentions. Laurens, his eyes laughing, had put it in her hands after they'd left the registry office in Ochagavia. He'd made a joke about entrusting it to her care because everybody knew that a woman's marriage license was one thing she would guard with her life.

Sure enough, as soon as she'd returned to the

pension, she had put it away carefully in her suitcase, wanting to have it with her on their honeymoon. She opened it now and admired its elaborate
calligraphy. Her eyes fell on Laurens's signature at
the bottom, next to her own. How strange that
she'd never seen his handwriting before. Like him,
it was strong, with bold strokes and no frills. The
loops of his *L* were angular and the *A*—

She blinked hard, sure that her eyes were playing
tricks on her. What on earth was *Pio*'s name doing
on her marriage license? She looked closer, but the
signature was unchanged. *Laurens Sebastian
Aquirre*, it read.

"But Laurens's name is Pelente," she said
aloud.

Feeling weak and dizzy, she sank down on a
small wooden rocker by the window. Was this some
kind of joke? No, it couldn't be. But there *was* a
logical explanation, a strange one linked to Basque
custom.

The village schoolmaster Señor Idiart, had once
told her that Basques were often known locally by
the name of the house they occupied rather than by
their family's legal name. When the daughter of a
family was chosen as *etcheko jauna* and her husband came to live in her house, he assumed the
name of his wife's house, though his legal name—
and that of his children—remained the same. Had
this happened to the Pelente family at some point in
the past? Was Aquirre their legal name?

But surely the people of Zubilibia would have

known this, thought Mayi. They must have recognized the name Aquirre when she mentioned it. But perhaps not.... Suddenly she remembered reading somewhere that a man often didn't find out his legal name until he registered for military service or for a passport.

Not only was it possible, it was probable that this was the explanation. Only what relationship was Pio to the Pelentes? He had said he had an older brother. Was it possible that Laurens was that brother? If so, why hadn't Laurens ever mentioned a younger brother?

Of course the Basques were so obsessed with privacy that they would never discuss such a tragedy with an outsider, especially since the circumstances of Pio's death had been so ambiguous. As Catholics, they would find it doubly painful to talk about. And later, after Laurens had asked her to marry him? Had he been reluctant to bring up a subject so tragic to his bride?

Mayi forced herself to look backward, and she realized that there had been signs. The sadness she'd sometimes seen in Engrace's and Tia Petra's eyes. A remark Engrace had once made about how difficult it was to be the only daughter in a family with two—and then she'd broken the sentence off and changed the subject. There were other things, too, things she hadn't questioned because of her own aversion to prying.

There had been signs of mourning, but she had thought they were for Laurens's father, who had been dead only a few years—things such as Tia Petra's black gowns and the empty chair at the table during family meals. "For the *aintzinekoah*, those who are gone," Laurens had said, and his eyes had shown such pain that she hadn't asked him any questions.

So she had located Pio's family after all, and now there was the problem of explaining to Laurens and his family her real reason for coming to Zubilibia. What would Laurens think when she told him that she had known his brother in Nevada, that Pio had asked her to marry him just two days before his death, and that she had refused? Would he believe that she had deliberately lied to him? She could only hope that he would understand the circumstances, that after she'd met him and fallen in love, her own happiness had been so complete that she hadn't been able to think of death and other sad things?

Mayi finished unpacking and stretched out on the bed for a nap, but her ears strained for the sound of Laurens's whistle as he approached the lodge, and she couldn't sleep. When the sun dipped low into the sky, she rose and went to the kitchen to put together a salad from the fresh vegetables in the cooler. She sliced the roast and the bread Constancio had sent, then set the table. When she had finished she changed into a silky blouse and a long skirt, instinctively choosing the most feminine of the clothes she'd sent ahead to the lodge.

She sat down to wait.

LAURENS FOUND IT ALMOST IMPOSSIBLE to keep his mind on business as he talked to the two revenue men. The controversy was an ongoing one concerning the semiannual advance estimate of winery profits. Although he always kept his records up-to-date, there was a discrepancy in one account that was open to differing interpretation. When the revenue men, both officious men who were filled with their own importance, finally accepted his explanations, he thought it prudent to offer them the hospitality of the villa, and it was late afternoon before they finally left for the village, where they had taken rooms for the night at the Bilbaos' pension.

Although his inclination was to rush back to the lodge immediately, he decided to glance through his mail first, since he hadn't touched it for the past three days. There was the usual assortment of letters; a couple were personal but most of them business. He read them quickly then set them aside, knowing there was nothing that couldn't wait a few days for an answer. The final envelope was large and bulky, and when Laurens saw the return address—Reno, Nevada, U.S.A.—he almost put it aside to be opened later. Only the knowledge that his curiosity might intrude upon his honeymoon made him decide to open it.

A moment later he was staring down at a picture that had fallen out of the envelope, fighting shock and disbelief.

The girl in the snapshot was Mayi. She was smiling into the camera, looking self-assured and at ease. A saucy little hat was perched on her red hair, and the costume she wore was brief, showing her long lovely legs. He guessed the outfit was meant to reflect a Robin Hood theme, but what the hell was Mayi's picture doing in a letter from the Reno detective he'd hired a month ago to look into Pio's death?

His hands were unsteady as he opened the detective's letter. It was detailed and couched in businesslike words, and the color slowly drained from his face as he read it. The detective apologized to Laurens for taking so long to get back to him, and spoke about an illness that had kept him off his feet for a while. Then it went on:

The woman who was involved with your brother worked at a Reno gambling house as a keno runner until a few months ago. Her name is Mayi Jenners and she is twenty-three, unmarried, a recent graduate of the University of Nevada. For what it's worth, she had a reputation for being a dependable worker, well liked by her co-workers—or so I was told when I interviewed her former boss, Earl Jenkins.

Miss Jenners quit work last summer, soon after she collected the insurance your brother left. Although she gave as her reason for quitting the fact that she would be seeking a job as a teacher, I can find no record of her present employment in the Reno area. She gave up her apartment about five weeks ago. Her landlady had the impression that she was going to do some traveling. When I checked with the university, I was told that there'd been some problem when your brother changed the beneficiary on his insurance because Miss Jenners was a non-relative. However, when he stated that she was his fiancée and they would soon be married, the objection was dropped. Originally, the beneficiary was Engrace Pelente, listed as Mr. Aquirre's sister.

As far as I can find out, Mayi Jenners met your brother when she began auditing the Basque language course he was teaching at the university. Although he was popular with his students, he seldom socialized with other faculty members and was considered something of a loner. In fact, Mayi Jenners was the only woman he was known to be involved with. I obtained the woman's photograph from one of her former co-workers, who stated that she was worried about Miss Jenners because she hadn't heard from her in the past few weeks.

As you requested, I am enclosing the police reports of the accident as well as statements from the two highway patrolmen who were the first to arrive on the scene. Although it was listed as an accident, as I told you in my preliminary report, there seems to be some small doubt in the mind of one of the patrolmen, who stated that it "seems funny" to him that the car was traveling at such high speed in the rain, and that the skid marks on the shoulder of the road showed that the car swerved at such a sharp angle that he must have twisted the steering wheel all the way to the right just before he went off the road.

Laurens's hand tightened around the letter, crushing it. He opened his hand and the letter dropped to the floor, but he didn't pick it up. Instead he buried his hands in his face, and the pain of betrayal, the knowledge that he'd been a fool, washed over him. Questions taunted him, shamed him. How had Mayi managed to fool him so totally? Was it her candid manner and openness? She had seemed so genuine. Had he been taken in by his first glimpse of her, running across the meadow with Topet at her heels, her hair flying in the wind, the grace of her body catching at his heart? Or had he been influenced by something as unsubstantial and romantic as an old dog's instant capitulation?

But how could he have guessed that Mayi had been lying almost from the first minute he'd met her? When she'd thrown Pio over and sent him into a depression before his death, had it really been because she'd discovered that the family money was in his older brother's hands? That was what Pio had written in his last letter, and why else had she come to the valley with lies on her lips?

When she'd decided to come here to find herself a wealthy husband, she must have planned it so carefully, every step of the way....

God, what an actress she was! He would have sworn she was inexperienced and had never been touched intimately by a man. She must have laughed when he'd curbed his almost uncontrollable passion the night he'd brought her back to her pension, and when he'd held back on their wedding day in an effort to make their lovemaking a beautiful experience for her, too. And the passion he'd thought was so new to her—had all of it been an act? Was she at the lodge right now, laughing at him, congratulating herself because she'd played him for a fool?

And what about Engrace and Tia Petra and the others she'd fooled? They all doted on Mayi. What would it do to them when they found out that she was a sham? He groaned aloud, wishing there was some way he could spare them disillusionment.

A light knock sounded on the door, and a moment later Engrace came into the library. She was wearing a smart traveling suit in preparation for the trip she and Tia Petra were taking to attend the wedding of a distant relative in Pamplona. Although she was smiling, there was an aloofness in her gray eyes.

As he looked at her, it occurred to Laurens for the first time that his sister was no longer a child. Had she grown up overnight, or had he simply been blind until now? How long before she would want what other women did—a man to love, a home of her own? God, he wanted her to be happy and never suffer the way he was now. He had promised their mother that he would always see to Engrace's happiness, and yet, while he'd been busy trying to straighten out village and family business affairs, she had grown up on him, and he had no idea what was going on behind that quiet manner and reserved smile.

"Tia Petra and I are about to leave, but since you're here, I wanted to say goodbye. The air-service plane will be here any minute now—" She broke off, staring at him, and he realized that the shock he'd had must have left its mark on his face. "Is anything wrong, Laurens?" she asked quickly.

Is something wrong? Oh, yes, little sister, something is very wrong. The woman I love is a scheming little bitch who probably caused the death of Pio, the brother you've always preferred to me. And your older brother, who is so quick to tell you what's best for you, is a gullible fool who was taken in by the oldest bait in the world—sex.

He opened his mouth to say these things aloud, but instead he was silent. God knew he wanted to share his pain with someone, but how could he tell Engrace, of all people, what a fool he'd been? Even before their father's death, he'd had to be the strong one, the mortar that held together the family. How could Engrace—how could *anyone*—respect his judgment once they knew that a scheming woman had made a fool out of him?

Forcing a smile, he said lightly, "The only thing wrong is that I'm getting a little bored with paperwork."

Engrace's face cleared. "So why are you wasting time here when Mayi is waiting for you?"

"Yes, Mayi *is* waiting, isn't she?" he said heavily.

"Then put away those papers and go to her. Oh, Laurens, I'm so happy for you! You waited so long to find someone like Mayi, but it was worth it. There's been too much sadness in this house. It will be different now. Mayi will change things—I know she will."

He managed another smile, and Engrace went off, leaving him sitting there with the ruins of his life around him. After a while he got up, picked up the snapshot and the report and put them in the pocket of his jacket. For a long time he stood there, staring out into the terrace, planning what he must do next. First he would talk to Mayi, and with luck, maybe, just maybe, he could salvage something out of all this after all.

MAYI'S HEART TURNED OVER when she heard Laurens's step on the stone patio outside the lodge. She was on her feet, a welcoming smile on her face when he came through the door, but she didn't run to him immediately as she had intended.

He looked like a stranger. His eyes were like ice, and his lips so rigid they seemed carved from stone.

"What's wrong?" she said quickly, starting toward him.

He gestured for her to stop. "Sit down," he ordered.

She wanted to disobey him and go to him anyway, but the chill in his eyes stopped her. Slowly she returned to her chair. "Has something happened?" she said.

"Oh, yes. Something has happened, all right. Today, I got a letter—from Reno, Nevada."

Her heart plummeted, leaving a sick feeling in the pit of her stomach. "I don't understand," she said carefully.

"Don't you? You have no idea what the letter was about?"

"How could I? Who wrote it, Laurens?"

"A private detective I hired to find out what really happened to my brother."

Mayi knew her face had changed color, but her eyes didn't waver as she met his stony stare. "I didn't realize Pio was your brother until just a little while ago when I came across our marriage license as I was unpacking. I thought your name was Pelente. How could I possibly know that it is Aquirre? I meant to tell you as soon as you returned—"

He stopped her with a gesture so violent that she gasped aloud. Only then did she realize the extent of the anger he was holding in rein.

"No more lies, Mayi! I've found you out and your tricks won't work now. You killed my brother. Oh, not directly, but you're just as guilty as if you had aimed a gun at his head and fired. He loved you—God knows you're an expert at manipulating men!—and after you threw him over he had no reason to go on living. He was a vulnerable, sensitive man—too much so for his own good, it turned out—but you didn't care about that, did you? When you found out he had no money of his own, you dumped him as if he were a piece of garbage, robbed him of his dignity as a man—"

"It wasn't like that. Please listen to me, Laurens! We were never that close. We were only friends."

"Friends? Are you saying he didn't ask you to marry him? That you didn't laugh at him, tell him that he was the last man in the world you'd marry—"

"Yes, he did propose to me, but he knew I didn't love him. And he didn't love me. It wasn't the way you said. I told him I couldn't marry a man I didn't love, and he agreed. You must believe me, Laurens! I swear I'm telling you the truth."

For a long moment he stared at her, and she felt bewildered and confused as she met the contempt in the eyes of the man who had told her just that morning that he would love her forever.

Laurens took another piece of paper from his jacket pocket. "I might believe you, if Pio hadn't written me a letter about you just before he was killed."

Automatically she held her hand out for the letter, but he jerked it away so roughly that for a mo-

ment she thought he meant to hit her. "Don't touch
it!" he snapped.

She felt so hurt she could only stand there, strick-
en and silent, as his relentless voice read Pio's letter
aloud. It was a long letter, and later she could only
remember part of it, but those few sentences were
engraved permanently on her brain.

"It was all a game to her, something to amuse
her. She let me think that she was my lady and
that she returned my love. Then, when I asked
her to marry me, she laughed at me. She told
me that I was a nobody, that I would never
amount to anything, living off the goodwill of
my brother, and that she had no time for no-
bodies. When I asked her how she could let a
man for whom she felt such contempt make
love to her, she said that any reasonably virile
man would do. She was a passionate woman
and she needed sex, but that was all it had
been. The man she married would be someone
who could give her all the material things she'd
missed in life. She might even be faithful to
him, provided he had enough money to make
it worth her while.

"And then she smiled—my lady has such a
lovely smile, Laurens! She looked so beautiful, like a wanton angel, with her beautiful
hair floating around her shoulders and her
eyes so dark. I still want her. I'd give up
everything else—my pride, my life—to have

her back. How can anyone so cruel and uncaring look so innocent? I tell myself that I hate her, but it's a lie, because none of this would matter if only she would give me another chance.

"You told me once that I was too trusting. Now I have to agree, but it's too late, much too late to change."

Laurens's grating voice stopped. He stared at Mayi with red-rimmed eyes, and the condemnation she saw there made her flinch. "It isn't true," she whispered. "That woman isn't me—Pio never called me his lady. It was someone else."

"The detective made a thorough investigation. The only woman Pio was involved with the last months of his life was you."

"Then he must have been out of his mind. None of it happened—not like that. He was my friend, yes, but he never said he loved me. He only proposed because he was worried about me, and maybe because he was lonely. When I told him I couldn't marry a man I didn't love, he didn't argue."

"You don't give up easily, do you? Well, the truth is that you played your little games with Pio, used him to satisfy your sexual needs, and then you dumped him in the cruelest way possible."

"That isn't true!"

"Tell me, Mayi, how did you talk Pio into making you the beneficiary of his insurance?"

"I—I didn't know anything about it until after—" Her voice faltered.

"After he drove his car off the highway? Was that your plan all along? To get him in such a state that he wouldn't care if he lived or died so you could collect his insurance? Well, you succeeded. And then you took your blood money and came here to find yourself a rich husband. You made a fool out of me, but you'll never profit from it. You'll leave here with exactly what you came with and not a penny more."

"I don't want your money. It never mattered to me." At Laurens's derisive laugh, she added, "Nothing else you've said is true, either. I came here hoping to find Pio's family so I could—"

She broke off, unable to go on. How could she tell Laurens that she'd come there in hopes that she could lay to rest her own ghosts by removing any doubts Pio's family might have that his death had been an accident?

"I didn't feel I had a right to his insurance," she said instead. "I wanted to make sure that his family wasn't in need. If I'm guilty of anything, it's of not being sensitive enough to realize how unhappy Pio was. I'm sorry about that. I am so sorry about that."

"Why do you keep on lying?" He bit off the words. "If you came here to find Pio's family, how is it you never mentioned him to me?"

"I did make inquiries before I met you, but everybody told me there were no Aquirres in Zubilibia."

"Why didn't you ask me?"

"Because by then I was convinced I had the wrong village. And after I met you, nothing else seemed important. It wasn't until today, when I saw your signature on our marriage license, that I realized Aquirre was your legal name."

Although the expression on Laurens's face didn't change, she drew some comfort from the fact that at least he was listening to her now and hadn't interrupted.

"I know I'm asking you to take a lot on faith, but how can you doubt that I love you after—after last night?"

"I believe in facts, and the fact is that you've been lying since the moment you came here. You said you came from Idaho—"

"I was born there, but I moved to Nevada later to go to school—"

"—but all the time you were lying so I wouldn't put two and two together and come up with the truth."

"The subject of where I went to school didn't come up. We never spoke much about our pasts because there were so many more important things to talk about. And you never mentioned your brother. Maybe if I'd stayed at the villa before we were married or if we'd had more time alone together, the truth would have come out, but we were so eager to get married that—"

"You don't know what truth is, Mayi. How careful you were not to mention that you'd worked in a gambling house." Laurens took a snapshot from his pocket and tossed it contemptuously in her lap. "This is the real Mayi Jenners, this half-naked tart in her cheap costume. Did Pio ever see you like that, or did you put on an act for him right up to the end?"

As she stared down at the snapshot, Mayi realized how damning it was. In Reno everyone took such costumes for granted. In fact, this one was conservative next to others she'd seen, just as the Robin Hood Club was a family-owned business where the employees were treated with respect.

"Pio knew that I worked as a keno runner," she said quietly. "He came to the club a couple of times to see me. Many of the University of Nevada students work part-time as keno runners and cocktail waitresses and even blackjack dealers. It's considered an acceptable way to work your way through the university. I'm not ashamed of it. I worked very hard—"

"I'll bet you did. The American expression is 'turning tricks,' isn't it?"

Until now Mayi had felt only shock and hurt. But Laurens's words, so contemptuously spoken, triggered off her anger.

"How dare you talk to me like that!" she demanded. "What happened to the faith you told me we must have in each other? This morning you swore that you would love me forever, and now, only a few hours later, you accuse me of being a prostitute! You of all people know that I'd never been intimate with a man before our wedding day—''

"A clever woman knows how to manage such a deception,'' he said in a hard voice. "What an actress you are, or was *all* of it an act? You told Pio that when you wanted sex, any man would do. Is that why you were so convincing when we made love?''

She started to answer him, but again he stopped her with a violent gesture. "This conversation is a waste of time. Since we did consummate our marriage, an annulment is impossible—at least for that reason. Divorce is also out of the question, which means I'll have to make the best of it for now. So I'm giving you two choices, and I want you to think about them very carefully before you make up your mind. You can leave, go back to America, taking with you only what you brought, and eventually an annulment on the grounds of desertion or misrepresentation can be arranged. Or you can stay on and enjoy the comforts of living in the villa.

"But if you do decide to stay, certain things will be expected of you. You'll be civil to my family and guests and take some of the burden of running the household off Tia Petra's hands. And you'll behave like a respectable married woman at all times. There'll be no lovers on the side, no taking off for Paris or Rome on your own, because I'll be watching you closely to make sure you don't fall into your old ways.''

Mayi discovered that she'd taken all she could of his insulting words. The rage, the hurt she'd been suppressing, finally came to a boil. She flew at him and slapped his face with all her strength. His eyes turned deadly cold, and she turned to run, suddenly afraid. But he caught her arm and brought it behind her back, forcing her against the back of a chair.

"It would be so easy to retaliate, but I'm not going to sink to your level." His voice was dangerously soft. "Instead, I'm still going to give you a choice. You can leave tonight, without saying any goodbyes, or you can stay and live by my rules. It's up to you."

As if he couldn't stand being close to her a second longer, he thrust her away so forcefully that she lost her balance and sat down hard on the floor. He stood over her, making no attempt to help her up. The mark of her hand was dark red against his pale face.

"You only have a few minutes to make up your mind. I'll be outside, waiting." His face twisted suddenly. "And one of the rules is that you will stay away from my sister. I don't want her being contaminated by you or learning any of your tricks."

He stalked from the room, and a few seconds later she heard the outside door open and close. Too crushed and humiliated to think straight, she struggled to her feet and then dropped down into the chair behind her. It had all happened so quickly. One minute she had been waiting for Laurens's return, anticipating their evening—no, their whole life—together. And the next—it was all so unfair! To be so sure of Laurens's love, only to have it snatched away in just a few minutes.

Well, she had no real choice. She would leave this place, put it all behind her and return to her old life. But how could she go on living without Laurens, knowing that she would never see him again?

If she went away now, any chance she had of proving that she was the wrong woman or that Pio had been suffering from a delusion would be gone. She was not the woman Pio called "my lady," but how could she convince Laurens of that if she returned to the United States? He had condemned her so quickly, and yet she couldn't really blame him; the proof had been overwhelming. Her only hope of regaining his trust was to stay and prove to him, day by day, that she couldn't be the woman Pio had described. Maybe in time he would learn to trust her again.

Mayi went into the tiny bathroom to smooth down her rumpled hair and renew her lip gloss. She wanted to look her best when she went to tell Laurens that she had decided to stay, to live by his rules—at least for a while.

CHAPTER NINE

FOR THREE MORE DAYS they remained at the lodge, days during which Laurens spent most of his time in the woods, returning only when the sun had dropped behind the trees. They slept in separate bedrooms, and Mayi's mood was one of grief, as if she was in mourning for the brief shining happiness that had been snatched away so cruelly. She wanted to talk to Laurens, to argue with him, but whenever she spoke, he walked away, and in the end there was only silence between them.

On the fourth day they returned to the villa. The decision was Laurens's, not Mayi's, and he didn't discuss it with her beforehand. All he said was, "Pack your things. We're returning to the villa. I'm going to tell the staff that you have a virus, so stay close to your room for a few days. It will save a lot of gossip."

During the days that followed, Mayi was glad she had an excuse to stay in her room. She felt no desire to talk to anyone, and wanted only to hide, like a wounded animal. Although she hated the game of deception her life had become, it was the only way to be near Laurens. She went through the motions of normalcy when Maria or Constancio brought food trays to her room, and when she finally emerged from her isolation, she presented a smiling face to the servants. Engrace and Tia Petra would be harder to fool, and she was glad that after the wedding they'd attended in Pamplona they had gone on their annual religious retreat to a convent near San Sebastián.

Even after she "recovered" from her virus, she still spent most of the mornings in her room, carrying on the pretense of recuperating from an illness. The truth was that she couldn't bear the smiles, the sidelong glances of the servants, knowing how wrong their assumption was that Laurens and she were passionately in love.

When she met Laurens for dinner, not only her heart but her pride took a beating. In front of Maria, who served them their meals in the family dining room, Laurens was unfailingly courteous to her, his mask never slipping. Even so, Mayi learned to stick to safe subjects—the weather, comments about the excellence of the food, which she ate so little of, and news from the village.

But there was no need to pretend when they were alone, which was as seldom as Laurens could manage. By the time Mayi came down to breakfast every morning he had already left for the village or the winery, or to take a walk across the meadows that surrounded the estate. When he returned to the villa he disappeared into the library and dictated innumerable letters and reports concerning the winery, the estate or the village co-op, of which he was chief director, to his part-time secretary, a young farm wife who had learned secretarial skills in Ochagavia before her marriage.

He joined Mayi at dinner, however, and these encounters became increasingly painful, something to be endured until she could finally leave the table and go up to her room. She ached for Laurens to return to her as her lover. Being with him was pure torture when she knew that beneath his polite words he had only contempt for her. Despite her love for him, she was relieved when the meals were over and she could hide herself in the bedroom he refused to share.

The alternate moods of despair and hope, coupled with a growing anger that he had so little faith in her, and the constant yearning for their lost intimacy soon took its toll. She seemed to have perpetual shadows under her eyes, and her skin took on a transparency that made her look fragile. Sometimes, when she glanced up from her plate, she caught Laurens watching her, and from the bleakness in his eyes she was sure that she had lost whatever beauty it was that had attracted him in the first place. Although she had always been a natural optimist and felt an innate confidence in herself, she seemed to have lost these qualities, and she grew to dread his glances, into which she read only distaste.

It was her pride that finally came to her rescue. After a particularly trying lunch during which

Laurens spoke to her only once, and then because she had asked him a direct question, she realized she was being a fool. After all, *he* was the one with so little faith that he had believed circumstantial evidence instead of trusting the woman he claimed to love. If the situation had been reversed and the evidence had been stacked against Laurens, she was sure she would have believed him, or, if that was impossible, she would have forgiven him almost anything. And yet, ever since their confrontation, she had been acting as if she was really guilty of his terrible accusations.

Well, it was going to stop. She would continue to play the game he had drawn up for them, but in the future she refused to act like a criminal—or a doormat.

That evening at dinner she forced herself to smile and to eat the food in front of her, and to her surprise she found that she was hungry. She ignored Laurens's silence and spoke to him warmly, asking him questions he was forced to answer. Her voice gay, just as if they really were lovers, she asked about the progress of the "crush," which was in full swing at the winery, and about the co-op he had helped the villagers set up to sell their crafts. She even offered to help him with clerical work on the days when his secretary was unavailable, adding that despite her self-taught, unorthodox three-finger style, she was an accurate typist.

Although he didn't respond with any great

warmth, Laurens did answer her questions in reasonable detail, and she felt a glow of victory when he forgot himself enough to tell her that he was concerned about Topet, who seemed to grow stiffer every day.

For the rest of the week, as she continued her tactics, she was sure there was a slow erosion in his hostility, but she also knew that she had a long way to go, and she was sorry that Engrace and Tia Petra would be returning to the villa before she'd had more time to penetrate Laurens's shell. Even his anger, she thought, would be better than his cold politeness.

When Engrace and Tia Petra returned, Mayi set out to win over her husband's aunt. Although the older woman's manner toward her was reserved, Tia Petra always greeted her courteously whenever Mayi sought her out in the family sitting room the Pelente women preferred to the larger, more elegant salon. After a few days, during which Tia Petra warmed to her gradually, Mayi offered to take over some of the responsibility of running the household. To her surprise, Tia Petra immediately agreed.

"I would appreciate that, my dear," she said. "I have to confess that sometimes—well, I'm not as young as I used to be. And with the weather so damp...." She looked uncomfortable and quickly changed the subject.

During the next few days Mayi discovered that the task of running a large household was not nearly as difficult as she had expected. To her secret amusement, it was her past jobs as a hotel maid and short-order cook in a fast-food place that prepared her for such things as counting linens and preparing menus.

At one point, while Tia Petra was showing her how to enter household expenses in a ledger book, she noticed the older woman had difficulties handling the pen. Although she said nothing to Tia Petra, she later sought out Engrace, who was reading in the sitting room.

"Does Tia Petra suffer from arthritis?" Mayi asked without preamble.

Engrace looked up from her book. "Oh, I'm sure she doesn't—" She paused, her eyes thoughtful. "You may be right. She's always been skilled at needlepoint, but it's been a long time since I've seen her working at her frame."

"I wonder if she's consulted Dr. Echahoun about it?"

Engrace shook her head. "I doubt it. Like Laurens, Tia Petra hates to admit to any human frailties."

"But everybody has weaknesses," Mayi protested.

"Except the Pelentes. They're expected to be perfect."

Mayi looked at her with sympathy. "It must be difficult, having to live up to other people's expectations all the time," she said impulsively.

"It is. I'm so *im*perfect, you see." She must

have thought her words sounded bitter, because she added quickly, "Please don't misunderstand. I'm not criticizing Tia Petra or Laurens. My aunt was in her forties when the responsibility of raising us was thrust upon her by our mother's death. And Laurens had to grow up so fast that he never really had a childhood. Our father was very seldom here. He preferred the—the bright lights of Madrid to the quiet of Zubilibia. Laurens had to be my father as well as my brother. He can seem so unbending at times, but underneath he is a different man, as you must have discovered by now. Of course, he's never been easy to understand." There seemed to be a question in her voice, and Mayi wondered how much of the tension between them Engrace had sensed.

"I love your brother," Mayi said. "There are a few problems, but I know we will work them out."

"I want you to be happy here, Mayi. I don't want Laurens to end up alone in this big house. He has so much pride. Sometimes I think the worst thing about the Pelentes is their pride. When Pio was killed—" Engrace paused and gave Mayi a quick look. "Do you know about Pio?"

Mayi hesitated, then said, "I know that you lost your younger brother a few months ago."

"So Laurens told you. I wasn't sure he would. I'm glad that he can talk about it now. For a while he wouldn't mention Pio's name. He took Pio's death so hard. For days he sat in his room, staring out the window. Well, I loved Pio, too, and I miss him terribly, but because I know that the last thing he'd want is for us to mourn too long, it's been easier for me. Laurens has such a load of guilt because he was always so demanding of Pio, so sure that he knew what was right for him—and me. Pio rebelled against it finally. He went away to school in Madrid and majored in education instead of taking the viticulture and business courses Laurens wanted him to take. I still don't know how he talked Laurens into letting him spend a year in the United States. Laurens blames himself for giving in, because that's where Pio was killed, you see. I—I planned to make some changes in my life, too, but after what happened to Pio, I just couldn't leave Laurens. But now that he has you, perhaps—''

She stopped herself, and when she didn't go on, Mayi asked, "Perhaps what?"

Engrace's eyes slid away from hers. "Things are different now that you're here," she said evasively.

Mayi didn't ask any more questions, but later, when she was alone, the conversation troubled her. Was it possible that Engrace was planning something, such as an elopement with Luis Hiribarren? But that would destroy Laurens, and it would mean that Engrace could never return to Zubilibia to live. Laurens was the patron of the village; no one would risk offending him by giving Luis a job or by associating with Engrace. And what other life did Engrace—and Luis—know? She had lived in the village all her life, except when she'd gone away to school in Barcelona, and if she eloped, she and Luis would be exiled for the rest of their lives. How long would their love last under those circumstances?

As she often did lately when she was deeply troubled or just feeling lonely, Mayi sought out Topet. She found the old dog sleeping in a patch of sun on the warm stones of the terrace. His tail thumped as she sat down beside him, and he raised his head to stare at her with clouded eyes, which she was sure saw very little these days.

"How are you today, my elderly friend?" she said, scratching the special spot under his chin. He groaned in ecstasy, and she laughed. "I wish you could talk. Maybe you could tell me what to do about Engrace."

Topet laid his head on her knee, gave a deep sigh and went back to sleep. She sat there for a while, her hand on his head, thinking. When her leg fell asleep, she eased the old dog's head off her knee and gave him a final pat. As she got up, her eyes moved upward to the library windows. Laurens was standing there, staring down at her, and her heart leaped as she saw the torment in his face.

He still loves me—or at least he wants me, she thought, and a quivering started inside her.

Since the day of their quarrel they hadn't slept together, and the slumbering desire that Laurens had awakened on their wedding day kept her rest-

less and awake at night. Although she was sure
that the servants must know that Laurens and his
young American wife slept apart, she in the master
bedroom and he in a guest room, no one had
shown their awareness of this state of affairs, including Tia Petra and Engrace.

Maybe they thought she was a restless sleeper
and that Laurens left her bed every night after
they'd made love. Or perhaps it wasn't unusual
for couples of the Pelentes' social class to sleep in
separate beds. Or did they blame her, thinking she
was so cold and unyielding that he'd quickly lost
interest in her? How strange if this were true when
it was just the opposite. Sometimes she felt she
would die if he didn't come to her and make love
to her again. She burned for his kisses, his hard
body....

Suddenly restless, she rose and went into the
house to get her sketch pad and pencils. Although
the afternoons were still unseasonably warm, she
knotted the sleeves of a heavy sweater around her
shoulders, knowing how quickly the wind could
come up in the late afternoon. She was passing the
door of the library when it opened and Laurens
confronted her.

"Where are you going?" he asked brusquely.

"To do some sketching."

"I know that. I want to know where you're going to do your sketching."

Although her temper flared, Mayi held it in
check—something she seemed to be doing an aw-

ful lot of lately, she thought angrily. But it was her suppressed anger that made her want to prick the control he maintained so rigidly. "I'm going to the grotto. I want to sketch the waterfall. I'm thinking of doing a pastel of it."

Laurens's mouth tightened, the only sign that he recognized her defiance. "Stay on the path and don't wander off into the trees. My men have more important things to do than search for someone foolish enough to get lost. And I prefer you don't take Topet with you. It's too damp in there for his old bones."

"I won't harm your dog," she flared.

Laurens's eyes narrowed. "I expect you back in two hours. That should give you time to make your sketch—and to recover your temper."

The unfairness of his remark exacerbated Mayi's anger as she hurried along the path, but when she reached the grotto, its serenity soon calmed her. She breathed in the pungent air, feasting her eyes on the lushness of the ferns and the sparkle of the water, and she wished she could lunge into that pool, so mysteriously warm, and wash away all her problems.

After she'd made her sketches, she stretched out on a moss-covered rock to rest, but the memory of the last time she'd been there, the joy and ecstasy of that day, tormented her, and when she returned to the villa she was feeling depressed and out of sorts.

At dinner that night Tia Petra reminded the

family that the following Friday would be the family's turn to host the monthly exchange of dinners with their first neighbors, the Carreras.

"Perhaps it would be a good idea to invite Father Ignatius, too. It's been a while since we've had him for dinner." She hesitated, looking at Mayi, then added diplomatically, "If this is agreeable to you, my dear."

Mayi knew this was Tia Petra's subtle way of acknowledging Laurens's wife as the new mistress of the house. "I think that's a wonderful idea," she said warmly, ignoring Laurens's frown.

"It's time we did a little more entertaining," Tia Petra said. "Let's see—the schoolmaster and his wife are good company, and since they've traveled in the United States, I'm sure they'd have many things to talk about with you, Mayi. Yes, I think we should invite them, too."

"Are you sure a large dinner party isn't too much trouble, Tia Petra?" Laurens said.

"Nonsense. I'd enjoy it, nephew. This house needs some new life." She turned to Mayi. "Is there anyone you'd like to invite, Mayi?"

Mayi hesitated and almost shook her head, but then she reminded herself that this was, after all, her home too. "I'd love to invite the Bilbaos. They've been very kind to me."

"Of course. That will make—let's see, that makes thirteen. We'll have to add one or two more—not that I'm superstitious, you understand. How about Dr. Echahoun and his wife?"

Mayi felt a warm glow. She had mentioned the Bilbaos impulsively, but they were, for all their warmth and good humor, of a far different class than the Pelentes. And yet Tia Petra hadn't blinked an eye. She caught Laurens's stare, but she ignored him. He was probably putting some dire motive on her choice of guests. Well, let him. She was tired of weighing every word, trying to please him.

"I'll work on the invitations in the morning and send Manuel into the village with them tomorrow afternoon," Tia Petra went on.

"Why don't I write them for you, Tia Petra?" Mayi offered, thinking how painful writing must be for the older woman.

Tia Petra nodded. "That would be very kind of you."

The rest of the meal was spent in planning the dinner party. Even Engrace, usually so silent at meals, joined in, offering to arrange flowers for the event. Only Laurens had nothing to say.

It was later, after Mayi had gone upstairs, that Laurens came to her room.

"What are you up to now?" he said, his voice tight.

"Are you talking about the dinner party? Do you disapprove of mixing classes? If so, you set a bad example by marrying a nobody like me."

"I'm not a snob. The Bilbaos are fine people. But it seems out of character for you to bother with them now that they've served their purpose."

"They were good to me and I want to repay them."

He shrugged. "I doubt that's your real motive, but we'll let it pass. I came here to warn you that I see through your tactics."

"Tactics?"

"Yes. Tia Petra always does the invitations. Are you trying to usurp her place as mistress of this house?"

The hurt was almost more than she could bear, but she faced him down, refusing to allow him to see how his words had wounded her. "Your aunt is suffering from arthritis. I only wanted to spare her the pain of extensive writing."

"There's nothing wrong with my aunt."

"No? When was the last time you saw her working at her needlepoint frame?"

There was a long silence as he stared at her. "Why would she tell you this when she's never mentioned it to me?"

"She didn't tell me, but I noticed how hard it was for her to handle a pen. Perhaps I'm around her more than you," she added, suddenly realizing that part of Laurens's reaction was anger at his own lack of perception. "You've been so busy. Don't blame yourself for not noticing. I'm sure she's been very careful to hide it from you."

"I don't need you to make excuses for me," he said coldly. "If you're right, then more reason not to have an elaborate dinner party."

"I intend to do most of the work, Laurens. Engrace will help, too. I promise that it won't be too hard on Tia Petra. And she's looking forward to having guests in the house again. Didn't you see how happy she was tonight, planning for the dinner party?''

He gave her a long cold look, and then, without another word, he turned and left the room. For a long time she stood staring at the door, wishing she hadn't lost her temper, wishing she'd handled the situation differently....

During the next few days Mayi welcomed the added duties. She left the menu planning for the party in Tia Petra's experienced hands, but she took on the other chores without fanfare. She supervised the two day women who came in from the village to do the heavy cleaning, she made decisions about which of the villa's ample supply of heavy, ornate silver and antique china and crystal and fine table linens to use, and she helped Constancio and Maria plan the marketing, following Tia Petra's menu. All the while she worked, she mentally scanned her wardrobe for just the right gown.

In the end she decided on an ice-blue silk dress that she hadn't worn before, knowing that the color and simple, classic style would create the image she wanted to project. Not that Laurens would notice, she thought, suddenly depressed. Since their last encounter he seldom spoke to her, maintaining only the barest facade of civility in front of his family.

She took her time dressing the evening of the party. She made up her face carefully, emphasizing her high cheekbones with blush, touching her lashes with mascara and outlining her mouth with pink lip gloss. She brushed her hair until it shone with highlights, then swirled it up to the back of her head, where she secured it with a sapphire hair clip that matched her gown.

As she examined herself in the mirror, she felt satisfied that she had chosen wisely. What had Laurens called her once—his American Rose Beauty? Well, tonight her smooth hairstyle and sleek gown made her look very continental. If she was a credit to him as a hostess tonight, would that make any difference?

When she went downstairs she found that the first guests were already arriving. The Carreras greeted her coolly, looking more than ever like two black crows in their somber clothing. But their daughter, Chartal, was a surprise. She was older than Mayi by three or four years, and she looked more French than Basque or Spanish. She was wearing a deep-red gown, and her dark hair was stylishly arranged and her eyes skillfully made up to emphasize their brilliance. When Tia Petra introduced them, Chartal studied Mayi openly, making no secret of her curiosity or her lack of warmth.

Her brother, Nicanor, was a different matter. He greeted Mayi with a friendly smile and told her how sorry he'd been to miss the wedding because of *"le flu."*

"I heard you sing at the festival," Mayi said. "You have a marvelous voice."

He looked pleased. "I love to sing. If things were different—" He gave his parents a sidelong glance, then shrugged.

"Well, you sing better than most professionals," she said.

She caught Laurens's disapproving glance and wondered if he could be jealous of the handsome younger man. The thought intrigued her, until Laurens took her arm and led her out of earshot of their guests on the pretense of asking her a question about the dinner wine.

"Nicky doesn't need that kind of encouragement," he said.

"Why is it wrong to compliment him?"

"Because he has some foolish ideas about becoming a professional singer."

"What's wrong with that?"

"He is *etcheko primu* of his house. If you want to be kind, discourage his unrealistic ambitions."

"The way you discouraged Pio's desire to be a writer?" she said hotly.

For a moment, until his face hardened, she saw pain in his eyes. "You're treading on thin ice," he said. "Be very careful or you'll be sorry."

She was glad that the Bilbaos arrived at that moment. Although they greeted her warmly, she knew at once that they were uncomfortable in the company of the Pelentes and the Carreras. She set out to make the older couple feel welcome and saw to it that they were supplied with glasses of wine and included in the general conversation. She knew she had succeeded when Señora Bilbao became involved in a lively discussion on needlework with Tia Petra, and when Señor Bilbao ventured a joke that made Father Ignatius's double chins shake with laughter.

But she was glad when dinner was finally announced by Maria, who looked pretty in a white blouse and dark skirt. The servants, a little to her surprise, had shown great enthusiasm for the party, and she was aware that the whole village would know within a day or so exactly what was said at the dinner table, since Basque, not English or Spanish, was being spoken. The thought made her wince. There was a price for living in such a tight, closed community, but after so many years of being completely on her own, it was one she was willing to pay.

During the first course Mayi realized that Chartal Carrera was watching her much too closely for good manners. She made a mental check of her appearance and was sure that she didn't lack in that quarter, so why was Chartal staring at her?

"I understand that you're from—Idaho, isn't it?" Chartal said, dropping the words into a lull in the general conversation.

"I was born in the state of Idaho, but I went to school in Reno, Nevada."

Chartal's eyebrows soared. "Reno. Isn't that a notorious gambling town?"

"I wouldn't call it notorious. After all, gambling is legal in Nevada."

"Didn't I hear that you were some kind of show girl?"

Mayi shot a quick glance at Laurens's impassive face. Had he been talking about her to Chartal? How else would the woman know that she'd worked in a casino?

"While I was attending the University of Nevada, I was a keno runner at one of the clubs."

"Really? Isn't that a rather—exotic occupation?"

"Not at all. It's very hard work, but also very respectable. Quite a few of the students at the University of Nevada supplement their income by working at the clubs when they turn twenty-one, some as blackjack dealers or cocktail waitresses or cashiers. Personally I was very grateful for the job. It paid far more than working in a fast food place or as a domestic or clerking, jobs I held before I turned twenty-one."

"Surely your family could have supported you while you went to school."

"My parents are dead. I was orphaned at an early age and raised in foster homes, which is why I am so happy that I have a family now," she said, not looking at Laurens.

"Bravo, my dear." It was Father Ignatius who spoke, his plump face sympathetic. "It must have been very difficult for you, going to school and working, and yet you learned to speak not only

Spanish, but Eskuara, too. You're a remarkable young woman."

"No, just a determined one," Mayi said, smiling. "My ambition was to be a language teacher, but my Basque studies were impractical—or so my student's advisor was always telling me. I had a dream of someday coming to Navarra because my grandmother had talked about it so much, you see. She—when she became ill, her mind seemed to slip back in time, and she sometimes forgot where she was. It was then that she talked about her childhood in Navarra." She stopped, realizing that her voice had thickened. Not wanting to disgrace herself, she looked away from Chartal into Laurens's eyes. For a moment she saw something there, a compassion perhaps, that made her heart skip a beat.

"This is very romantic." The schoolmaster, Señor Idiart, nodded his head vigorously. "You came here to find your grandmother's roots, and now you'll be making Zubilibia your home. You must be proud of your wife, Laurens."

Laurens hesitated briefly before he said, "Mayi has many good qualities."

"Well, I think Señora Pelente is very brave," Nicky Carrera said, his eyes admiring. "To follow her own dreams and do it without help from anybody else—that takes a lot of courage."

"And of course your story does have a happy ending," his sister said smoothly. "How lucky for you that you met the most eligible man in the valley. It almost makes one believe in fairy tales.''

"But I have always believed in fairy tales,'' Mayi said, laughing. "It was my dreams that kept me going so many times when things got rather bleak.''

"Now I understand why you seem so mature for such a young woman.'' Tia Petra turned to Señora Carrera. "It's amazing how quickly Mayi grasped the principles of keeping household accounts. She organized the rotation of household chores, too, something that I'd never thought of doing, so that too much heavy work isn't piled upon Constancio and her helpers at one time.''

"Not so amazing,'' Mayi said dryly. "One of my part-time jobs was hotel maid, and another was keeping books for a gift shop. And working in the chemistry laboratory at the university gave me a healthy respect for organizing regular chores.''

"You worked as a laboratory assistant?'' Engrace asked.

"No, as the lab janitor. I cleaned out the animal cages, too.''

"Oh, dear. You really have lead a varied life so far, haven't you?'' Chartal drawled.

"I've held many jobs, yes.''

"Why on earth didn't you try for scholarships?''

For a moment Mayi hesitated. It seemed the Basque aversion to prying didn't apply to asking questions of an outsider. "For various reasons,'' she said finally.

But Chartal wasn't about to let her off the hook. "What reasons?"

"Because I'd had enough of other people's charity. I preferred to earn my own way."

Tia Petra gave Chartal a long hard look. "I think Mayi must feel like a bug under a microscope with all these questions. Since Maria is waiting to clear the table, why don't we have our brandy in the salon?"

During the next half hour, Mayi noticed a warmth in the Carreras that hadn't been there before. Even Chartal, as if she'd had second thoughts about her own rudeness, came over to tell her that she looked marvelous in her blue dress and to ask her if she'd bought it in Pamplona. Only Laurens stood aloof. As the conversation swirled around him, he responded in monosyllables, and when the guests finally left, he disappeared immediately.

Although obviously tired, Tia Petra declared that she was too keyed up to go to bed without a cup of tea, and Engrace and she started a lively conversation, declaring the dinner party a huge success. They were so busy dissecting it, in fact, that neither of them noticed how quiet Mayi had become.

By the time she went to her room, she felt so depressed that it was all she could do to get ready for bed. She had changed into one of the white silk nightgowns from her trousseau and was brushing her hair at the small poutré table in her dressing room when there was a sound at the door. She turned, startled, to meet Laurens's eyes.

Conscious of the sheerness of her gown, she wanted to reach for a robe to protect herself from his hard, probing stare, but pride prevented her.

"Yes? Did you want something?" she said.

"How cool you are—and how clever. You know just which buttons to push to put them all in your pocket, don't you? Poor little orphan, making her own way so bravely in a cruel world. It was quite an act."

She rose and faced him squarely. "I was myself. That was enough for you once. I've never pretended to be anything else, and I don't intend to pretend in front of your friends. Chartal was obviously goading me with that question about being a show girl, hoping I would lie about my past so she could humiliate me. Well, your little scheme didn't work."

"I have no idea how she found out that you once worked in a gambling casino. I suspect it was a lucky guess, that she was fishing for information."

His words were so startling that she could only stare at him for a few seconds. She nodded slowly. "I'm sorry. Of course you wouldn't tell her. You're too proud to have it known that your wife once worked in a gambling casino. Well, I'm proud, too, but not of my family's history or their name. I'm proud that I worked hard, got an education completely on my own—and what's more, I don't intend to let that education go to waste. Tonight Señor Idiart was feeling me out about helping at the village school, teaching English to the children. I told him that if you had no objections I would accept—without pay, of course.''

Laurens was silent, as if weighing her words. Finally he shrugged. ''Do as you please. I expected you to become bored with the quietness of life here sooner or later.''

''I'm not bored. But I was trained to be a teacher. I want to keep up my skills.''

''How noble. You do that so well, you know.''

Suddenly she was tired of his insults, tired of trying to reach him and not succeeding. ''Get out of here,'' she said, pointing toward the door. ''I don't have to listen to this.''

But Laurens only smiled, a thin, humorless smile. ''Oh, but you do,'' he said softly. ''Have you forgotten that you're my wife, that you're living by my rules? You're a very beautiful woman. In that dress you wore tonight, you looked like a princess. And I have a normal man's drives and needs. I see no good reason why I should abstain from what's rightfully mine.''

When she realized what he meant, a flush flooded her face. She wanted him, but not like this.

She turned away. ''I'm sorry. I'm much too tired. If you haven't anything else to say—''

She felt his hands on her shoulders. Before she could speak he had swung her around and his lips were enveloping hers, silencing her. She started to struggle, but his arms were too strong, and then, with humiliating swiftness, she didn't want to get away. A dizziness, a delirium, swept through her, negating the pain of knowing that to Laurens she was only an available body. She felt his hardness against her soft stomach and knew that he was aroused. Her knees grew so weak that only his arms kept her upright.

He swept her up and carried her to the big bed. As he placed her on a nest of cushions, his face was so close to hers that she could see the tiny lines beside his eyes and the taut white line above his mouth. He kissed her again, this time a long, lingering kiss that sent small waves of pleasure through her body. Without any thought of tomorrow, she clung to him, desperate for more intimacy, and when his hands found her breasts and he began the long slow movements of seduction, the last of her defenses came tumbling down and she was lost in the whirlwind of desire that his touch had evoked.

She had expected that he would be rough and demanding in his lovemaking, but he, too, seemed to have forgotten the distrust between them. His touch tender, he caressed her until she was trembling, until she begged him with her pliant body and her own caresses to take her, and when he did, when he entered her, her surrender was complete.

A wild rushing sounded in her ears, as if a gale had invaded the room, and her whole body felt energized, while at the same time her limbs trembled and the blood in her veins seemed to have turned to molten honey. Wildly she met the demanding thrust of his body with her own frenzied demands, and she knew he felt the same depth of ecstacy because his cry of release echoed through the room at the same moment that hers did.

Only afterward did reality intrude again. As she lay in Laurens's arms, she knew the exact moment when his mind took over from his emotions. His body, still entwined with hers, stiffened, and his arms seemed more like metal restraints than flesh and blood. She knew then that nothing had changed. Now that Laurens's passion had been appeased, his suspicions had returned. Tomorrow everything would be the same and he would treat her with cold politeness again.

But she didn't pull away or leave his arms, and after a while, when he began caressing her again, she responded with the same fervor as before. Even this, she told herself, the bitter taste of tears in the back of her throat, was preferable to facing the long night alone.

AT SOME POINT during the night, Laurens left her bed. When she awoke in the morning and found she was alone, she wasn't surprised. In her heart she had known that he wouldn't spend the whole night with her.

Later, when she went down to breakfast, she ate alone in the sunny solarium the family used as a breakfast room. Engrace and Tia Petra were sleeping in after their late hours, and Constancio, who served Mayi her breakfast, told her cheerfully that the master had eaten earlier and then gone for a morning walk.

Laurens came in as Mayi was having a second cup of coffee. He asked her to come into the library, and after she'd followed him there, he told her, his voice cold, that in the future he wouldn't be "bothering" her again, that they would each go their own way.

"But that doesn't mean you are free to take a lover," he went on, speaking in English as he always did when they were alone. "As long as you remain *etcheko andre*, the mistress of this house, you will conduct yourself as a virtuous wife. The only reason I'm willing to continue with this charade is because Tia Petra and Engrace are so fond of you. If you leave now, it's bound to hurt them. However, I expect you to—restrain your instincts. If that's too hard on you—" his eyes moved over her and she knew he was thinking of the night before "—then you are free to leave."

It was all Mayi could do not to scream at him, to tell him that his memory was selective. Had he forgotten that it was *he* who had come to her bedroom, who had been the seducer, who had kissed her until she was helpless in his arms?

"Very well," she said evenly. "I'm very fond of your aunt and sister, and I'll stay for their sake. But I'm tired of being treated as if I have the plague. In front of other people I expect you to act as if you had human blood in your veins. No more cold looks or slighting remarks. When we're alone—

well, that's up to you. But as your wife I demand respect. Under those conditions I'll stay.''

For a moment she thought he would tell her to pack her things and get out, but he nodded indifferently, turned on his heel and left the room. It was only after she was sure that he wouldn't be back that she finally allowed herself to cry.

CHAPTER TEN

IT WAS TWO DAYS AFTER THE DINNER PARTY that Mayi came upon Engrace and Luis in the grotto.

She had awakened that morning for the fourth day in a row with a raging headache and nausea, brought on, she was sure, by the constant pressure of living in a fishbowl. In this case it was the aftermath of lying awake most of the night, living over and over her latest encounter with Laurens and its disastrous and humiliating ending.

When she finally got up she took two aspirin tablets, but they seemed to upset her stomach even more. She dressed and went downstairs, and since she was too late to have breakfast with the family, she had Constancio fix her toast and coffee, which she only played with. Later she returned to her room, took off her clothing and slid into the freshly made-up bed, intending to close her eyes for a while and rest. But she fell asleep instead and slept for more than two hours.

This time when she awoke, the headache and nausea were gone, but not her depression. That seemed a permanent part of her these days. As she lay there, staring up at the ceiling, she seriously considered giving up and leaving Zubilibia, putting her marriage behind her.

How much more can I take? she asked herself. *How can I go on seeing Laurens every day, knowing that he will never love me again.*

When her thoughts grew too disturbing, she got up and dressed in jeans and a warm sweater and went downstairs. Since she was still not in the mood for conversation, she was glad that Engrace was in town shopping and that Tia Petra was resting in her room. Laurens, too, had disappeared, for which she was thankful. She had no desire to face him.

Although she wasn't interested in sketching, she decided to take her pad and pencil to the grotto. She had been going there often lately in search of solitude. Although she was treated with respect by the servants, who consulted her about all household matters these days, she sometimes found it difficult to cope with the knowledge that she was never alone in the villa.

As she passed the kitchen she heard voices, someone's laugh, and she felt a dull envy. At least Constancio and Maria had a purpose in life, a job to do every day. More and more she was beginning to feel useless, a parasite. If she stayed there, she must find something to do. Maybe she should talk to Señor Idiart again about helping out with his English classes.

If she stayed there....

She winced, realizing how insidiously the thought had slipped in. Was she really ready to give up and go home in defeat? If she did she would never see Laurens again, never again know his kiss or the lovemaking that had turned her into a woman.

Suddenly weary of her own thoughts, she hastened her step, eager to reach the grotto. Even so, she paused along the path to laugh at a feisty squirrel who was so intent upon fitting an acorn into each of his fat cheeks that he didn't notice her.

Farther along she stopped again, this time to watch the slow procession of a black-and-yellow caterpillar as it moved along a bare twig. A white bird, a snow dove, arched across the sky above the nearly bare branches of a chestnut. She followed it with her eyes as it headed south and rejoiced that it had escaped the cruel nets of the Basques. The bird was luckier than she was. It could fly on, never knowing the danger it had missed, while she was trapped there, trapped by her love for Laurens and her need to be near him at any cost to herself.

Sighing, she went on, her step light on the leaf-covered path. Just before she reached the final stand of trees she heard voices ahead, and she stopped, debating whether to turn back. She decided to go on. If it was Laurens talking to a woodsman or a shepherd, so be it. Eventually, she had to face him again. If he had any more recriminations to toss at her, it had better be where they wouldn't be overheard. Yesterday she had been stunned by his words. Today she just might give him a surprise and point out a few painful truths to him.

A moment later, when she realized that she had interrupted a rendezvous between Engrace and Luis Hiribarren, she would have retreated, but it was too late. Engrace, who was in Luis's arms, had already seen her. For a moment there was panic in her gray eyes, but when she realized that the intruder was Mayi, her face sagged with relief.

Mayi approached, forcing a smile. "I'm sorry. I had no idea anyone else came here."

Luis, his broad face rigid with embarrassment, stepped away from Engrace. "I was just leaving," he said. His eyes were burning as he looked at Engrace. "Goodbye, Engrace—and good luck."

With a nod at Mayi, he stalked off. The set of his shoulders was stiff, and Mayi suspected she had interrupted a quarrel.

She put her sketching pad down on a rock, trying to think of something innocuous to say.

Engrace spoke first. "You're wondering if we do this often, aren't you? Well, the answer is yes." She tossed her head defiantly. "And now I suppose you feel you have to tell Laurens."

Mayi shook her head. "No. I won't lie about it if he asks me a direct question, but I won't volunteer any information about seeing you and Luis together."

Engrace's eyes filled with tears. "I know it's dangerous and stupid, but we can't stay away from each other. And it's all so hopeless. Laurens will never allow me to marry Luis, and the Hiribarrens are just as set in their ways. Sometimes I wish I were dead!"

"I'm sorry. I'm so sorry, Engrace."

Engrace wiped the tears from her eyes with the back of her hand, and suddenly she looked very young. "You really mean that, don't you?"

"I know something of what you're going through, Engrace."

"How could you? You're so lucky. How could you possibly know what I'm feeling?"

"Because things aren't always the way they seem."

Engrace studied her closely. "I know it's none of my business, but is something wrong between you and Laurens?"

"We have—well, as I told you once before, we have some problems to work out," Mayi said evasively. How could she tell Engrace the truth, that Laurens thought his wife was responsible for the death of his—and Engrace's—brother?

Engrace sighed. "Laurens is stubborn. When he decides on a course, he seldom turns aside. It will take time for him to accept that you're different from us."

"Why do you say that?"

"You've been answerable to no one but yourself for so long that it must be hard for you to adjust to Laurens's—Luis calls it a 'medieval attitude.' Luis is very progressive in his thinking, you know."

Mayi smiled at the pride in Engrace's voice. "It isn't just because I'm independent, though that has something to do with it."

"If only Laurens wasn't so rigid and unbending!'' Engrace burst out, and Mayi knew she was thinking of Luis and herself. ''Just because he's *etcheko jauna*, he thinks he should make all the decisions for us. It doesn't help any that he's used to being the judge in village disputes, too. It doesn't seem to matter that he's human and not always right. Even with the elders of the village he usually has the final say.''

Her words were sobering. Maybe Engrace was right. Even without the misunderstanding between them, adjusting to life in a different culture would have been difficult. There was the insurance money she'd inherited from Pio, for instance. After she'd had it transferred from her Reno bank account to the local bank owned by Señor Carrera, she'd been astounded to discover that she would need her husband's signature on any checks she drew on the account.

''Well, Zubilibia is still a man's world, but I wouldn't advise any man here to criticize his wife's cooking or try to tell her how to run her household,'' Engrace said, a gloomy satisfaction in her voice.

The two of them exchanged smiles. ''Luis wants me to go away with him,'' Engrace said abruptly. ''I told him that I couldn't, and now he's going alone. He has a job as a gardener at a resort in San Sebastián.'' Her eyes filled with tears again. ''It's easy for him to make the decision to leave. He's a man, and the third son of his house. No one will think it strange if he finds work somewhere else, and when he comes back home to visit or even to stay, he'll always be made welcome. But if I run away I can never return home, not even for a visit. I'll never love anyone else, but it isn't easy.''

"I can see that. You would be giving up so much. It's a decision you might regret all your life," Mayi said carefully.

"I don't know what to do. I will miss him so, and what if I'm pregnant—" Engrace stopped, her cheeks flooding with color.

"Is there a chance you may be?" Mayi asked quickly.

"I don't think I am, but of course it's possible." Engrace's face fell. "I don't know what Laurens would do. He's so proud, and he would blame Luis. He thinks I'm still a child. He wouldn't even consider that I wanted Luis as much as he wanted me."

"Don't worry about it now," Mayi advised. "Maybe things can still work out for you and Luis. Have you tried talking to Laurens?"

"Oh, no! I can't do that! When someone finally told him that Luis had chosen me for the *aurresku*, there was such an uproar. You were in the village visiting the Bilbaos that day, or you would have heard him shouting at me. If he finds out that I've been meeting Luis behind his back, I don't know what he'll do. Besides, it's too late. Luis is leaving this afternoon. I guess I'll just have to learn to live without him.''

She sounded so hopeless that Mayi decided it was

time to change the subject. But she couldn't help thinking there was something wrong with a culture that allowed a man to have complete control over the life of his sister.

Engrace and she were both silent as they returned to the villa, but when they reached the flagstone terrace, Engrace stopped Mayi. "Thank you for being my friend," she said shyly. "I'm glad someone else knows. If—if I need to talk to someone, may I come to you?"

Mayi answered her with a hug. She started to tell Engrace that she was glad they were friends, too, but a sound behind her made her turn. Laurens was standing there, his face grim. He stared at them for a long moment before he wheeled and stalked away.

She realized Engrace's face was pale. "Did he hear?"

"All you said was that you were glad we were friends," Mayi reassured her.

"Then why did he look so angry?"

"That was because Laurens and I had a quarrel the night after the party. He's angry at me, not you."

"A quarrel? But he went upstairs early, and since you don't sleep—" Engrace broke off, looking flustered.

"You know that we don't sleep together?"

"It—it isn't anyone else's business. And besides, everybody knows that you're very restless at night, so it seems sensible to sleep in separate bedrooms."

"Well, you're right about one thing. It isn't any-one else's business," Mayi said.

After Engrace went into the house, Mayi sank down on a stone bench. So it *was* common knowledge that she and Laurens slept apart. How many other things were whispered behind her back? That Laurens seldom spoke to her, even in the company of others? That they were never alone together?

Laurens's hard voice spoke behind her. "I want to talk to you."

She rose stiffly to face him. "What is it?"

"I want you to discourage this attachment my sister has developed for you. She's a very impressionable girl who has led a sheltered life. I don't want her to pick up any of your North American ways. It can only lead to trouble."

The hurt welled up inside Mayi, sharpening her voice. "And maybe she might start wondering why it is that you have the right to direct her life?"

"Our ways are different from yours. We live by our own code of behavior."

"I'm not going to argue with you, Laurens. But I will say that I have no intentions of making your sister any more unhappy than she already is. She needs a friend, and I value friendship very much. Which is why I came to Zubilibia. Pio was my friend, too. So if you're asking me to suddenly start ignoring Engrace, you must know that this would hurt her far more than contact with my 'North American ways.'"

He stared at her silently, his eyes narrowed. Suddenly she was remembering how tender he'd been when he'd made love to her two nights ago. A hot flush rose to her face, and rather than risk his seeing it and interpreting it wrongly—or rightly—she whirled and started off. His hand on her arm stopped her.

"I haven't finished—"

"Take your hands off me," she said, furious.

"You'll stay here and listen to me."

"I'm not your slave, and besides, you've already said enough. You used me like I was a whore, and then, when you had satisfied your needs, suddenly you want no part of me. I can't forgive you for that, Laurens. In the future I want you to stay away from me. Until the day you can honestly say you believe me, *leave me alone*!"

She jerked her arm away and ran into the house, down the hall and up the service stairs. When she reached her room, she turned the lock in the door and then flung herself face down on the bed. But she didn't cry. The frustration and anger were too deep, and the tears she shed were internal.

At that moment she made the decision to give up. In the morning she would tell Laurens quietly, without emotion, that she was leaving. She would ask him to release the insurance money that she'd transferred to the local bank. After all, it belonged to her. Then she would pack her suitcase and send a message to Señor Roche to come for her. She would put the past few months behind her and never look back.

That night she slept fitfully, waking up several times to plan the conversation she meant to hold with Laurens. When she awoke for the final time, just as dawn was filling the room with a gray light, the nausea that had been plaguing her was back, so strong that she barely made it to the bathroom in time. Even after she had washed her face with cold water, she felt disoriented and dizzy. She told herself that it was the residue of the emotional storm of the past months, but when she started to dress, the tenderness in her breasts could no longer be ignored, and she was forced to admit something she had been trying to deny for the past two weeks.

The nausea was morning sickness. She was pregnant with Laurens's child.

CHAPTER ELEVEN

DURING THE NEXT FEW WEEKS, Mayi sometimes felt as if she was losing her mind. While she went about her daily routine, attending a few village events, going to church, following the low-key social life expected of the wife of the valley's most influential man, the conflict raged inside her. Up until this point her only desire, the reason she had stayed in Zubilibia in the face of Laurens's hostility, had been to convince him that he was wrong about her and regain his love. Now something else had priority, the welfare of the baby she carried.

Already the baby filled her thoughts, evoking a wonder, a hope for the future and even a cautious joy. Except for the years she'd spent with her grandmother, she had always been alone, an outsider looking in at other people's lives, Now she was carrying another human being under her heart, someone who could give her life new purpose.

Even though she was sure that her love for Laurens was hopeless, she would still have a child to love and protect, a buffer between herself and loneliness. She knew what it meant to be completely on her own in a world that could be indifferent and uncaring, and she was determined that she would give her child the same kind of love and understanding her grandmother had once given her.

As the days went by she put off telling Laurens, postponing the inevitable. For one thing, there never seemed to be an opportunity to talk to him alone these days. He no longer pretended, even in front of others, that their marriage was a happy one. In fact he seldom spoke to her, and when they met by accident, he ignored her and stalked on. With all pretenses gone, there was no opportunity to talk to him without seeking him out. If she did that, she knew instinctively she would be at a disadvantage.

Mayi vacillated from day to day, unable to decide what to do next. Winter set in with a blast of cold rain that turned to a light snow, and she welcomed the change. The gray skies that hung over the valley reflected her mood more closely than the brilliance of fall had done.

Christmas came and went. Although mainly a religious holiday among Basques, there was an exchange of presents, and to Mayi's surprise, Laurens gave her an ornate emerald necklace. At first she was deeply touched, until she caught his sardonic smile and realized the gift was an insult, his way of labeling her as a greedy woman who craved expensive jewelry. She wanted to tell him that since she didn't have his love she would prefer no gift at all, but she knew he wouldn't believe her. Instead she thanked him with dignity and then put the necklace away in a drawer, knowing she would never wear it.

Her own present for Laurens, which she'd purchased with the last of the cash she'd brought with her to Spain, was a tiny gold tie pin in the shape of a dove. For a moment she thought he would refuse to accept it, but he thanked her in a perfunctory way and then he turned to smile at Engrace, who was whirling around the room, showing off the exquisite silk-lined lace robe he'd bought her. Mayi looked away to hide the tears that smarted her eyes. When she turned back she found that he was watching her, his lips tight, and she stared at him, too proud to look away, even though she knew he must see the hurt on her face.

After Christmas the days seemed to drag. Because of the persistent nausea, Mayi lost her appetite and found it hard to sleep. She was torn by conflicting emotions. Part of her was sick with apprehension that she must eventually confront Laurens and tell him that the woman he scorned was carrying his child, a child who could be a replacement for Pio, his appointed *etcheko primu*.

But another part of her rejoiced in the baby she carried, who was already so dear to her. Sometimes, despite her worries, she would think of holding her baby in her arms, and she would find herself humming a lullaby.

One possibility she refused to consider was simply to leave. Despite his treatment of her, she knew she could never deprive Laurens of a child that could mean so much to him, even though he despised its mother. She wondered if sharing a child with him would make any difference in their marriage. Would it soften him, make him realize that despite his belief that she'd driven his brother to his death, he still had some feeling for her? Oh, she was sure about that. When he'd made love to her after the party he had forgotten his anger, and he had been the tender lover of their wedding night. However hard he might fight it, he still felt desire for her. But if he turned to her in the future, could she endure knowing that once he'd made love to her, he would reject her again?

Since there was no answer to that question, she tried to put it out of her mind. To keep herself occupied, she decided to accept Señor Idiart's invitation to teach English to the village children, provided it didn't cause additional conflict with Laurens.

She left a carefully worded note on Laurens's desk, telling him what she planned, and adding that if he had any objections she would abide by his decision, since she didn't want Señor Idiart to be caught in the middle. When he ignored her note, she called the schoolmaster and told him that she would be delighted to help him out.

During the next few days some of the tension left her. Because she had worked hard all her adult life, sometimes at two jobs at a time, her recent idleness had become increasingly burdensome. Now she felt useful again, and the children—those handsome Basque children with their luminous eyes and sturdy bodies and red cheeks—won her heart. Although very reserved with her at first, they gradually warmed and accepted her.

She decided to offer to teach English to any adult in the village who dealt with the tourist trade, and she went to the Bilbaos first. To her surprise, both of them signed up immediately. A short time later she was approached by Señora Idiart, the schoolmaster's wife, who sometimes clerked in the town's co-op gift shop during the summer. She told Mayi she wanted to learn English so she could better deal with the occasional American and British tourist who found his way to the village.

The class of three became six when Dr. Echahoun and his wife joined, followed by Father Ignatius, who declared that he'd always wanted to learn to speak "American." Mayi started them off with conversational English first, gradually introducing a few rules of grammar and spelling. As she explained such mysteries as syntax, Señor Idiart, who admitted freely that he had no affinity for foreign languages, shook his head. He told her that the Basque language was said to be so difficult that the devil himself, after seven years of study, could master only two words, *bai*—yes—and *ez*—no. This accursed English, which had a dozen spellings for words that sounded alike but had different meanings, must be the devil's own language.

To Mayi's satisfaction, others soon joined the class, among them Nicky Carrera. He had a lively intelligence and already possessed a rudimentary knowledge of the language, so he was soon able to carry on simple conversations, a skill he was very proud of.

Mayi was driving home after her afternoon adult class when the small car Laurens had put at her disposal broke down. The road was a lonely one, used only by a few families, and she prepared herself for a long walk to the villa. To her relief she saw Nicky's car, a Land Rover, approaching.

"Is something wrong?" he called to her in English.

She smiled her relief. "My car has conked out on me."

"Conked out? This is an Americanism?"

"This is an Americanism," she said, laughing.

"Ah—I'll make note of that," he said, nodding. He came over to her car, lifted the hood, then shook his head. "I think this is more complicated than an amateur can fix. Why don't I drive you home and then you can call the mechanic in the village to pick up your car."

She accepted his offer gladly, and as they drove off, she studied his profile. He was far better looking than the stocky, rather plain Luis, and she wondered why Engrace hadn't fallen in love with him. Was it forbidden fruit that made Engrace and Luis so attractive to each other, or was it lasting and true love?

"You think that I can learn English well?" Nicky asked.

"Yes, I do," she said truthfully. "You're picking it up faster than anyone else in my class."

"That's because I have so many American records," he said, sounding complacent. "The words don't seem strange to me as they do to the others."

"Well, it would certainly be a help if you ever decide to make singing your profession," she said without thinking.

His face lit up. "That's my dream. All my life I have wanted to be a professional singer but—" he shrugged "—it cannot be. I don't have the resources to pay for music lessons, and I am *etcheko primu* of my house and must learn banking. Someday I will take over the responsibility of running the family bank from my father."

He sounded so dispirited that Mayi's sympathy stirred. "If you had the money, would you strike out on your own?" she asked curiously.

"But that question has no meaning since I have no money of my own. And my father won't consent to my leaving Zubilibia, not even to go away to school. He's afraid that if I get a taste of the outside world, I will never return. So I will sing in the *bertsolari* contests and eventually become a banker, like my father."

Mayi wanted to point out that she had managed to acquire an education without any help from her family or anyone else, but she bit her lip and was silent. In Nicky's world family was all-important. How did she know what problems existed for a Basque student trying to get an education without, as Nicky had put it, resources?

But Nicky's wistful face haunted her, and it was

only when she realized that Nicky reminded her of Pio that she understood why she'd taken a personal interest in him. Both of them had the same sensitivity; they were both dreamers. They shared something else, too. Both of them were unhappy. Pio had been a very unhappy man, even though he'd smiled a lot, joked and teased her. Would Nicky become so unhappy that one day he too would—

No, she would *not* think such a thing! Pio's death had been an accident, nothing more, and Nicky was much more at ease in his own world than Pio had been. After all, there was one very large difference in their situations. Nicky was the heir of his house, not a second son. He didn't have that particular demon to fight.

After their conversation, Nicky began to stay behind after class to talk to her, and though she knew it was unwise, she couldn't help showing her sympathy for his dreams of becoming a professional singer. When she found herself feeling disappointed the times when he went off right after class, she knew that she was treading on dangerous ground, and she finally told him that since she was married, perhaps it would be best if he didn't stay after class with his questions.

He accepted her edict with a quiet dignity, but she could see his hurt. It was then an idea came to her. After all, she reasoned, the money in her bank account had been left to her by Pio, and she felt sure Pio would be pleased if some of it went to help one of his friends.

After agonizing over the idea for a few days, she sought out Laurens.

As she knocked on the library door, her palms were wet and her mouth dry. When had this happened, she thought with self-contempt, this dread of any kind of a confrontation with Laurens? She'd never feared anything or anyone in her life before she came here, so why was her heart hammering and every muscle in her body tense?

"Come in," Laurens called.

She opened the door and went in; only her resolution not to be intimidated kept her face impassive as she met his unfriendly gaze.

"What is it?" he said, not bothering to conceal his impatience.

"I want to talk to you."

"Well, shut the door and sit down."

She chose a chair halfway across the library from his desk. "It's about Nicky Carrera. I want to help him."

"Help Nicky? What the hell are you talking about?"

"He wants to go to Madrid for voice training."

"What business is that of yours?"

"It isn't my business, but the money that Pio left me is just sitting in the bank. Nicky told me that he and Pio had been good friends, and—"

"When did he tell you this?"

"Nicky is enrolled in my afternoon English class for adults. That time my car broke down, he gave me a lift to the villa. He mentioned then that he'd been close friends with your brother. That's why I thought Pio would have liked some of his insurance money to go to help Nicky—"

"Have you said anything about this to Nicky?" Laurens interrupted.

"Of course not. I wanted to talk to you first."

"Well, don't. Have you any idea the trouble this would stir up with the Carreras? It's enough that you've been trying to worm your way into the good graces of the villagers. What they don't need is your interference in their personal lives."

Mayi felt the nausea churning in her stomach, making her feel dizzy. Laurens gave her a sharp look. "What's wrong with you?"

"I—it's something I ate," she said weakly. "Excuse me. I need to lie down for a while."

"If you're ill, then call a doctor. If this is some trick to get your own way—"

A blind rage came over Mayi, as it had once before. She jumped to her feet and reached out for the nearest thing at hand. That it happened to be a heavy book didn't register. She threw it at him, her face twisting under the force of her fury, but he dodged it easily. In a minute he was beside her, grasping her arms and pushing her back against the chair. She struggled to get up, but he held her there easily, scorning her efforts to escape.

"I'm not impressed by temper tantrums," he grated. "And if you're staying on in hopes of becoming a rich widow, you can forget that, too. My heir is Engrace. She will become *etcheko jauna* if anything should happen to me. And forget any plans you might have to seduce Nicky. He's a decent young man, and if you try any of your tactics on him, I promise you'll suffer for it. You made your choice. Now you'll live with it—unless you've changed your mind. If so, you're free to leave. I'll pay your fare back to Reno—but Pio's insurance money remains here.''

She wanted to rage at him, to hurt him as he'd hurt her. Only the knowledge that any more emotional storms might harm the child she carried kept her quiet.

She was also tempted by his offer. To be gone from there, never again to have to endure his contempt—she longed for that with all her heart. She knew now that he would never change.

But again, it was the baby that stopped her. Maybe, just maybe, when Laurens found out about the baby, he would decide to stop these painful encounters with her. In time he might even treat her with the respect due the mother of his child. And besides, how could she take away their baby's only chance for a normal life surrounded by a family, by security, a security that she could never give him?

She knew she could earn a living for them on a teacher's salary once she found a teaching job. But what would she live on when she first returned to Reno? Laurens had made it plain that his responsibility would end with her return fare; he didn't intend for her to profit from Pio's death. She was almost four months pregnant, and it was a miracle that she hadn't already begun to show. Who would hire a woman in the advanced stages of pregnancy? The alternative would be welfare, public charity, and she would never submit to that humiliation again.

"Well? Have you made up your mind?"

She looked into his cynical eyes, and the desire to lash out at him with angry words was almost overwhelming. The nausea was more acute now, and she felt as if she'd reached her breaking point. She started to get up, but he held her there, so effortlessly that the rage rolled over her again. It built and built until something inside her snapped, and everything around her began to revolve, including the sudden consternation in Laurens's face.

She never completely lost consciousness, even when her eyes rolled upward and she could no longer hold herself erect in the chair. She slid forward, and only Laurens's quick movement kept her from hitting the floor. He picked her up, swearing under his breath, and the room around her became gray. She felt something solid under her body and realized that he was putting her on the leather sofa. She started to get up, but he pushed her down again, and to her surprise, the hand he laid against her forehead was gentle.

"Your forehead is very hot," he said, and she knew he was speaking to himself, not her.

She tried to focus her eyes on his face, but it seemed to be bobbing around, making her dizzy, and she gave up trying. "It's something I ate," she managed finally. "I've felt strange all day."

"Well, don't move. I'll call Dr. Echahoun."

"I don't need a doctor," she said quickly. "I'm fine. I'm already better."

Exerting all her willpower, she sat up. He studied her closely, as if trying to judge her sincerity. "Very well. But I want you to stay in bed for the rest of the day. I'll tell Constancio to bring you something light for your dinner later. In the morning, if you aren't better, I'm calling Dr. Echahoun."

He picked her up before she could protest, and as he carried her up the stairs to her room, she discovered that the strength of his arms, the closeness of their bodies, the male scent she associated only with Laurens was stirring her physically.

Afraid that he might guess her feelings, she buried her face in his chest, and only then realized that their closeness was also affecting him. She listened to the quickening of his heartbeat under her ear, and when she opened her eyes and stared into his face she saw a sheen on his forehead and a familiar tautness in his face, as though he was holding himself in check with great effort.

Impulsively she reached up and brushed the back of her hand across his damp forehead. His eyes bit into hers, and when she saw the hunger there, a trembling started inside her own body. She wanted him, wanted him so badly that she felt no shame when she lifted her lips for a kiss.

His mouth came down upon hers, and suddenly

she was transported back to another day, another time. She felt the sweet ache washing over her as the kiss deepened, and their tongues, molten and pliable, touched. She shuddered with desire, wanting him to make love to her, to love her with the tenderness of their wedding night.

Then she was slipping out of his arms. She fell upon her bed, not gently but with jarring force. "You never give up, do you?" he said in the hard voice she had come to dread so much. "Well, your tricks won't work on me. Why do you keep trying?"

She stared up at him, hurt and bewildered. Hadn't he felt anything at all? Had she read something in his eyes that wasn't really there? No, his eyes still burned and his lips had a swollen look. He wanted her all right, but his pride, his stiff-necked Basque pride, was even stronger than his desire.

"I've never made any secret of what I feel for you," she said wearily. "You say you don't want me? Well, I say you're a liar. But you're right about one thing. I don't want you to make love to me for the wrong reasons. I want you to love me and trust me, as I still love you. But I know now that it's impossible. So in the future, I promise that I won't try to—to corrupt your principles."

If she had hoped that her bitter words would shame him, she was disappointed. His face remained aloof as he said, "You can always leave, you know."

She shook her head. "No, I'm not going to leave.

But don't worry. I won't embarrass you. I'll run your household, and I'll make sure that my behavior is acceptable to your neighbors and friends. But I want something from you, too.''

"I thought you would," he said cynically. "What is it? A personal allowance? Or perhaps you'd like some more jewelry? A little something for a rainy day?''

"I don't want your jewelry. I don't care for gifts that have no personal meaning. But I want you to stay away from me, to stop tormenting me. You've already made your opinion of me very clear. I can see now that it was a mistake, trying to talk to you. In the future I want you to continue to ignore me. It's much easier that way."

Laurens nodded his head jerkily. "I prefer it that way, too."

He turned on his heel and was gone. Mayi closed her eyes and slumped back against the pillows. The nausea was back, but she knew she must fight it. In the morning she would appear for breakfast at the regular hour, looking as normal as possible. She didn't want Laurens to call Dr. Echahoun. If he examined her now, he would realize immediately that she was pregnant, and he would say something about it to Laurens.

It still wasn't the right time for that. After today's quarrel, Laurens would be even more suspicious of her. What if his hatred for her, his suspicions, were so strong that he demanded that she stay only long enough to have the baby and then leave—alone? He was all-powerful here. There was no way she could fight him without money, without influence, a foreigner in a foreign land.

She had been foolish to antagonize him. In the future she would be wiser. From now on she would hold her tongue, no matter what he said, and treat him as if he was a casual acquaintance. Perhaps then, when she told him the news, he would see that their marriage could work out, even though they never made love again.

MAYI'S CLASSES BECAME ESPECIALLY PRECIOUS to her during the next few weeks. They provided an outlet for her energy and gave her an excuse to be away from the villa for a few hours every day.

Her class expanded to fifteen, then twenty, and still Laurens hadn't ordered her to stop them, as she had half expected. In fact he never mentioned them, but she noticed that he seemed to be listening with more than usual attention at the dinner table when Engrace asked her questions about a knotty pronunciation problem.

Engrace, who seemed to be seeking ways to forget her own worries, had enrolled in the class and was a faithful student. She and Mayi rode to and from the village together, which eliminated the problem of Nicky staying alone with Mayi after classes.

At first, after Luis had left Zubilibia, Engrace had lost weight and drifted around the house like a restless ghost. In the past two weeks, however, she had shaken off her depression, and once again her cheeks had color and she was in constant good spirits, laughing at the dinner table and driving off every morning to visit friends in the village and neighboring farms, returning in time to have lunch with the family.

Mayi was relieved, if a little surprised. Engrace had recovered with such ease that her love affair with Luis must have been infatuation after all. Then Mayi noticed that although Engrace went to see her friends often, few of them returned her visits.

On her next visit with the Bilbaos, Mayi listened with unusual interest to Señora Bilbao's array of village gossip. Her suspicions were confirmed when she learned that Luis had returned from San Sebastián.

"He found city life not to his liking," Señora Bilbao said, wagging her head. "And being a sensible man, he returned where he belongs. It is not easy being a third son, but luckily his hands are needed at his father's farm, and he is very strong, a hard worker." She gave her husband a sidelong look. "Perhaps there is another reason for his return to Zubilibia. Who knows, eh?"

His face roguish, Señor Bilbao hummed the fragment of a tune. Then, with the lack of self-consciousness the Basques had about singing, he sang a few lines of a song Mayi wasn't familiar with.

"The nightingale sings beautifully,
It charms the whole neighborhood.

Last night in a hedge
There were two of them.
They were beautiful and charming
In every kind of way.
And they were very taken with each other.''

Although she applauded and pretended not to catch the significance of both his wink and the words of the song, Mayi went home in a deeply troubled mood. So this was the explanation for Engrace's good spirits lately. Luis had returned and they had resumed their affair. Yet nothing had changed. Marriage between her sister-in-law and Luis, the son of the Pelente family's enemy, was impossible as long as both families remained traditionally bound to the past.

She waited until the following day, when she and Engrace were driving home after class, before mentioning Luis's name. Engrace's smile faded.

"So you know about Luis's return," she said. "Yes, we're lovers again. While he was gone, we discovered that we couldn't live without each other. No matter what it costs us, we intend to stay together. Since it's impossible for us to live in Zubilibia, we are going to San Sebastián to live. Luis is sure he can get his job back at the resort hotel where he worked before. We're only waiting until after the celebration of his parents' wedding anniversary next month.''

Mayi, who knew the heartbreak of losing someone you love, felt a deep sympathy for the star-crossed lovers. But this wasn't a simple case of parental disapproval. Not only would Engrace and Luis be giving up their families, but they would also be outcasts in Zubilibia. They would spend their lives in exile, and to a Basque, his family and home, his village, were everything.

"Is there no other way?" she asked.

"Life doesn't mean anything to us without each other," Engrace said. "We found this out while Luis was gone. I think that I would have died if he hadn't returned when he did, and Luis feels the same way. So we have no choice. All my life I've done what other people told me to do—my father and Laurens and Tia Petra. I didn't mind because it is our way to be obedient to our elders and to do our duty. But to live without Luis—no, I can't do that."

She looked at Mayi with anxious eyes. "You won't tell Laurens, will you? You promised that you would keep my secret. It won't make any difference if he finds out. We'd still go off together. But it would mean we must go earlier than we planned, and that would ruin his parents' anniversary celebration."

"I won't tell. We never speak alone," Mayi said wearily.

"Things between you two haven't improved, have they?"

"No, nothing has changed."

"I hope that in time it will be better. Surely when you tell him about the baby—" Engrace bit her lower lip as if to punish it for allowing the words to slip out.

"You know that I'm pregnant?"

"Constancio guessed. She has a sixth sense about such things. I'm sure no one else knows. She only told me because she was worried that you haven't announced it yet. She's convinced that because you've never had a mother to instruct you about such things, you aren't aware that you're carrying a child."

"I haven't announced it because I still haven't told Laurens. At present things are even worse between us."

"He loves you, Mayi. I see him watching you and there is such unhappiness in his eyes. Whatever the quarrel between you, can't it be mended?"

"I once hoped it could be, but lately I've almost given up."

"Perhaps the baby will make a difference. It is strange that he hasn't suspected. You've changed so much in the last weeks. It won't be long before others guess."

Mayi's heart sank. Was it possible that others had noticed? Had it been only their respect for Laurens that prevented them from teasing him about becoming a father? Well, that made it even more pressing that she tell him herself before he heard it from someone else.

After Engrace had gone up to her room, Mayi went to the terrace to seek out Topet, her mood somber. She seemed to do her best thinking while sitting beside the old dog. She found him, as usual, curled up on the rush mat that was kept there for his daytime use. Lately, except on sunny afternoons like this, Topet spent most of his time in his comfortable and warmly insulated doghouse, and she couldn't help wondering if he would survive the winter.

The thought saddened her, and her eyes were blurred with tears as she stroked his silky head. Lately, she thought, suddenly cross with herself, she seemed to be on the verge of tears so often. Was it the hormonal changes of her body, or simply that her defenses, which she'd always thought were so strong, were finally wearing thin?

Although the day was clear, the wind was chilly, and suddenly she felt very cold as she sat there, assaulted by her own random thoughts:

I must tell Laurens soon...but what words should I use? Should I be casual or flippant or simply honest, laying all my cards on the table and telling him how much I want this baby? And just how will he take the news that he has fathered a child by the woman he considers little better than a whore? Will he send me away—or will he allow me to stay, to raise his child and remain his wife?

CHAPTER TWELVE

LAURENS STOOD BY THE LIBRARY WINDOW, staring out at the terrace. He knew the afternoon sun was in Mayi's eyes, and she couldn't see him, and he also knew it was a mistake, watching her like this. She was sitting beside Topet, her legs curled under her, an azure sweater knotted around her shoulders. As she bent her head to pet the old dog, her hair drifted over one cheek, and he felt an absurd desire to push back the strand of hair, to kiss those full, sweetly curved lips until she melted in his arms.

Lately, Mayi had changed. He had noticed because he couldn't stop watching her and thinking about her. Her figure had filled out, as if overnight she had changed from a girl to a woman, and her skin had taken on a luminescence, her eyes a new glow, startling in its intensity. Even her hair, that marvelous hair that he dreamed about at night, seemed more alive these days, and he felt a sudden pang, remembering how it had clung to his fingers when he'd stroked it after they'd made love.

And this new radiance—it was so unlike her paleness in the days following their wedding. Had she found another lover? The only young man she saw with regularity was Nicky Carrera. Was she meeting that poor, bedazzled boy secretly and letting him make love to her, twisting and gasping under the weight of his body?

Jealousy, painful and humiliating, arched through Laurens, and he brought his fist down hard on his open palm, trying to repudiate both his suspicions and his jealousy—and the sudden rush of memories.

Mayi, her nude body pearl pale against dark-green moss, against his own brown body...Mayi, holding out her arms to him, shyness warring with the deeply sensuous look of longing on her face... Mayi, her eyes startled and wondering but unafraid as she felt the full force of his passion for the first time, just before she yielded herself to him in complete surrender...Mayi, lying in his arms afterward, her face buried in the warm hollow of his shoulder, her heart still hammering beneath his... and, best of all, the wonderful feeling of rightness, of togetherness, the knowledge that he was no longer alone, that now he had someone who would always be there by his side, sharing the good and the bad, his lifelong companion as well as his lover....

His face twisted as he remembered how thankful he'd been that day. He'd been so sure of Mayi's love. How could she have fooled him so completely that he'd had no doubts at all? Surely, at least for that moment, her feelings had been genuine. As she'd lain in his arms, had she forgotten her scheme to marry a wealthy man? If so, it didn't change things. He had never doubted that Mayi returned his passion. Such things couldn't be faked. But it didn't matter, because he could never forgive the rest of it, that she had been the cause of Pio's agony of spirit just before he'd died.

Another memory, one etched in pain, came back to him—the moment when he'd realized that Mayi had been the woman Pio had loved. God, it had been the worst time of his life, even worse than the day he'd learned about Pio's death. And it shamed him that even the knowledge of what she'd done and what she was hadn't changed one thing—he still wanted her.

For the past few weeks, the sight of her had been a constant torment to his flesh, and that was why he had kept away from her. He didn't want to punish her, as she obviously believed. He wasn't in the business of punishment. He would leave that to a higher authority.

But for his own self-preservation, he couldn't afford to get into any more situations like the last one. When he'd held her in his arms, he'd been tempted almost beyond endurance. He had almost made love to her then, had almost lost his head under the force of his lust for her.

His eyes brooding, Laurens watched Mayi. She was talking to Topet; he could see her lips moving. Topet's ears were alert, and his head was tilted to one side as if he could understand what she was saying. Maybe, in some mysterious way, he could. What did she say to Topet, those times when she sat beside him in the sun, brushing out the burrs in his long silky coat or simply stroking his head? The dog adored her, but then dogs weren't hard to win over. A warm hand, a kind voice, and they were slaves for life.

He wouldn't fall into the trap of constantly finding excuses to trust her again. Yet it was strange how well she'd kept up the facade of being the woman he'd loved, right up to the moment when he'd seen the damning evidence against her. Why did she continue to play that game when she knew he would never be taken in again?

And those English classes. Teaching a foreign language to a group of adults who had little academic experience was hard, grueling work and demanded a lot of preparation. If he was honest, he had to admit that the village would profit from them. But what did Mayi get out of them? He had accused her of wanting to ingratiate herself with the villagers, but wasn't that an acceptable ambition for a new bride who meant to make her home among her husband's people?

Her friendship with Engrace was a puzzle, too. The two of them seemed like sisters, which was another sore point. Engrace had always treated him with respect, but never with the warmth she'd shown Mayi almost from their first meeting. Yes, Mayi had a knack for making friends, for winning over people. Was that how she'd won Pio's trust?

The pencil in his hand snapped in two, and he realized that his fingers had tightened around it, breaking it at the very moment that an insidious image of Mayi's white body in Pio's arms had slipped into his mind. With a curse, he turned his back on the window and returned to his paperwork, and that evening at dinner he was careful not to look at Mayi any more than was necessary.

Luckily they had guests to keep him occupied—Father Ignatius, Dr. Echahoun and his wife and their grown daughter, Dolores, a shy, lovely brunet who was one of Mayi's students.

"Engrace tells me that you've chartered a plane to take you to Guernica next week," Father Ignatius said, helping himself to his third portion of Constancio's justly famous *pollo vascongado*, a succulent casserole of chicken and shrimp in wine sauce. "Is it business or pleasure?"

"I'm meeting an Italian wine buyer there. With luck he'll make a large purchase of our wines. He's a Basque on a pilgrimage to Guernica, which is why we're meeting there. I also have an appointment in Bilbao to look at some winery machinery. If we want to compete with other wineries, we need to modernize the plant. Unfortunately my two appointments are a day apart, so I'll be away three days."

He smiled at Engrace and his aunt as an idea struck him. "Would you two like to come along? You could shop in Bilbao—and I understand there's going to be a singing contest between Joseba

Oiherrant of Soule and the Guernica *bertsolári*, Augustin de Mendiburu. It's being billed as the contest of the century, which may or may not be true. Even so, it's something worth attending."

Engrace hesitated, then shook her head. It seemed to Laurens that she was avoiding his eyes as she said, "I have to attend the christening of Therese Jaurreguy's new baby."

"And unfortunately, I don't feel up to a trip at this time." Tia Petra smiled at him. "I'm sure Mayi would love to see Guernica, especially with such a knowledgeable guide. She's never witnessed a *bertsolari* contest. Why don't you take her, Laurens?"

Laurens decided that his aunt's voice was just a little too ingenuous. He was sure Mayi would make some excuse and was completely nonplussed when she said, "I'd love to see Guernica, and I've always wanted to attend a *bertsolari* contest."

Laurens knew he was neatly trapped unless he canceled his own appointments. There was nothing he could do about it. He had already let it be known that he had a free day between his business meetings.

"If you'd like to go, you're welcome, Mayi," he said reluctantly. "However, I won't be able to spend much time with you."

"I'm sure I can manage on my own," she told him quietly. "And I do need to do some shopping for winter clothing."

She didn't explain further, and he let the subject drop. He was in for it, but he would see that they were alone as little as possible, and he would take a suite at the hotel to make sure they weren't forced to sleep in the same bedroom.

Three days later they left for Guernica. As he often did for business trips, he had arranged for a private plane from an air-service company in Pamplona to pick him up, and he was thankful that there was no opportunity to talk to Mayi during the bustle of getting their luggage on the plane and settling in their seats. Once they were airborne, he was grateful that the engine of the prop-driven plane made conversation difficult, though not impossible.

Despite himself, he couldn't help noticing how well Mayi looked in her trim, but very feminine suit. She had once told him that most people considered it trite for a redhead to wear green, but she loved the color so she wore it often anyway. As she stared out the window, watching the countryside below with the complete absorption she gave to anything that interested her, his eyes kept straying toward her, and he thought she looked like a forest nymph, fresh and vibrant and incredibly appealing. The next three days would be a real test of his willpower.

When the copilot, a young Italian who was obviously smitten with Mayi's long slender legs, came back to the small cabin to ask if they would like coffee, Mayi smiled at him, nodding. Laurens felt a primitive desire to plant his foot in the young fool's rear, but he accepted the coffee, too, and they sipped it silently, side by side.

The silence between them was so strained that Laurens felt a sudden rebellion. Before he thought it through, he said, "Look, since we've been forced into each other's company for the next three days, let's make the best of it."

"Your aunt was the one who suggested I join you," she pointed out.

"You could have refused, made some excuse."

"Told a lie?" Her lips twisted, then straightened out. "But you abhor lies—and liars, don't you? Or so you've told me many times."

"A social lie is hardly in the same category as a destructive lie like—" He broke off, then tried again. "As I was saying, we were forced into each other's company—for whatever reason—and it would be more comfortable for both of us if we simply pretend that we're casual acquaintances, two people who have just met. That way we can at least be civilized about it and make a bad situation endurable."

"Yes, let's be civilized. Let's forget that a Basque never forgives or forgets an insult, even if it's all in his mind," she said evenly. "Let's forget that we're married and that for a while I thought—" She stopped and took a ragged breath. "And you're right, of course. We'll pretend we've just met, and we know nothing about each other. We just happen to be going to the same place. You'll be busy with your business and I'll do some shopping and sightseeing." Her face softened. "I do want to see Guernica. Sometimes I have this crazy feeling that I lived through the attack on Guernica, maybe because I've read so much about it.''

"I know the feeling. Did you know that my father was there that day—April 26, 1937? He lost the partial use of one hand, and there were other scars, mental ones that never healed. He talked about it so often that I feel as if I lived through the attack, too.''

"How did it happen that he was there?''

"He had gone to see a friend who was very ill. Just as he was passing through the marketplace—it was market day, a Monday, you know—the first German planes flew overhead. He told me once that he'd always felt guilty because so many died and he was spared. He ws pinned down by a falling chimney, and he couldn't help the wounded. For almost twelve hours he was forced to watch—that horror. After that, he drank, increasingly so in his later years. That's why—''

"That's why the responsibility of raising Engrace and Pio fell on your shoulders. That's why you were more like Pio's father than his older brother and why—''

She stopped then, and he knew that if she had gone on, she would have said that this was why he was so set in his ways.

"I had responsibilities, yes, but none I wasn't willing to take on,'' he said shortly.

"And your mother? You never speak of her.''

"She died when Engrace was born. She was twenty years younger than my father but she wasn't very strong—except for her willpower and her spirit. She knew our father's weaknesses, and she made me promise that I would look after Pio—and the baby. I've always tried to do that. Sometimes I haven't handled things right, but I always tried to do my best.''

"Pio knew that,'' she said, her voice so low that it was hard to hear her above the roar of the engines. "Once, when I told him I'd always wanted a brother, he told me that he'd been lucky. Not only did he have a brother, but he had someone to take the place of his father, who seldom was there."

For a long moment he stared into her eyes. His skin tingled, as if the air between them was highly charged, and he had a feeling that in another minute something important would happen, some revelation would take place. Then Mayi looked away, her face pale, and he took a long breath and said stiffly, "Thank you for telling me that. I've had my doubts."

She nodded, then said quickly, "I want to see the Tree of Guernica. I understand that the trunk was left standing as a symbol of Basque unity."

"There's a superstition about the tree that as long as any part of it still remains, the seven provinces and the Basque people will stay a united people. I just wish all Basques would remember that we kept our identity as a people for thousands of years by means other than anarchy."

"The innocent always suffer when ruthless men try to force their will upon others," she said sadly.

"But I hope the superstition about the tree is true—
and that it's guarded well to make sure nothing
happens to it."

"It really matters to you?"

"I'm Basque, too. Only half-Basque, of course,
so maybe I have no right—"

"If you have only a single drop of Basque blood
in your veins, you're still Basque," he said gruff-
ly.

"Well, I feel that I belong here. Maybe it's because I never belonged anywhere else. Even when
my grandmother was alive, we weren't really part
of the Uncetas, the family who owned the boarding
house where we lived. Then later, the foster homes
were always temporary. Adoptive parents seldom
choose children older than seven. I moved around a
lot while I was in school, too. I always had this
dream of someday living in my own little cottage."
She paused, a faraway look in her eyes. "There's a
Basque song about a house on a hill."

He nodded. "I know the song. 'Do you see, in
the morning, at the first light of dawn, on a hill, a
small house, white fronted, in the midst of four oak
trees, a white dog in the doorway, a little fountain
at the side? It is there that I dwell in peace—' "

He stopped, realizing that her eyes were bright
with tears, and he wasn't sure if he was glad or
sorry that the copilot chose that moment to gather
up their cups—and, Laurens noticed, to take
another long look at the redheaded American
woman.

Half an hour later the plane was dipping down toward a small private airport in the outskirts of Guernica. Laurens had arranged for a rental car to be waiting, and as they drove through the quiet streets of the town he pointed out landmarks. There were few signs of that long-ago day the Basque people would never forget.

"It looks like any other small European town," Mayi said with obvious disappointment. "Not at all like Zubilibia, which is so Basque."

He started to remind her that the town had been almost totally rebuilt after the bombing. Instead he pointed silently to a broad-shouldered elderly man, wearing the blue blouse and flat beret of the Basques, who was riding in a two-wheeled cart pulled by a pair of oxen. The backs of the oxen were protected by a heavy canvas sheet edged with red and blue, and the cart was piled high with sweet potatoes. The farmer ignored the traffic, his eyes aloof. He was obviously convinced that he had the right of way over pedestrians, cars and the occasional bus that passed him by.

Mayi laughed, and he found himself smiling, too. She listened intently as he told her more of the history of Guernica and how the Parliament Building and its famous oak tree had survived the bombing when so little else had. Occasionally she asked him a question and commented that she was glad the town's school and the Convent of Santa Clara had survived that terrible day. Later, when they pulled up in front of the modern hotel where he'd taken a suite, she gave him a smile that made his mouth go dry.

"Thank you for telling me about your father," she said.

Laurens nodded silently, but the alarm bells inside him were going full blast again for the simple reason that he found it almost impossible not to bend his head and kiss her upturned face. After he'd registered and arranged for their luggage to be taken to their suite, he reminded Mayi that he had a business appointment. Since he would be having dinner with his client, she should have her own dinner sent up to their suite.

She didn't argue with him, though he expected her to point out—rightfully—that she was perfectly capable of dining alone in the hotel dining room. Instead she murmured, "I'll see you in the morning," and followed the porter toward the elevators.

Laurens spent a profitable evening with the Italian wholesaler and came away with a new outlet for the winery's estate wines. Although he didn't stay out late after all, the living room was empty with only a single lamp burning when he let himself into the suite. He hesitated, staring at the closed door of one of the bedrooms, but he didn't knock, even though a sliver of light showed under the door.

The extent of his disappointment that Mayi hadn't waited up for him alarmed him, however, and he decided that in the morning he would make some excuse, tell her that business had unexpectedly come up. He would suggest that she spend the day shopping and perhaps take a tour if she wanted to do any sightseeing. He'd also find an excuse to stay away that evening, thus avoiding temptation. It was humiliating to discover just how vulnerable he was, but if he allowed himself to forget again, it would only end in disaster.

In the morning he overslept, mainly because he'd had so much trouble falling asleep. He heard Mayi moving around in her room next door. Still half-asleep, he lay there smiling, idly wishing she would come back to bed and curl up against him.... He awakened fully with a wrenching start. Angry with himself, he got up and put on his robe. When he saw that the bathroom they shared was empty, he took a fast shower and dressed quickly, hoping to leave the suite before Mayi came out of her bedroom.

He was writing a note at the bleached mahogany desk in the sitting room when Mayi spoke from the doorway. "I ordered coffee and croissants to be sent up," she said. "Would you like something more substantial for breakfast?"

"Thank you, but—" He intended to tell her that he would eat later and that he would be busy the rest of the day. Instead he heard himself saying, "Croissants are fine. Why don't I take you to see the tree today? You can go to Bilbao with me tomorrow and do your shopping while I'm busy with the winery supplies salesman."

"I'd love that," she said, then added, "I have a

favor to ask you. You said something about a *bert-solari* contest. If you have time, I was hoping that you would take me to it. I understand it's not something a woman alone would go to.''

He hesitated, then nodded. "I can arrange that. Of course, one of the *bertsolaris* is French and doesn't speak Spanish, so you won't be able to follow the words. However, I can translate for you—''

"Oh, but I know French," she said, and then flushed at his incredulous stare.

"You speak French as well as Spanish and Basque?''

"I majored in languages. That's what I hope to teach when—someday. Why are you so surprised?''

"Few Americans seem interested in learning foreign languages.''

"Perhaps because it isn't as necessary to speak other languages in the United States as it is in Europe," she said. "As for me—well, languages come easily to me. I even thought that if I'm still in Zubilibia next year, I might teach a class in French, too—if anyone is interested. It could be useful for anyone who deals with French tourists.''

He started to ask what she meant by "if I'm still in Zubilibia next year" and then thought better of it. The conversation was verging on the personal again.

Mayi went to finish dressing, and when she came out of her room, he saw that she'd made a special effort to dress up for the occasion. His throat tightened as he took in her silver-gray suit, which emphasized rather than minimized her curves. She must have put on a little weight recently; her figure, which had been almost too slender, was softly rounded now. He wanted to tell her she looked wonderful, but he was afraid to open up any more doors that he wouldn't be able to slam shut easily. He compromised and praised her suit instead.

His opinion was reflected in the eyes of the men they met as they walked down Calle de la Estación toward the railroad station plaza where the first German bombs had fallen in 1937. Her hair seemed to draw masculine eyes like a magnet, and yet he would swear that she was unconscious of the attention she attracted.

On their wedding night, when he'd told Mayi she was the most seductive woman he'd ever met, she had smiled indulgently and said that that was because he loved her. He'd been thankful for her modesty, but now for some reason it annoyed him. The feeling was so perverse that he tried to track it down. Maybe it was because her unawareness of the effect she had on men didn't match Pio's description of the woman he'd called "venal and amoral and provocative."

An hour later they stood before the circle of cement that held the remains of the Tree of Guernica. "It bloomed late that spring in 1937," he told Mayi. "A bad omen, the people said."

The sheen was back in Mayi's eyes, and he felt a twisting pain that the emotion wasn't for him. His own reaction dismayed him, and his voice was curt as he commented, "Do you need to borrow my handkerchief?"

She looked away. "I'm sorry. I seem to cry a lot these days. I guess that's because of—" She broke off. "When is the *bertsolari* contest?"

He glanced down at his watch. "At six this evening. I thought we'd spend the rest of the day sightseeing and taking a drive up along the coast. The hotel arranged for our tickets to the contest, so that's no problem. Most of these contests are held in cafés, even private homes, but Oiherrant and de Mendiburu have such large followings and the rivalry between them is so bitter that something larger was needed this time. The contest is being held in the municipal pelota *fronton*. It won't have the intimacy of a café, but on the other hand, it's a once-in-a-lifetime chance to see two of the best troubadours in the country locking horns. There's such a demand for tickets in the galleries that we'd better be there on time, or we may lose our seats and have to stand in the back of the court."

"Surely they wouldn't do that to Laurens Pelente," she teased.

"They wouldn't dare," he said darkly, then added, "But let's get moving anyway."

As they left the plaza to return to their car, Mayi asked him questions about the *bertsolaris*, which he answered as best he could. Although the troubadours were not as popular as they'd been before the advent of radio, movies and tape recorders, they still existed as a prime source of entertainment in small villages, especially those in the mountain regions.

They spent the early part of the morning exploring the town, walking the tree-lined streets, which held a serenity that belied the history that had been made there. Later they drove along the Bay of Biscay's wild, breathtakingly beautiful coast. Mayi confessed to a fascination as well as an uneasiness with the ocean, and Laurens told her that it was the result of having always lived inland.

When they returned to Guernica, they lingered over their lunch in a small workman's café near the Church of Santa Maria. The café's proprietor told them that on the day of the attack the bell had pealed continuously. Later they drove up the winding road to Luno, stopping once to read a road marker that honored those who had fallen there, gunned down as they'd fled the bombs.

That evening when they arrived at the pelota stadium, it was already so packed that Laurens was surprised to find their seats, in the third row of the lower gallery, still empty. Mayi's eyes were bright with excitement as she watched the rowdy crowd around them, and she laughed whenever an *irrintzina* cry split the air. The audience was wildly partisan. Most of the customers were men, but there were a few couples, too, ruddy-faced men and sturdy sharp-eyed women who seemed intent on exchanging good-natured insults and making private bets with others nearby.

The clapping of hands and a fresh wave of the high-pitched *irrintzinas* announced the entry of the contestants. In the manner of such contests, the *bertsolaris*, both large muscular men with burly shoulders and the build of woodsmen, were given a subject; each was assigned an opposing side of the controversy. Laurens explained to Mayi that the way they marshaled their arguments, pro or con, the ingenuity and persuasiveness of their improvisations and the quality of their singing would decide who was the victor. The judges, a row of elderly men dressed in black suits and immaculate linen with black berets worn squarely across their heads, sat on the front-row bench. From the gravity of their expressions, they were quite aware of their own importance.

The subject was nonpolitical—a wise decision, Laurens privately thought. The singer from Soule defended the advantages of following a sailor's life, while the local man, who had the largest claque of fans, exhorted the joys of being a farmer. Since the subject was so tame, Laurens expected Mayi to quickly lose interest in the contorted and often nitpicking arguments, but she listened intently, laughing at the contestants' dry, acidic wit, the pricks of irony and the subtle insults, always couched in mock complimentary terms, as first one man, then the other, took the floor to sing his improvised arguments.

The voices of both of the *bertsolaris* was so extraordinary and their improvised arguments so inventive that Laurens wasn't surprised when the judges, after wrangling a long time, finally declared the contest to be a draw. Groans of dissent and catcalls rose among both factions, but especially those who had come to cheer for the local champion.

Since Mayi favored the man from Soule and Laurens favored the Guernician, they argued good-naturedly most of the way back to the hotel, then continued the argument over dinner in the lobby restaurant, finally declaring a truce when their menus were presented by a bereted waiter.

Although the restaurant had been highly recommended to Laurens, the hotel had been built since his last visit to Guernica and he wasn't personally familiar with the quality of the food served there. He kept his fingers crossed as he studied the menu, especially since their lunch—the open-faced sandwiches of sardines and pimientos that Guernica was famous for—had been several hours earlier. Mayi asked him to order for her, and he chose seafood from the Bay of Biscay, chicken-and-rice paella, a salad of lettuce and endive, with flan for dessert. To his relief, the food was excellent, and they both ate with healthy appetites.

As she had all day, Mayi was treating him as though he really was someone she'd just met. He realized she was making a sincere effort to honor their agreement when she told him some of the problems of working as a keno runner and trying to juggle a full school schedule at the same time. Although she presented the incidents to amuse him, he realized they couldn't have been anything but difficult, and yet she treated those years of struggle with humor.

As they sat there sipping cognac, Laurens saw Mayi's face soften, and he realized that the restaurant's small combo was playing a medley of Basque folk songs. The vocalist was a young man with a pleasant voice, and Laurens stiffened when he finished a lullaby and began singing another song. "White snow dove, whither are you flying? All the passes into Spain are full of snow."

His eyes met Mayi's and he saw that her eyes were shimmering again, but this time he knew that the tears were for what could have been. A rebellion against the past, against honor and guilt and all the other things that had ended the sweet communion of their wedding night, welled up inside him. Without thinking of the consequences, he reached out and took Mayi's hand. Against his brown skin her hand looked white and fragile as he pressed it to his lips, then turned it over to kiss the palm.

"Let's get out of here," he said hoarsely.

He threw several bills on the table, not waiting for a check, and got to his feet. Mayi rose, too, looking dazed, and he knew that she felt the same urge to put aside the past. He didn't allow himself to think. All that mattered was the call of his flesh, the strong pull of his emotions. They didn't speak as they crossed the lobby and took the elevator to their floor. His hands shook so that the key to their suite rattled metallically when he inserted it in the lock.

Then they were inside, and the door closed behind them. Wordlessly they went into each other's arms. Laurens felt Mayi's body tremble as his arms tightened around her. As if he was soothing a child, he kissed her forehead, then her closed eyelids before he finally claimed her soft, warm lips.

As his desire for her deepened, he felt a moment's uncertainty, but it was too late to turn back. He put his doubts aside, subjugating them under the hunger, the need. He lifted Mayi and held her high in his arms, and the fragrance of her heated body filled his nostrils, making him light-headed. She clung to him, her face buried against his shoulder, as he carried her into his bedroom and lowered her to the white spread.

While he undressed her, she lay there quietly, not trying to help him. She was watching his face, her eyes telling him that she knew he was acting out his fantasies of undressing her like this, removing each garment lingeringly, touching and kissing and stroking the creamy skin that he exposed inch by inch.

Under his hands and lips her flesh was incredibly soft and supple, and he watched with fascination as her breasts swelled in response to his touch, each mound like carved ivory; even the areolas and the small erect nipples were pink, not dark like most women's. He explored them with the tips of his fingers, then kissed their softness, gently teasing the small erections with his teeth. Her lips were full and moist and he kissed them hungrily, then buried his face between her breasts, inhaling deeply. The scent of her body, subtle and fresh and faintly musky, was like an aphrodisiac, arousing him until he was afraid he would lose control.

Mayi's hands stroked his tousled hair, then moved down to his shoulders and the nape of his neck. Spreading her fingers wide, she stroked his back. When he lifted his head to stare into her eyes, he saw that her pupils were dilated, and her body arched against his as if she was too hungry for deeper intimacy to wait.

He ran his fingers through the strands of her thick hair, then lifted her chin so he could kiss her mouth, her throat and then the underside of her breasts, the softest of all female flesh. Her skin was like silk, an invitation for further exploration, and he caressed her rounded stomach, lingering at the deep indentation in the center, then moving to the soft triangle below. At the slow stroking of his hand, she called out his name urgently, and the sheen of perspiration that formed on her skin seemed incredibly erotic to him.

He tasted her then, and when she moaned and twisted under him, opening herself to him, the heat from her body set him on fire. He buried his face in her hot, fragrant flesh, his whole body trembling under the force of his own need.

"I love you," he said, his words muffled.

Her caressing hand stopped, and there was a sadness in her voice as she murmured, "You only want me, Laurens, but for now—oh, God, for now, that's enough. Make love to me, Laurens. Make me forget—"

His kiss cut off the rest of her words. As his tongue plunged deep into the moist softness of her mouth, the need inside him became a torment, but still he continued to stroke her—her face, her throat, the softness between her thighs, and when he felt a slow quivering beneath his hands, he knew that she burned for him as he burned for her. Her eyes were moist, not from the wash of tears this time but from the fire he had kindled. As his caresses became more intense, she moaned and twisted like something wild and untamed, and he gloried in the knowledge that he had aroused her almost to the point of no return.

"Touch me," he said hoarsely, sinking down beside her. He groaned as she bent willingly over him, her loosened hair forming a veil around them as it fell, silken and cool, against his feverish skin. She ran her fingertips along the bridge of his nose, and then around the edge of his mouth and down to his throat, lingering for a long time at the place where his pulse throbbed erratically. Her fingers, those supple fingers that knew so well what drove him wild, traced a pattern through the hairs of his chest, stopping to caress his hard, masculine nipples as he had caressed hers. She stroked the taut muscles over his rib cage, his muscular stomach, and then the proud shaft of his manhood, making him aware as never before of his own virility. He breathed her name as she touched his throbbing flesh with her lips, and with a twisting movement, he rose above her, his body covering hers.

"Take me—take me now, Laurens," she moaned. He slid deep into the hot moistness of her flesh, and she yielded beneath his first frenzied thrust, her breath warm against his face. A primitive force drove him now, demanding that he satisfy himself without further delay.

But still he held back, wanting the pleasure to be shared. He watched her as he moved, gently now, against her. Her face was flushed and her lips were parted, as if in mute appeal for him to bring her to the brink of paradise. A surge of power moved through him and he lost all control; he sank into her fully, moving frantically now. She writhed beneath him, her body accommodating his every movement, and then they were both climbing to the ultimate intimacy together, two people joined in the greatest sharing of all.

When she came back to earth again, Laurens lay there holding her, their bodies still joined in the act of love, and a truth came to him. He loved Mayi—loved her even more than he had the day of their wedding, and the thought of life without her was unendurable.

He was sure now that she was in love with him, at least physically. She couldn't possibly have faked what had just happened. Even now her heart was racing in the aftermath of their lovemaking.

Maybe this was all that mattered. Maybe the rest of it—his pride, his honor, the debt he owed Pio for not being wise enough to understand his needs because they were different from his own—wasn't important. He wanted desperately to believe that Mayi had changed, that the woman who had tormented Pio to the edge of madness and then rejected him so cruelly no longer existed. If this was true, surely he could forgive Mayi and forget the past and go on from there.

Since she had come to Zubilibia, she had shown none of the venality that Pio had written about. Was it possible that part of her denials were true, that she simply had been too inexperienced to realize her effect upon Pio? Had she merely been thoughtless, a girl-woman stretching her wings and experimenting with her own sexuality, not really aware of her power over a rather naive young man?

And yet she had claimed Pio's insurance money without any qualms, and she had lied about her reason for coming to Zubilibia. When he had confronted her with Pio's letter, she had admitted that she already knew he was Pio's brother and that she felt guilty for Pio's death.

But what did he really know of the kind of pressure that had driven her? What did he know of being alone in the world with no one to give a damn if you lived or died? Wasn't it possible, no matter what her motive for coming to Zubilibia, that Mayi had really fallen in love with him and wanted a strong marriage as much as he did?

He raised up on one elbow and looked down into

Mayi's eyes. There were shadows in them as she stared back. She seemed uncertain of what he would say or do now that his passion was spent. He felt a wave of tenderness for her. If she really loved him, then the past few months must have been hell for her—as they had been for him. So why must she—and he—suffer anymore? What purpose would it serve? Revenge? He was sure Pio wouldn't want that.

"We have to talk, Mayi—"

"I know. I have something to tell you—"

"But not tonight. Let's forget the outside world tonight. Tomorrow we'll talk and make decisions, but right now I just want to make love to you again."

For a moment he thought she hesitated, but then she was smiling up at him. She pushed back the damp hair on his forehead and kissed the corner of his mouth. "Tonight we're just two people who met in Guernica and fell in love," she said huskily.

He kissed her then, and as he touched her, the passion began to stir again. This time when he made love to her, he moved slowly, savoring every caress as he brought them both to the peak of passion. And afterward he held her in his arms while she slept, the way he had done on their wedding night.

Tomorrow, he thought, just before the mists of sleep overwhelmed him, too. *Tomorrow we'll settle our differences. I'll listen to what Mayi has to say and try to believe her. And if I can't, then I'll learn to live with my doubts, because, God help me, I can't live without her. And maybe, if we're very lucky, we can build a real and lasting marriage, after all....*

CHAPTER THIRTEEN

MAYI AWOKE with exquisite slowness, knowing that something wonderful and exciting was about to happen, and then she discovered that it was already happening—Laurens was kissing her with the hunger of a man whose desire had gone unsatisfied for far too long. Wanting the sweet sensation never to end, she pretended to be still asleep and gave herself up wholly to the sweetness that moved through her limbs. Then his caresses grew bolder and her own body betrayed her. She moaned softly, and he gave a soft laugh.

"What a fraud you are, you little tease! Well, now you must pay the penalty. I'll make you happy, but only if you promise not to move an inch. That'll teach you not to play tricks."

With exquisite slowness he caressed her. The blood rushed to her skin, and waves of delight rippled up and down her body. When he brushed his lips against her breasts, she couldn't restrain herself any longer, and she lifted her arms to encircle his neck and lifted her body toward his. With mock anger he flung himself on his back, his arms folded across his chest. He looked so ridiculous that she had to giggle.

"Okay, you just blew it—to use one of your barbaric American expressions. No more loving today."

Mayi was enchanted by this playfulness from a man who was usually so serious. Using her fingertips, she explored the long length of his body, stroking him intimately. Since there was no way he could conceal his arousal from her eyes or her hands, he groaned finally and gathered her up in his arms, pulling her on top of him. As she felt his hard, virile body beneath hers, a surge of energy went through her. With an aggressiveness that seemed to surprise both of them, she initiated the next step of their lovemaking, accommodating her own body to his, then prolonging the exquisite sensations. She moved slowly, letting the tension, the throbbing sweetness build and build until it finally exploded.

"Oh, God, how I love making love to you, Mayi," Laurens whispered, and when she looked into his eyes and saw no censure, no suspicion there, she sighed with contentment.

"Did you know that there are tiny specks of gold in your eyes?"

"And your eyes are the color of mink," he replied, nuzzling her throat. "I think that after I've rested awhile, I'm going to lose myself in them again. In fact, if you keep looking at me like that, I just might forget about taking that rest."

He pulled her across his chest, but before he could carry out his threat, the phone beside the bed rang. With a muttered curse, he freed one arm and reached for it. She snuggled against him, liking the male scent of his body and the crispness of his chest hair against her face.

When his body stiffened, she moved away reluctantly, knowing their interlude of lovemaking was over. But there would be other days, other times for love now, she thought. Somehow they would work the ugly suspicions and the hurt of the past few months out of their relationship and return to what they'd lost.

Laurens cradled the phone, frowning. "Dammit. That was Sabino Echeberri. It seems that the regional tax-revenue man found another irregularity in our bookkeeping. He's at the winery now, demanding to see me." He ran his hand over his hair as if to clear his thoughts and change gears from lover to businessman. "I have no choice. Sabino is a fine wine master, but he's not much of a diplomat and if he antagonizes the man, it could tie up our shipments for months. So I'll have to handle this myself, I'm afraid."

Mayi struggled to hide her disappointment. She still hadn't told him about the baby, the one thing that could cement their new understanding of each other. "I'll pack," she said, sitting up.

"No, that isn't necessary. Since I chartered the plane for the next two days, they can fly me to Zubilibia and back in a matter of a few hours. With any luck at all I'll be back late tonight. Do your shopping while I'm gone, and we'll extend our visit for a few more days. Maybe we'll drive to San Se-

bastián and have that honeymoon we've never had.
I think we deserve that, don't you?''

Absurdly happy, she nodded so eagerly that he
laughed and kissed her. ''About that talk—there'll
be plenty of time for that. All the time in the world.''

There was a promise in his words and in his eyes,
and Mayi settled back against her pillow, smiling
up at him. Just yesterday she had been so full of
doubts, knowing that she must tell Laurens about
the baby. Now everything had changed, and her
news would be a joyous sharing with the man she
loved so desperately.

After Laurens was gone she fell asleep again. A
couple of hours later she awoke, ravenously hungry. She ordered a breakfast of mammoth propor-
tions, telling herself virtuously that she was eating
for two. She indulged herself further by eating in
bed for the first time in her life, propped up by
pillows. Her contentment continued as she dressed
and went shopping for the maternity clothes she
would soon need.

Although her pregnancy was barely apparent,
Constancio had already guessed her secret, which
meant the whole valley would know soon. They
would be delighted that another generation of Pelentes would be occupying the villa, and no matter
whether the baby was a girl or boy, her child would
be the next *echeko primu* of the Pelente house. She
felt a twinge of pain as she thought of Pio, who had
been the last *etcheko primu*. She had to believe that
he would have liked knowing that she'd put down

roots in Zubilibia and that Laurens's and her child would carry on the Pelente name.

The day passed quickly. Although the local shops were small and rather old-fashioned, she found several maternity outfits that pleased her, and she returned to the hotel late that afternoon, her taxi laden with store boxes. She was getting dressed for dinner, which she had decided to eat in the hotel dining room, when the phone rang. She hurried to pick it up, sure that it was Laurens calling from Zubilibia to tell her he was on his way. Laurens broke into her warm greeting and when she heard the remoteness in his voice, the happiness inside her burst like a pricked bubble.

"I've sent the plane back for you, and I've made arrangements for a rental car to pick you up and take you to the airport. Be ready in an hour," he said brusquely.

"What's wrong, Laurens?"

"I'll talk to you when you get here." The click in her ear told her that he had hung up.

For the next hour, as Mayi hurriedly packed, a thousand possibilities for disaster went through her mind. Had something happened to Engrace or Tia Petra? If so, why hadn't Laurens said so on the phone? Or had something very serious resulted from the inspection of the winery books? Laurens had sounded furious, as if he were holding on to his temper with only partial success. But surely he wasn't angry at her. She had done nothing that could possibly provoke his anger.

She put the mystery out of her mind for the present and hurried to shower, then dress in slacks, a silk shirt and a warm, wool jacket. Since there wasn't room enough in her small overnight bag or in Laurens's suitcase for all the maternity outfits she'd bought, she packed the overflow back into one of the store boxes. On the trip to the airport she sat staring out the window; she hardly noticed the rows of neat houses and apartment buildings that had been of such interest to her on the trip to the hotel.

During the flight back to Zubilibia, Mayi was thankful for the talkativeness of the copilot, who seemed to feel it was his duty to keep her entertained. She let his conversation flow over her, responding with monosyllables at appropriate times. Although she couldn't have said later what he talked about, at least it diverted her troubled mind.

But after a while his chatter and extravagant compliments began to grate, and she closed her eyes, pretending to doze. When he finally took the hint and returned to the cockpit, she did drift off, worn out by her lack of sleep the night before and the endless questions to which, as yet, she had no answer.

She awoke as the plane was settling down on the small meadow that served the village as an airstrip. Laurens was waiting for her, standing beside the Jeep that was used to haul supplies for the winery. As the copilot helped her down the retractable stairs, Laurens made no move toward her, his expression stony. Mayi felt confused and bewildered. For a few minutes he talked to the pilot, then waited while the copilot loaded their luggage and the store box into the back of the Jeep. When he motioned silently for her to get into the front seat, not even offering to help her up the high step, Mayi wanted to scream at him and demand he tell her what was wrong. But so much was at stake that she was silent as she climbed into the Jeep.

During the ride to the villa she sat staring straight ahead. Stubbornness prevented her from asking him any questions.

When they reached the villa he spoke to her for the first time. "Go into the library. I'll be there in a few minutes."

"Where are Engrace and Tia Petra?" she asked.

His eyes moved over her, cold and expressionless. "Don't add hypocrisy to your other sins, Mayi. Since you haven't had your dinner, I suppose you'd like a sandwich or something?"

"I'm not hungry," she said angrily.

He shrugged and turned away. "I'll order some coffee."

A few minutes later as she stood in the middle of the library, staring at his cluttered desk, she heard Laurens's voice in the hall and knew he was ordering coffee to be brought to the library. She expected him to join her immediately, but it was a good fifteen minutes before he appeared. To her surprise he was carrying a tray. "I sent the servants to their rooms. I'm sure you don't want them to hear what I have to say to you.''

Her blank stare seemed to anger him, and the muscles of his face tightened ominously. He poured coffee into two cups, set one beside her chair, then carried the other to his desk. Although she didn't want the coffee, she sipped it anyway; it gave her time to prepare herself for what instinct told her would be an ordeal. There could be no doubt now that Laurens's anger was directed at her; though she could think of no reason for it, she braced herself as if expecting a blow.

While she finished her coffee, she was aware of his eyes on her, brooding and cold. Finally she set her cup down.

"What is it, Laurens?" she said.

The quietness of her tone seemed to trigger off a rage he'd been holding in check and he made a chopping gesture with his hand. "So you intend to brazen it out, do you? Well, it won't wash. You should have told Engrace to lie for you."

"What do you mean?" she asked, in complete bewilderment.

In answer he took a piece of stationery from a desk drawer, brought it over to the chair where she was sitting and thrust it into her hands. "Read this before you dig yourself in any deeper with your lies."

Although she found it hard to concentrate, Mayi read the brief letter. As its words sank in, her bewilderment changed to dismay. Engrace had written:

I am going away with Luis. By the time you
return from Guernica, we'll already be married, so there's no way now you can keep us
apart. We've been in love for almost a year,
and we can no longer go on without each
other. Mayi will tell you how hard we tried to
stay apart. We failed because we were so
miserable. If I hadn't had her to talk to these
past months, I think I would have gone out of
my mind. I hope you will forgive me someday,
or at least that you will understand.

The letter dropped from Mayi's hand and came
to rest in her lap. She looked up into the condemnation in Laurens's eyes.

"They've eloped," she said stupidly. "Engrace
and Luis are married."

"And now you've had your revenge, haven't
you? How long have you planned this, working on
Engrace's mind, filling her full of romantic ideas,
corrupting her? Oh, you were so clever! First you
tricked me into taking you to Guernica, and then
you kept me busy so Engrace could run off with
Luis without interference. You must have been in a
panic when I got the call to return to Zubilibia. But
you needn't have worried. They were already gone
by then. You really could earn a good living as an
actress, you know. You were so convincing that I
never suspected a thing."

"You're wrong—so wrong. I didn't know—"

"Don't lie to me. It isn't necessary now. I know

you for what you are—a liar and a hypocrite and a cheat."

"I'm not lying. Engrace will tell you that I tried—" She broke off, realizing that Engrace wouldn't be able to tell him anything. From this day on, she wouldn't exist for Laurens. For a moment she felt envy for her sister-in-law, who had put her love for Luis above everything else but who also had the love and trust of the man she loved.

"What happened to all your fancy words, Laurens?" she said bitterly. "It was only lust, after all, wasn't it? If anyone here is a liar, it's you. If you were speaking the truth last night, then you would trust me, not condemn me automatically."

"Give you a chance to tell more lies? You must think I'm stupid. Why did you do it, Mayi? Was it revenge? Did you use Engrace in your scheme to get even with me?"

Despite his harsh words, there was more disillusionment than anger in his eyes. A feeling of hopelessness swept through her as she realized that it would be useless to talk to him. Silently she rose and started to leave the room, only to stop when his strong hands on her shoulders swung her around. Instinctively she jerked away, and his grip on her tightened painfully. As pain lanced up the back of her neck, she gave a choking cry, afraid for the baby she carried.

Her cry seemed to bring him to his senses and he pushed her away, breathing hard. "Get out of here," he said thickly. "I can't stand the sight of you."

Her head high, she faced him, knowing that she must have her say for the sake of her own self-respect. "For the past few minutes you've been hurling accusations at me. Now it's my turn. I didn't know anything about Engrace's elopement—"

"Are you saying my sister was lying, that she didn't confide in you about her relationship with Luis and that you weren't in on her elopement?"

"I knew they were seeing each other, but—"

"And still you didn't tell me what was going on?"

"I—I couldn't. I promised Engrace that I wouldn't. She was my friend. How could I betray her trust?"

"You betrayed *my* trust, and I'm your husband."

"It wasn't like that. It wasn't a conscious choice between you and Engrace. For one thing, she didn't confide in me, not at first. Of course I suspected something was going on during the festival when Luis chose her for the *aurresku*, but—"

"You knew about that?"

"I wasn't alone in—in wanting to keep it from you. Most of the village was there. Are you going to accuse all of them of betraying your trust because no one told you about it for a long time? They didn't want to hurt you or cause trouble by stirring up that old feud again."

"I don't need you to explain my own people to me. But you're my wife. Your first loyalty is to me, and yet you didn't tell me what was going on behind my back."

"I tried to get Engrace to go to you and tell you that she and Luis wanted to get married. They really do love each other, you know."

"Engrace is a child with a child's romantic notions, and for that, she will pay for the rest of her life," he said coldly.

"She's a woman, and love is all-important to a woman. We've always been willing to follow the men we love, even into exile."

Her impassioned words seemed to startle him. For a fleeting moment she thought she saw a flicker of belief in his eyes, but his voice was contemptuous as he said, "Marriage between a Pelente and a Hiribarren is unthinkable. Engrace has thrown away her family, her home, her people. And so has Luis Hiribarren. He'll never be welcome in his house again, not with a Pelente wife."

"But it doesn't have to be that way. Can't you put aside your bitterness and welcome Luis into the family? Can't you find a way to end the feud, once and—"

He stopped her with an angry gesture. "I've had enough of your interference in my affairs, you little tart—"

Mayi's temper had reached the boiling point. She drew herself up to her full height and stared into his eyes. "Don't call me that again," she warned. "Don't *ever* call me that again!"

"Would you prefer another word—such as bastard?" he said, his nostrils flaring. "You don't even know for sure who your own father is, do you? Is that why you're so full of hatred and envy? Do you get some perverse satisfaction out of manipulating people, stirring up trouble? You encouraged Engrace in this insanity of hers, filled her full of romantic notions, and then helped her run off with a man who is totally unacceptable. Are you happy that you made a fool out of me again? Well, it will be the last time you do. From now on I'm keeping a closer eye on you. And I'm warning you, I won't stand for you spreading poison among my people. And don't plan on any more little tête-à-têtes with Nicky Carrera. He's beyond your reach now. I talked his father into packing him off to school to learn modern banking practices. If I find you even talking to another man, I'll lock you in your room, and no one here will blame me. We Basques know how to handle an unfaithful wife."

"You're a monster, and I'm not going to stay here any longer than it takes me to pack my things and arrange for transportation home."

"And what if I decide that I want you to stay? After all, you're still a beautiful woman. You may as well service me when I need a woman."

His voice cut her like a whip. Blindly she backed away, and when he followed her, she turned and ran out the door and down the hall. She heard his footsteps behind her, and she darted around a corner and then, almost immediately, into the corridor that led to the kitchen. His footsteps ceased, as if he was listening, and she crouched behind the door, her hands pressed tightly against her chest.

He called her name, softly at first, then louder, but she didn't answer him, and it was only after she heard his footsteps on the service stairs that she moved silently down the passageway to the kitchen and out through the back door into the gray moonlight.

The night shadows of the garden beckoned her, and she felt a primitive urge to hide among them, like a wounded animal seeking the dark. She stumbled across the fieldstones of the rear patio and into the garden, running between the barren hedgerows. When she reached the wall that surrounded the gardens she climbed over it, not bothering with the gate. Moving by instinct, she crossed a narrow strip of meadow and plunged into the trees, following the path that led to the lodge.

The patches of moonlight that filtered through the bare branches of the trees were silver gray, as cold as her heart, and for a while it was easy to follow the path even under the trees. But the sameness of the terrain and the layers of withered leaves that encroached on the path soon betrayed her, and suddenly she realized that the pale stones had disappeared and she was wandering blindly through the forest.

She stopped, hunching her shoulders inside her

warm jacket against the night chill. There was no sound except the sighing of the wind through the branches overhead and the distant call of a night-flying bird.

Was it a snow dove, she wondered dully. A snow dove who had started back too early to its summer home in the north, only to lose its way through the mountain passes. If so, it would be trapped here in this valley, waiting for summer—and so would she if she didn't find a way to escape. Although she was sure that Laurens's threat to use her as a sexual object was only his way of showing his contempt, she knew that he would never let her go once he found out she was carrying his child. Before this final confrontation she might have had a choice, but not now. Now his hatred for her would outweigh everything else, and he would use this to punish her for yet another crime she hadn't committed. Once again Laurens had turned his back on her, and although she knew there was no malice in Engrace's letter, it had been just as damning as Pio's had been.

There was a bitter taste in her throat, but she wouldn't allow herself to cry. There would be time for tears later, when she had found her way out of there. Meanwhile she must think of her safety and the safety of the baby she was carrying.

Cautiously she moved forward, taking care not to stumble. The ground was still soggy from the winter snows and made progress difficult, but she struggled on. Half an hour later when she found herself under the same oak tree from which she'd started, she had to admit that she was lost and had no idea where to go next. She tried to remember where the moon had been when she'd plunged into the woods, but she'd been too upset to focus on anything except her desire to escape from Laurens. Fear stirred and set her heart racing, but by clamping down hard on the panic that made her want to run blindly through the trees, she managed to stay calm enough to make a plan.

First she must find shelter for the night. It was too cold simply to huddle under a tree somewhere or wander around in the dark, and in the morning she would have a better chance of finding her way out of the labyrinth of trees.

She attempted to stay in the patches of moonlight as she went on, stopping now and then to get her bearings as best she could, but it was only by pure accident that she stumbled upon the shepherd's cabin.

It stood in a small clearing, dark and forbidding in the moonlight. When she drew closer she saw that it was derelict; it no longer had a door, and its one window was a square of blackness. But she knew its stone walls would provide shelter from the rising wind, and she finally mustered up the courage to go inside. She was met by a dank odor tinged with musk, and images of wild creatures filled her mind as she stood there, hugging her chest with her arms.

After a while, when nothing stirred and she

heard no sound except the wind whistling through a gaping hole in the roof, she edged her way forward. Her knee bumped against something solid. She felt it with her fingers and discovered it was a wooden cot. There was no bedding, not even a mattress but the slats were close together and she knew the cot would keep her off the damp ground until morning. Carefully she lowered herself onto the slats and huddled there, determined not to sleep. She was afraid of what might sneak up on her in the dark.

But her fatigue was stronger than her fear, and at some point during the night she fell asleep, awaking only when a faint light filled the doorway and the high square window.

Her body stiff and her muscles aching, she sat up and looked around. In the cold gray light the hut looked more dilapidated than she'd suspected, and she shivered convulsively. She'd been so exposed and vulnerable as she slept, oblivious to anything that might have harmed her during the night.

When she went to the door and looked out, a thick mist lay over the forest, and the morning wind seemed to whisper to her, telling her she was no longer welcome in Laurens's world. For a moment she felt a stirring of grief; once more she'd lost a home. She put the thought behind her and returned to the problem of finding her way back to the villa.

Logic told her that where there was a cabin, even one that had been abandoned for decades, there should be some kind of path. She studied the edges of the clearing, and when she found what looked to be an opening that didn't seem natural, she followed it for a few yards, only to lose it among the encroaching shrubs and clumps of dried ferns. But she went on anyway, hoping to pick up the path again soon. Once she thought she heard a dog barking off in the distance, but when she paused to listen, the only sound was the wind and the pounding of her heart.

She was pushing her way through a thicket of blackberry bushes, trying to avoid a patch of muddy ground, when she heard a rustling nearby as if a large animal was moving toward her. She froze, trying to remember if there were any dangerous animals in these woods. Deer and pottok, the shaggy little horses that roamed wild in the mountains—and wild boars. Weren't boars dangerous if they decided to attack? Well, maybe she could climb a tree—if she could find one with branches low enough for her to reach.

She waited, hardly daring to breathe, but the rustling sound stopped, and after a while she went on, her step quicker now. As if the spirits of the forest had taken pity on her, she stumbled upon the path again a few minutes later.

It led downward through a growth of mature beech, and she was sure now that it would lead her to another cabin or perhaps even to the villa. She was hurrying along when she heard a familiar whirring sound overhead. When she realized it was a helicopter, she dashed forward toward a small break in the trees up ahead, waving her arms.

A row of shrubs blocked her way and she pushed through them hurriedly, eager to reach a clearing where she would have a better chance of being seen. She realized too late that what she had thought was a clearing was in fact a drop-off into a deep gully. Frantically she tried to stop her momentum by snatching at a shrub, but her shoes slipped on the wet earth, sending her over the edge. She hurtled forward, rolling and tumbling down the steep sides of the gully.

She landed with a jarring shock that sent a lance of pain through her whole body. For a long moment she was too shocked to move, and when she finally did, the agony was so intense that she was forced to lie still again. Fighting against panic, she tried to assess the pain, and finally decided that she must have broken a rib and possibly her left leg, as well. She changed her position cautiously, and the pain came surging back. Suddenly everything around her seemed to be moving away from her, as if she were looking through the wrong end of a telescope.

Part of her was glad that the pain, too, seemed to be retreating, but the realization that she must remain conscious gave her the strength to fight the shadows that were closing in around her. She tried to move again and managed to drag herself forward through the muddy earth so that she was lying out in the open. Then she realized that the whirring sound of the helicopter had disappeared.

Tears filled her eyes, but she blinked them away.

Gathering all her strength, she called out for help, hoping that someone would hear her—a shepherd or a woodsman or a hunter. When no one came, she refused to give up. For the next hour she alternately called for help and then stopped to listen. But it was no use. No one answered her; no one stepped out of the woods to help her.

Her voice grew hoarse but she persisted, afraid that she couldn't survive the cold of another night. She drifted in and out of consciousness, but the moments of awareness grew increasingly shorter as the day wore on. She longed for numbness, for the cessation of pain, and only the realization that she was fighting for the life of her baby as well as her own kept her struggling against the seductive voice that whispered how easy it would be to give up and sink permanently into the blackness.

During these feverish, pain-filled hours she made a vow. If she survived, if the baby survived, she would put aside selfish concerns. No matter what the personal cost to her pride and self-respect, she would make peace and strike some kind of bargain with Laurens so that their child's welfare would come first.

The sun moved overhead in jerks and starts, dropping a little lower in the sky each time she drifted back to consciousness. When she opened her eyes yet another time to stare groggily up at the patch of sky above, elongated shadows were spreading out from the trees that surrounded the narrow gully. She tried to call out again, only to find that all that came from her throat was a croaking sound. But she persisted, husbanding her strength, until finally a few words escaped her raw throat.

"Help me . . . please help me . . . ."

At first she thought she was hearing things, that the voices that had whispered to her so insidiously earlier were back. Then she heard a crashing in the underbrush above her, and a few pebbles tumbled past her. Someone called her name and she closed her eyes, knowing she had been found. She and her baby wouldn't die in this lonely place.

She held the darkness at bay a little longer, wanting to see the face of her rescuer so she could thank him. Then someone was touching her, and she felt a hand against the pulse in her wrist. She opened her eyes to find Laurens bending over her. His face was so ashen that she was sure she was hallucinating again, and in her disappointment she shook her head weakly and drew back. The expression on his face became guarded and wary, but his hand was gentle as he brushed the tangled hair back from her face.

"Laurens?" she said questioningly.

"You're safe now, Mayi," he said, and at the sound of his voice she knew he was real. "Don't move until we find out how badly you're hurt."

"I fell. I heard a helicopter and I was running and I fell—"

"Don't try to talk. I'll take care of you," he assured her, and she closed her eyes and let go, knowing that it was safe to sink into the darkness now.

FOR ONE OF THE FEW TIMES IN HIS LIFE Laurens felt completely helpless. He was standing beside the canopied bed where Mayi slept, staring at the wife he both distrusted and loved, and even though he knew that nothing had changed, something within him had been resolved during the long night when he'd hunted for her so desperately through the darkness of the forest.

He had tried to make a bargain with God during those terrible hours and had vowed that if he found her safe and unharmed, he would release the insurance money Pio had left her, provide her with a generous settlement and let her go. But now that she had been returned to him, he wasn't sure he could keep his side of the bargain. He wanted her to live, to grow strong and well, even though it meant she would leave him. But when she did, how long would it take him to get over her, how long before he stopped thinking, dreaming, wanting her?

He realized that Dr. Echahoun was talking, explaining about the cracked ribs and the bruises, the sprained ankle and wrist, which were more painful than serious.

The words only partially sank in as Laurens continued to brood over Mayi. She had been sleeping ever since the doctor had treated her scratches and bound her ankle and wrist, and her bandages were no whiter than her colorless face.

Her hair, unrestrained and spread out on the pillow, was a flame that seemed both to warm him and to warn him away. He wanted to touch her, to reassure himself that she was really alive, but he was afraid that if he did he would lose control and gather her up in his arms and say foolish things. If she should awaken, she would know his secret, that he still loved her and would gladly humble himself before her if he thought there was a chance she would stay.

He realized that Dr. Echahoun had asked him a question. He answered it, and he must have made sense because the doctor nodded and set a bottle of pills on the nightstand next to the bed.

"I'm leaving these pain pills. She'll need them later, although the shot I gave her should be effective for several hours. Right now she's probably still in shock—not anything of lasting seriousness, but she needs rest and absolute quiet. No excitement of any kind." He snapped his bag shut, smiling at Laurens. "Cheer up, man. Things could have been a lot worse. Luckily she seems to be very strong even though she looks frail."

"She told me once that she'd never been ill in her life," Laurens said absently, aware suddenly that Mayi was conscious and listening to their conversation.

"Well, she's a very lucky young woman, and you're a lucky man. Her fall could have had serious consequences. Sometimes a first child is more susceptible to physical traumas. I'm sure the baby hasn't suffered, but even so, I advise complete rest for a few days, just to make sure. A fall like that with the baby only four months along...one never knows.''

Laurens heard his words, but it was a few seconds before they registered. "Four months along?'' he repeated.

"Give or take a few weeks. Of course, this is just my educated guess without a complete examination and tests." He gave Laurens a curious look. "Did you think her pregnancy was further along? I could be wrong, of course.''

But Laurens had stopped listening. Somehow he responded correctly when Dr. Echahoun offered to arrange for his wife, who was a practical nurse, to stay with Mayi for a few days. The doctor assured him Señora Echahoun would be only too glad to have a patient to fuss over, and then he left, after congratulating Laurens again.

After he was gone Laurens sank down on a chair beside the bed. He met the fear in Mayi's eyes, and as if she had spoken aloud, he understood the reason for her fear. *She's afraid I'll take the baby away from her,* he thought.

A child—Mayi was carrying his child, a child they had created between them. If her pregnancy was four months along, then she had known about it for at least two months. Why had she kept it from him? From some desire to make him suffer? Or had it been fear, the same fear he saw in her eyes now? In his country, laws gave priority to a father, so he would have no trouble getting custody of his child, something Mayi must realize. From the panic on her face, he could tell that she wanted the baby; otherwise she could have returned home months ago and had it aborted. That she had stayed on proved—what? That she wanted the child to know its own father?

"Why didn't you tell me you were pregnant, Mayi?" he said heavily.

"I didn't know how you would react to my having your child." Her voice was hoarse, and it was hard to make out her words. "I wanted to be alone with you when I told you. That's why I went to Guernica with you."

"But you didn't tell me, and we were there two days."

She moved restlessly, her eyes feverish. "I tried to tell you, but you said we should wait until morning to talk."

He brushed her words aside. "Who else knows? I suppose you confided in Engrace? You two have been thick as thieves lately."

"I haven't told anyone. But Constancio suspects it. She has a built-in radar about such things. She told Engrace that she thought I was pregnant."

His mouth tightened, but he didn't point out that probably half the village already knew that he would soon have an heir. Mayi must know that. Had she postponed telling him to cause him humiliation?

"If you don't want this child, I'll go away," she said.

Anger swept over him and he stood up, frowning down at her. "You'll stay here until the baby is born. I'll see that you get good care, and the rest and quiet Dr. Echahoun recommends for you, but there'll be no talk of you leaving. This child is mine, too. Someday, he'll be *etcheko primu* of the Pelente house."

"What if the child is a girl?"

"It makes no difference. You know that much about our customs. We don't practice Salic law in Zubilibia. A daughter can inherit as well as a son. When she marries, her husband will take the Pelente name and the line will go on."

"Is that all a child means to you? An heir?" she said, her voice bitter.

"I don't have to explain myself to you. I want this child—that's all you need to know. I intend to do a better job with him that I did with Pio and Engrace, and because a child needs his mother's love, you're welcome to stay as long as you like."

For a long while she stared at him. When she spoke, her voice had a dull, dead sound.

"The day we were married, I was so much in love that I would have given up anything, done anything, for you. All I wanted was to be your wife, to live with you in this peaceful valley for the rest of my life. Even after you turned on me I stayed, because I hoped that someday you would change. But that hasn't happened. Even if you found out tomorrow that I had nothing to do with Engrace's elopement, you would still suspect everything I do.

I would spend my life proving myself, over and over again, being careful what I said and who I talked to, always afraid that you would find some new reason to distrust me."

He started to speak, but her rasping voice over-rode his. "Hear me out. For God's sake, just for once, hear me out! When I was lost in the woods, certain that I was going to die, that I had killed my baby because of my stupidity, I made a vow that if we both survived, I would put the baby's welfare first, no matter about my own desires or feelings. I don't want to live in an atmosphere of hostility and suspicion where everything I do is measured against some yardstick in your mind. But I, too, believe that a baby should have both his parents.

"I've lived as an orphan, and I know what it's like to belong to no one, to face every little problem alone, with no one to rejoice at your triumphs or grieve with you when things go wrong. So I'll stay here, even though this place has become a prison to me. But I'm warning you—don't push me too far, Laurens, or I may not be able to keep my vow. If I stay, there'll be no more recriminations and accusations. You'll treat me with respect or I'll leave you. And no barbaric code of law can keep me from taking my child with me."

She closed her eyes. "And now I want you to go. I'm very tired."

For a long moment Laurens stared at her pale face, then her trembling hands. Without a word, he turned and left the room.

CHAPTER FOURTEEN

EVERY MORNING unless it was raining, which it did with great frequency that spring, Mayi and Topet took a walk along the road that zigzagged downward toward the village. Mayi no longer went to the meadow or took the path through the forest. These days she avoided anything that might arouse her from her strangely peaceful lethargy.

Sometimes Laurens walked with her, and their conversation was pleasant, impersonal, like two strangers who had fallen into each other's company for a while and were making polite conversation to pass the time. They spoke of the weather, of village affairs, about books and music, about Tia Petra's arthritis and Topet's growing blindness, about the vineyards, where the vines, gnarled and thickened with age, were greening against the brown earth of the hillsides. Sometimes they even talked about politics and the state of the world, about everything and anything as long as it wasn't personal.

Occasionally Mayi wondered a little about the change in Laurens, but she never let her thoughts dwell on him too long. Although she knew his concern for her was because she was bearing his child, the child whom he hoped would replace Pio as his heir, she responded to his new gentleness as if it was natural, never questioning it or analyzing it too deeply. That would be painful, and she had no tolerance for pain these days. It was enough to take each day as it came, to observe with wonder the changes in her own ripening body and look forward to holding her baby in her arms.

This morning as she stopped to give Topet's old legs a rest, she sat on a small pile of fieldstone beside the road and took pleasure in the wild flowers that grew so profusely along the ditches. To her surprise, Laurens had named them for her as they'd begun to appear, telling her what various wild herbs were used for, and she discovered that he had a deep interest in floriculture, something she wouldn't have suspected in such a pragmatic man.

Or perhaps he wasn't pragmatic. These days she was seeing a third side to the complex man she'd married. He was no longer the ardent lover of their wedding day or the harsh man who had hurt her so cruelly with his lack of faith. There was a mellowing in his attitude toward her, one that she responded to with relief if not complete trust. When he checked with her daily to make sure she had taken the vitamins and iron pills Dr. Echahoun had prescribed, it was almost possible to believe that theirs was a normal marriage, that the bitterness between them had never occurred. At the dinner table she would often look up to find that he was watching her, his face sober, and she couldn't help noticing that his face had a drawn look, as if he was having trouble sleeping at night.

Topet, who was dozing at her feet, his nose anchoring down her foot, shifted his position and brought her thoughts back to the present. She had just decided to move on when she heard a car climbing the steep grade from the village. She bent to put a restraining hand on Topet's head, even though she knew he was too wise to wander out into the road in front of a car. When she saw it was Laurens in his Maserati, she waved, and he pulled up alongside her.

"Do you want a lift back up to the house?" he asked.

"No, I'm not tired. I thought Topet could use a rest. I'm about ready to start on again."

"Then I'll join you. I need to stretch my legs after being in my stuffy office at the winery all afternoon."

He parked the car and got out, and for a moment, until she put a check on her thoughts, her heart jumped as she noted the easy grace of his body and the play of muscles across his arms as he tossed his suit coat onto the seat and slammed the door.

He turned, and some of her feelings must have remained on her face, because he asked her quickly, "Is something bothering you, Mayi?"

"I was just thinking about—about Topet. He's been acting like a puppy lately. Frisky and full of beans, I mean."

"Full of beans—very expressive, you Americans." His voice was so dry that she had to laugh. "You should do that more often, Mayi," he added. "You seldom laugh out loud, you know."

Unexpectedly she felt a thrill of anger. "I laugh when I have reason to."

"There haven't been too many occasions for laughter in your life, have there?" he asked softly.

"My childhood wasn't all that bad," she said defensively. "In fact, it could have been a lot worse. Most of the people I stayed with were kind. They were impersonal, but that's to be expected. Foster parents can't possibly invest their emotions in every child they take in, so they learn to develop a protective shell, the way doctors and nurses do. Even when I was a youngster, I understood that. And I was very lucky because I had my grandmother until I was nine. Okay, I was lonely at times, but who isn't? People can be lonely in the middle of a large family or a big city. And it gave me an incentive to—to make something good of my life. There are worse things than being alone, you know."

"You're right. You had more than I did, for all my Pelente background. My mother didn't have time for me—she had her own problems. Pio was a sickly child who took all her attention, and then she died having Engrace. My father was a cold man, very much the disciplinarian except where his own excesses were concerned. When he was drinking he was verbally abusive. Pio and Engrace learned very early to keep out of his way when he was drinking, but I had too much pride, so I got the brunt of his abuse. Luckily he was seldom here. I hated him, and that's a very abrasive emotion, hating your own father so much that you wish he were dead.''

"Is that why you tried so hard to make it up to Pio and Engrace?'' she said, speaking her thoughts aloud. When he didn't answer her, she added, "I know you're hurt because Engrace seems to have turned on you, but she loves you almost as much as she loves Luis. She tried to give him up—that's why he went away to San Sebastián. It didn't work because what they feel for each other is genuine love. Otherwise Engrace never would have eloped with him. And Pio loved you, too, enough so that he was coming back to Zubilibia despite his own desire for a different kind of life.''

She stopped, sure that she had said the wrong thing, but there was no anger in Laurens's voice when he spoke.

"I was wrong about a lot of things. I know now that I demanded too much from them. After my father's poor management depleted the family holdings, I was determined to put the estate back on its feet. I wanted Pio beside me, helping me with the winery, but he didn't want that kind of commitment or responsibility. He wanted to leave the valley and see the world, live among strangers and become a writer. Eventually I made a bargain with him. He was free to go off on his own at any time, but if he wanted me to continue his allowance, there was a time limit—one year. Then, just when I

was sure he was coming back, I got word that—''
He stopped, his face bleak.

"Pio didn't commit suicide," she blurted. "He told me once that he was ready to grow up. I know he meant it. That's why I'm sure his death was an accident."

He was silent a moment. "I want to believe that."

Topet, who had been making side trips into the tall grass at the edge of the road, came prancing up, his tongue lolling and his eyes roguish, as if he were laughing at some canine joke. Laurens bent down to scratch the small indentation behind his ear. "I see what you mean about him acting like a puppy. Well, even old dogs get frisky in the spring. I hope this isn't—'' He broke off, and when he went on, he changed the subject. "If we had some food, we could have a picnic."

With the second sense that sometimes existed between them, Mayi knew that he had intended to say, *I hope this isn't his last spring. . . .*

She felt a tightening in her throat, but she said lightly, "As it happens, I did bring along a cheese sandwich and a candy bar for Topet and me. How about sharing it with us?"

They settled down on a patch of grass in the sun. With meticulous care Mayi divided the sandwich into three equal parts, gave one to Laurens and fed the second to Topet. The retriever devoured his portion in one gulp, then sat there quivering, his ears alert, watching as she nibbled on her third. She produced a candy bar from her jacket pocket and again divided it, laughing when Topet forgot his manners and gave an impatient bark.

"Did you take off work early because you had spring fever?" she asked Laurens.

"What's that?"

"It's what you get in the spring when it's too nice outdoors to stay inside working."

"So that's what I have. I suspect the whole valley has it, too. There won't be much work done today. Everybody seems to be out picnicking or taking a walk or strolling in the sun."

"All except Tia Petra. She's sitting on the terrace, crocheting like crazy on something she calls a belly warmer," Mayi said ruefully. "I pointed out that I was going to have a late-July baby, but she just smiled and kept right on crocheting."

They exchanged amused glances. Tia Petra had appointed herself guardian of Mayi's health and had taken charge of preparations for the baby, including its wardrobe. In the past few weeks, despite her arthritis, she had turned out enough crocheted sacques and receiving blankets to take care of a dozen babies.

"I'm afraid she's going to spoil our son or daughter terribly," Mayi said.

"A little spoiling from a great-aunt never hurt a child."

"This is Laurens Pelente speaking?" she said, feigning shock.

"I've learned a lot since my efforts at being a surrogate father," he said. "I think I'll do better this time."

"I know you will," she said, and meant it.

They walked home slowly, talking easily, and Mayi felt a lightness of spirit that remained with her during the following days. Although she found it increasingly difficult to get around, she took her daily walks and watched her weight religiously. As a result, she'd never felt better in her life and she eagerly waited for the last week of July and the birth of her child.

But the baby didn't wait until then to be born. In early July, when the grapes were ripening in the vineyards, Mayi felt the first labor pains. Twelve hours later, in the same bed in which Laurens had been born, Mayi presented him with a son and heir.

THE DELIVERY HAD BEEN NORMAL. Mayi was delirious with relief that her son was a sturdy baby with lusty lungs even though he'd been a bit premature. He was a beautiful baby, with a full head of dark-red hair and fair skin like his mother's. When Mayi held him in her arms for the first time and felt his searching mouth at her breast, she knew that the worry and fears of the past months had been worth this moment.

She had known that Laurens would be proud of his son; what she hadn't expected was his complete capitulation the moment he was allowed into her bedroom to view the baby. As if he'd been a father a dozen times before, he seemed to know instinctively just how to hold his son. Mayi saw the tenderness in Laurens's face as he looked down at the baby sleeping in his arms, and a strange jealousy stirred inside her.

"He looks like you," Laurens said huskily. "He'll have your eyes, too, I expect."

"Well, it's too soon to tell," she said, holding out her arms. Although he relinquished the baby immediately, she knew he was reluctant to give him up.

"What shall we name him?" he said.

"I know it's the custom in your family to name a baby after his maternal grandfather," she said, "but since I'm not sure of my father's name, would you like to name him for your father?"

For a moment he was silent, and she knew he was remembering the words he'd flung at her so angrily that day in the library. "I've never told you how sorry I am about that, Mayi. I am, you know—very sorry. As for naming the baby after either of his grandfathers, let's start a new tradition. Any ideas?"

"How about Michael? St. Michael the Archangel is the patron saint of the village, and I've always liked that name."

"It's a good, strong name." Laurens touched the sleeping baby's face. "Michael it is."

During the next weeks Michael thrived. He was a contented baby, as if he knew that he was surrounded by love. For Mayi it was a strange, dreamlike time. For the first time in her life someone was completely dependent on her, needing the sweet milk that flowed so abundantly from her breasts, needing her care to keep him warm and dry and comfortable. She devoted herself to him, pushing aside her personal worries.

"Michael is my child," she told Tia Petra when the older woman suggested that she needed help with the baby. "I want to take care of him myself."

Although Tia Petra didn't argue with her, Mayi knew that she was disappointed. When it finally dawned on her that Michael's great-aunt wanted more time with Michael herself, she reluctantly relinquished some of the strings and allowed Tia Petra to watch him a few hours a day, knowing that her own total absorption in her child was unhealthy.

During the last weeks of her pregnancy, when she'd become so ungainly, she had stopped her English classes. Now, knowing that she should find some outside activity, she decided to resume them, especially since she'd had feelers from several of her former students.

She discovered that her status in the village had soared since she'd provided the Pelente family with an heir. *What's good for the Pelentes is good for Zubilibia,* she thought, paraphrasing the old American saying about business and the government. That she could accept such a belief as normal brought home to her something she hadn't realized until now: during her months in Zubilibia she had adjusted to so many of the new ways, new mores, just as she had once adjusted to the rapid changes of her childhood.

During these days, as she devoted herself to her son, she often thought of Engrace and wished she could introduce Michael to his aunt. From time to time she heard news of Engrace and Luis, always in the form of offhand remarks that Constancio, who kept in touch with them, dropped into conversations. Luis and Engrace were happy, but they both wanted to come home, Constancio told her, sighing. Although they had tried to adjust to city life, it was difficult, and they both missed the valley and their families and friends.

When she learned that Engrace was expecting a baby, Mayi went to Laurens, even though he had given orders that Engrace's name was not to be mentioned at the villa.

She found him working in the library, doing some of the endless paperwork that his secretary, who was on maternity leave for the third time, usually took care of.

"My offer to help still stands, Laurens," Mayi said, smiling at his messy desk. "I'm a passable typist, and with Michael on a regular feeding schedule, I have plenty of spare time."

Laurens leaned back in his chair, flexing his shoulder muscles. "You already have your hands full."

"But I like being busy. In fact I've been thinking about starting up my English classes again. Several of my students have asked about it."

"Not yet. As long as you're nursing Michael, you don't need any additional strain."

At one time Mayi would have argued with him and pointed out that his own secretary was expected to be back on the job within weeks of the birth of her child. But she had learned that there was a double standard where the Pelentes were concerned. As village patron, Laurens might work himself to the brink of exhaustion for the village co-op as well as settle disputes and keep the bickering factions of the village council from killing each other. Nothing was expected from his wife except that she be a good mother to the Pelente heir. Even her teaching came under the heading of pastime or hobby, because the Pelente women did not hold down paying jobs.

"Very well," she said. "I'll postpone the class until Michael starts on solid foods and I stop nursing him." She paused a moment, then said resolutely, "And that isn't why I came here. It's Engrace—I've heard some news about her that will interest you."

His face sharpened. "What is it?"

"She's expecting a child."

"And why do you think that would interest me?"

"She's your sister. She may need you."

"She made her choice. I don't want to talk about her."

Mayi turned away and went to stand by the window, not wanting him to see the anger on her face. How strange that he could be so protective toward the mother of his own child, despite their very real differences, and yet still harbor such hostility toward Engrace, whose only crime had been to love a man of whom he disapproved.

Unexpectedly she felt Laurens's hands on her shoulders, turning her to face him. "Mayi, Mayi—always trying to change us. This is our way, and it's as important to us as your American way of life is to you. Engrace knew, when she went away with Luis, that she would never be welcome here again. It was her choice. She made it, not I. And there is no future for them here, even if I permit her to return. Can't you see that? To welcome them back to this house would only stir up our old feud with the Hiribarrens."

At her silence he sighed, then added, "I didn't give orders that her name not be mentioned in this house through cruelty, but because I knew it would hurt Tia Petra to hear endless speculations about Engrace. You must make an effort to understand, because this is your life now. I'm not claiming that our ways are always right, but adhering to them keeps us strong. We've survived as a people only because we never deviate, never give in to pressure. Can't you try to understand that?"

"All I know is that Engrace is alone in a strange city, that she's pregnant and may need help. I was surrounded by people who—who were supportive when I was carrying Michael."

He was silent for a moment. "Very well, I'll give a little. When Engrace is ready to deliver, I'll per-

mit you to go visit her for a few days to help with
the baby. Will that make you happy?''

She started to thank him, to tell him that yes,
he'd made her very happy, and then impulsively she
kissed him instead. It was meant to be a fleeting kiss
on the cheek, but his hands tightened on her shoulders and he pulled her close, holding her there while
he kissed her thoroughly.

She knew immediately that she'd made a mistake. The old feelings were stirring through her
body, which had been without love for so long.
She wanted to stay in his arms, to have him make
love to her again, but she had been disappointed
too often. He had softened toward her before,
made love to her, brought her hope, only to reject
her and dash away those hopes once his own passion had been appeased. Three times now she had
suffered when he'd reverted to his old hostility
and suspicion. Could she endure it if it happened
again?

As his hands slid down her arms, pulling her so
close that she could feel the hard strength of his
body against hers, she knew that she wasn't strong
enough for another disappointment. During the
past months she had found a certain peace in his
impersonal kindness, a contentment just in being
friends with him. But if their old relationship was
renewed, how long would it last? The fear that he
would reject her again would always mar her joy.
What if his feeling for her was only lust? Lust
wasn't enough. She wanted Laurens's love and his

trust, which, she was painfully aware, she would never have again.

Carefully she extracted herself from his arms. Just as if it had been a casual kiss, she said, "I'll go tell Tia Petra the news, unless you want to tell her yourself?"

It was a moment before he spoke. She wouldn't look at him; instead she pretended to be straightening her blouse, smoothing down her skirt. "No, you can tell her. But you do understand, don't you, this is not a prelude to any kind of reconciliation?"

Mayi nodded and left him, closing the door behind her, but it was a long while before she sought out Tia Petra. Instead she went to her room and flung herself on her bed. She cried, muffling her sobs in the pillow, until finally there were no tears left.

DURING THE NEXT FEW DAYS, Mayi became aware of a deep restlessness that even invaded her hours with Michael. Knowing that she must keep busy, she renewed her interest in painting and ordering supplies from Pamplona. She was unpacking the order, a pleasant chore, when an idea came to her for something that would keep her busy until she could start her English classes again.

Laurens's thirty-third birthday was in September, and since she'd met him just after his last one, there were no bad memories connected with the day to haunt either of them. She and Tia Petra were planning a surprise dinner party for him, and it occured to her that a portrait of the baby would be an acceptable present, one that held no hidden dangers.

Although her art studies had been casual, she had been told by her teachers that she had a natural talent, especially for portraits. She was confident that she could produce a portrait of their son that Laurens would like—maybe even treasure. After all, Michael was her own baby. Who else could capture that intent look in his eyes when he was absorbed in one of his games, or the way his mouth curled upward, more on one side than the other, when he was amused?

It would also be her way of apologizing for the scene in the library, a scene she had precipitated by her kiss. Since that day Laurens had been courteous, but his old reserve toward her had returned. Although she knew she never again dare open herself to the dangers of resuming their physical intimacy, she yearned for the uncomplicated give-and-take of the days of her pregnancy and wanted them to return.

In her search for a place that would enable her to keep her plans secret from Laurens yet provide a suitable background for Michael, she finally settled on the grotto and arranged for Manuel to carry her easel and paints there. But when she was walking up the path, carrying Michael in a back sling, she wondered if she'd made a mistake. Would the grotto where she and Laurens had consummated their marriage evoke too many painful memories for him? What if he thought she'd chosen it on purpose to taunt him? Or would he even notice? Maybe by now he had forgotten their wedding day.

Well, it was time she forgot it, too. She couldn't go through life always treading carefully because of old memories. She and Laurens would have to live with the past, and maybe it was healthier to simply go on as if it hadn't happened.

When she reached the grotto, she put Michael down on a mossy spot near the waterfall. The rays of the late-September sun, oblique and golden, filtered through the leaves of the trees and turned Michael's hair to a golden-red halo around his face. As if he knew how important it was to her, he chose to be cooperative. As he watched the play of light and shadow on the rocks, Mayi worked feverishly, trying to capture the essence of his personality with her pastels.

How like his father he was, she thought, so alert and interested in everything around him. He would grow and thrive there, fitting comfortably into his Basque heritage, and Laurens would have the son he wanted, someone to take over the reins someday. So she had given Laurens that much. Was that why he was different toward her these days? As long as Michael had a happy childhood, did it matter that she would grow old never again knowing the full passion of the man she loved?

She was still working on the portrait when she heard footfalls coming up the path. It was probably Manuel, she thought. He had promised to return in a couple of hours to carry her equipment back to the villa. She began cleaning her brush on a bit of cloth, satisfied with her work for the day. When she looked up, Nicky Carrera stepped out of the woods from the second path.

He was wearing work clothes and was carrying a small metal toolbox. His smile was warm as he examined Michael, who immediately transferred his attention to the stranger.

"So this is the Pelente heir," Nicky said. "Laurens must be a very proud man these days."

"He is. How nice to see you again, Nicky. Are you back for good?"

"I am—and glad to be back, too. Now that I've had a taste of the outside world, I appreciate what we have here."

As he smiled at her, she saw that he had changed. The past months had matured him and given him a new assurance.

"Even so," he said, "I would've stayed for another semester, but the family needs me to take some of the burden from my father's shoulders. He's not too well, you know."

She nodded. The state of Señor Carrera's health was a matter of concern to his first neighbors. "Then you've given up your plans for a singing career?" she couldn't help asking.

He threw back his head in a laugh. "Oh, that was a boy's dream. Now I'm a man. I would've been miserable, living among strangers and learning their ways. In the future I'll do my singing at festivals and to my own children, God willing.''

"You're serious, aren't you?"

He looked surprised. "Of course. My dream was unrealistic, but we all have our youthful dreams. Even if I still wanted to pursue a singer's career, I couldn't let my family down. It isn't right to be happy at someone else's expense." He paused for a sly grin. "But when I get the chance, I'm going to challenge a certain *bertsolari* in Ochagavia to a contest—and I'll win, too, and earn money for my friends."

Although she smiled at Nicky's cocky words, Mayi was thinking how uncomplicated he made it sound, and how right and proper. "When you left so suddenly, I couldn't help wondering if Laurens had anything to do with it," she said.

"But of course. Didn't he tell you that I went to him, as I always do when I have problems? I told him that I wanted to go away to school to learn modern banking methods, but my father wanted me to stay home. 'What's good enough for my father,' he said, 'is good enough for me and you.' But Laurens talked to him and got him to see that I'd be much more useful at the bank if I had some formal training. Laurens has a friend who's a don at the University of Barcelona, and even though the course I was interested in had already started, he arranged for my enrolment. I have a lot of ideas that will be helpful when I take over my father's bank. Of course, they're much too progressive for my father to accept now, but—all in good time."

He went on to explain some of the innovative bookkeeping methods he hoped to introduce to his father's bank, but Mayi was only half listening. Instead she was struggling with an uncomfortable realization. She had been so angry the times that Laurens had misjudged her, but she had been quick to jump to conclusions, too. Knowing Laurens had taken a hand in sending Nicky away, she had assumed it was because of jealousy or to keep Nicky from being influenced by her enthusiasm about a singing career. She had judged Laurens without knowing all the facts, and it was sobering to realize that her suspicions had been wrong. How many other times had she misjudged him in the past year?

"There's another reason why I came home early," Nicky was saying. He reached out and took Mayi's hand. "The banns for Dolores Echahoun and me will be announced next Sunday by Father Ignatius. The wedding will be in November."

He looked so smug that she had to laugh. Nicky laughed, too, his eyes sparkling, and impulsively she pulled his head down and planted a kiss on his cheek. "I am so happy, Nicky—"

A voice interrupted her before she could add that she was happy for both of them. It was Laurens's voice, savage with raw anger. "What the hell! So you're up to your old tricks again, Mayi!"

LAURENS HAD JUST RETURNED from a harrowing morning with the warring factions among the elders of the village. As he always did when he'd been away from the villa, he immediately went in search of Mayi and Michael. He knew Mayi believed it was Michael he came to see, and he was careful to sustain this belief, not wanting her to guess the hunger that was so strong inside him.

These days they were so polite with each other, so careful never to say anything to evoke the searing emotions that lay just below the surface. Sometimes when he took his long nocturnal walks, trying to make himself so tired that he would sleep, the hunger was sexual, so strong that he was sure he would explode with it. Other times, like now, it was a gentle hunger just to be with Mayi, to watch the grace of her body as she bent over their child's crib, to see the expresions that crossed her mobile face, to hear her soft, husky voice.

During the past days he had come to realize so many things, and not the least of them was that things between them must change. He—both of them—must put the past behind them and go on from there. Whatever changes the future brought, they must become husband and wife again—for Michael's sake, if not for their own. To continue to live permanently under the same roof as strangers—no, it couldn't go on.

But the opportunity to talk to her privately never seemed to occur. There was always someone else nearby. Perhaps Mayi made sure of this. When he suggested that they take an evening walk together, she always had an excuse. Was it because she couldn't stand to be alone with him these days? Or was it fear—fear that another corrosive scene would erupt if they were alone?

Laurens's frustration grew when he went to the nursery and discovered it was empty, as were Mayi's bedroom and the patio where she often took Michael on sunny afternoons. He searched the house and found his aunt placidly reading a book in the small morning room. After he'd kissed her cheek, he asked if she'd seen Mayi and Michael, but she only smiled and said—rather mysteriously, he thought—that perhaps they had gone for a walk.

Too restless to make polite conversation with Tia Petra, he excused himself and went out into the garden. There he spotted Manuel, who was bending over a flower bed, removing tulip bulbs from the brown earth and replacing them with tiny green starts of petunia. When Laurens asked if he had seen Mayi, Manuel's smile broadened.

"She took the young one to the grotto to do some painting," he said importantly. "I myself carried her easel there earlier, and I'm to return soon to carry it back to the villa."

An idea came to Laurens. He had been trying to get Mayi alone so they could talk. What better place than the grotto, which held so many good memories for him—and, he hoped, for Mayi?

He told Manuel not to bother since he would be joining his wife at the grotto. From Manuel's smile he knew that his gardener suspected a romantic encounter was in the offing. Maybe, Laurens thought, it just might work out that way, if Michael was cooperative about taking an afternoon nap.

Half an hour later he was approaching the grotto when he heard a woman's laugh up ahead. He smiled to himself, knowing how Mayi loved to talk to Michael when they were alone together. Then he realized that he was listening not to one voice, but to two. One of them was Mayi's, but the other was deeper, male.

Unconsciously Laurens slowed his step, and when he came to the end of the path, he stood in the shadow of a tree, watching Mayi and Nicky. Although he couldn't make out their words, the scene before him was enough to send the blood roaring to his head and to make his hands clench into fists. Mayi was smiling up into Nicky's face, her eyes sparkling. Nicky was smiling, too, talking a mile a minute. His expresive hands emphasized his impassioned words while Mayi listened intently, her face alive with interest.

Dark suspicion came to Laurens; he tried to fight it, to tell himself that no matter how bad it looked, it had to be an innocent encounter of some kind. But why would Nicky, who had just returned to the valley, come to the grotto on the very day, the very hour, that Mayi had decided to paint there?

Reason intervened and he started to turn and walk away, knowing it would be impossible to hide his suspicions from Mayi's discerning eyes. Then Nicky reached out, took Mayi's hand and said something in a low voice. He looked so smug that

Laurens felt his own muscles tighten. And Mayi—Mayi gave a throaty laugh; she reached up and put her hands on each side of Nicky's head, pulling his face down so she could kiss him. "I'm so happy, Nicky," she said in a lilting voice.

Anger exploded inside Laurens; he stalked forward, into the clearing.

MAYI'S FIRST response when she heard Laurens's explosive words was disbelief. Even before she turned to meet the fury in his eyes, she felt a wave of nausea.

With an effort she kept her voice level and her eyes steady. "I was congratulating Nicky on his engagement to Dolores Echahoun," she said quietly, "As usual, you've jumped to conclusions, Laurens."

Laurens didn't answer her. He directed an angry glare at Nicky, who looked bewildered and disbelieving. "You'd better leave while you're still able, Nicky."

"But surely, you don't think this is some secret rendezvous! My father sent me here to do some repairs on the tower of death. He noticed some rotten boards on the ladder last year, and since it's almost hunting time again—"

"You don't have to lie for Mayi. I know who's to blame. And I want you to leave. I have some things to say to my wife—in private."

"You're wrong if you think—"

"Get out of here now or I won't be responsible for what happens!"

Nicky's face paled, but still he didn't move. When Mayi realized that he was afraid for her, she said, "Please go, Nicky. He won't hurt me—not physically. Laurens uses words instead of his fists for punishment."

Nicky gave Laurens a long, considering stare. "All my life I've looked up to you, Laurens Pelente, not just because we're first neighbors, but because you're my friend. But I have to tell you that I think you're a fool. I hope Mayi can forgive you for your insult. I know that if I were in her place, I couldn't."

He stalked away, leaving behind a silence that was broken only when Michael gave a cooing laugh. Mayi wanted to go to him and pick him up, but she couldn't seem to move.

"It's time we had this out," Laurens said, his voice rasping. "You've let me know very plainly that you don't want our marriage to be a real one. I didn't push it because you were still nursing Michael—and because I thought we both needed time. But that wasn't the reason at all, was it? How did you and Nicky keep in touch while he was gone? And how did you arrange this little—rendezvous? Why did you bring Michael along? He must have gotten in the way." He paused and his face twisted as an ugly suspicion struck him. "Or did you bring him here to show him to his real father? Is *that* it, Mayi?"

He took another step toward her. "No wonder Nicky broke off his studies to return home. Well, you corrupted him thoroughly. Are you satisfied? He called me a fool and he's right. How long after our wedding did you start meeting him, or were you lovers even before that? Is he a good lover? Is he the one who taught you how to tempt a man, how to make him want you so badly that he doesn't ask any questions?''

His hard words beat against her ears, but she didn't defend herself. Too sick at heart to speak, she picked up the baby and turned her back on Laurens's angry face. She was afraid that he might stop her, but he was silent as she walked away. When she reached the path at the edge of the clearing, she looked back to find that he hadn't even waited until she was out of sight to disappear up the path that led to the hunting lodge.

As Laurens plunged up the path, he was only dimly aware of the shadows that were thickening under the trees. Wanting only to be free from the sight of Mayi, he headed toward the one place where he knew he could be alone. By the time he reached the lodge it was almost dark, and he lit several lamps, hoping that light would banish the darkness inside him. But the rage still devoured him and he couldn't sit still. He prowled through the lodge, fighting jealousy and his own sick thoughts.

During the past months his feelings toward Mayi had mellowed, and he'd reached a compromise with his suspicions. Now the demons were back, raging and insatiable, and he was afraid of what he might say or even do to Mayi if he returned to the villa before he'd gotten his anger back under control.

He spent the night at the lodge, a sleepless night, and when his mood still hadn't improved by morning, he went for a long hike in the woods, following the route that led to the border. He wouldn't admit to himself that his real goal was the tower of death.

It was when he saw the raw new boards halfway up the tower ladder that a small doubt began to stir. For a long time he stared at the pile of sawdust at the foot of the stairs, evidence that Nicky had been working there—work that it must have taken several hours to do.

Other things came to him, like the pleased expression on Mayi's face as she'd pulled Nicky's head down so she could kiss him, a chaste kiss on the cheek. It hadn't been a lover's kiss—God knew he was familiar with her kisses of passion. She had touched her lips to Nicky's cheek as one friend kisses another.

And Nicky—he had been covered with sawdust and was wearing rough clothes. Would a lover come to a rendezvous dressed like that? But why hadn't Mayi defended herself? She was capable of standing up to him. If she was innocent, if his accusations were untrue, why had she simply stood there, heard him out, and then turned and walked away?

Laurens returned to the lodge, but he was too

restless to stop for food. He continued on down the path and eventually arrived at the grotto. Mayi's easel, still standing near a rock, attracted his attention, and he went over to have a look at the painting she'd been working on, expecting to see a landscape of the grotto.

But the canvas showed a portrait of his son, done in pastels. Michael was sitting in a pool of sunlight, playing with a leaf. As if Mayi had just called his name, he was looking up, half smiling, and even though his eyes were still the bottomless blue of a newborn, she had made them brown with tiny amber specks.

Laurens sank down on a rock with a groan. He'd made a terrible mistake. Was it an irreversible one? Had he ruined any chance Mayi and he might have had to put their marriage together again? And if he went to Mayi, told her that he was sorry—God, he was so sorry!—and willing to forget and forgive the past, would she take him on those terms?

He rose finally and went back to the lodge. There were still things he had to work out, reservations he must cleanse himself of before he went to her. If they were to have a chance at happiness, he must come to her with an open heart. Only then would they be able to build a real marriage.

It was the next morning before he returned to the villa. Feeling more relaxed than he had in months, he came home prepared to make his peace with Mayi, to ask her to forgive him as he was willing to forgive her. But when he reached the villa, he discovered that she was gone.

She had taken their son with her, giving Tia Petra the excuse that she was going to visit Engrace in San Sebastián. She'd left behind the emerald necklace and other presents he'd bought her, everything but her wedding ring and the tiny bell he'd given her on their wedding day.

She had also left a note. He found it pinned to the pillow of his bed.

I thought I could live with your suspicions in order to give Michael a father and to be near you, but now I know that it won't work. Michael needs a father, but not one who isn't sure about his parentage. So I am going away. Since I have no access to the money in my bank account, I've borrowed plane fare from Tia Petra, which I will repay as soon as I find work and can save up the money. Do whatever you like with Pio's insurance money—I don't want it. You can get an annulment, saying that I married you under fraudulent conditions, that I lied about my virginity—or anything else you like.

I'm starting a new life. Maybe in time I can forget all that has happened and be happy again, or maybe not. That isn't important. What really matters is that Michael not be surrounded with the kind of suspicion that could poison his life. I intend to do everything in my power to see that he grows up strong and healthy, believing in himself and in his own worth.

The note was simply signed with the initial *M*.

CHAPTER FIFTEEN

MAYI HADN'T EXPECTED TO MISS ZUBILIBIA so much. She had known when she left Laurens that she would be leaving part of herself behind with him. She'd known that for the rest of her life there would be nights when his face would haunt her dreams and she would awaken with tears on her pillow. But the thing that surprised her was how alien she felt in her own country.

She yearned for the emerald green of the Valle de la Añara, so different from the dry sterility of the Nevada desert. She longed for the serenity of Zubilibia with its red-tiled roofs and stone houses, nestled so snugly along the banks of the Río de la Añara. And for the Pyrenees, with their wealth of deciduous trees, so unlike the sameness of the Sierra Nevada's pines.

And she missed the people who had come to accept her as one of their own. She hungered for the brisk, clicking sound of Eskuara, for the lilt of a Basque voice singing a song that was a thousand years old. Most of all she grieved for the stability of knowing that tomorrow and the next day and the day after that she would be living in an ordered world, that her son and her son's son would live out their lives in the same place, and that perhaps in time the story of an American girl who had won the heart of a Basque would become part of legend along with others that had been passed down through the years.

Her longings were even stronger than she'd expected, and she almost welcomed the problems that awaited her, because at least when she fell into bed at night, she was too tired to do anything but sleep.

She had gone back to Reno, where she still knew a few people. The air fare had taken most of the money she'd borrowed from Tia Petra, so she had pawned her wedding ring almost immediately at one of the pawn shops that catered to gamblers who had spent all their "going home" money on the slots or at the blackjack tables. She had no problems with guilt. After all, she'd left behind the insurance money, which was rightfully hers. After she'd sent back the money she'd borrowed from Tia Petra by international money order, there was enough left to buy the things she needed for the baby and to keep her going while she looked around and tried to decide what to do next.

She stayed in a hotel the first night and the next day rented a mobile home that was on a bus line. The single-width structure was old and shabby and not very clean, but the rent was affordable, and there was a coin-operated washer and dryer in the mobile home park that she could use for Michael's diapers.

Before she looked for work, she knew that she must find a trustworthy babysitter. To her relief, she found one almost immediately—an elderly widow who lived in one of the mobile homes and who was a grandmother several times over. Her name was Mrs. Oldsfield, and she was delighted to be earning a little money to supplement her pension and, Mayi suspected, grateful for the chance to have a baby to rock again.

Although it was too late in the year for a teaching position, Mayi put her application in for substitute-teacher work, then applied for a keno runner's job at the same casino, the Robin Hood Club, where she'd worked before. Because of her past work record, she was hired immediately and was working within two weeks of her return to Reno.

The next few weeks were so hectic that she seldom had time to think, much less do something as impractical as read a book or newspaper. She lived in a kind of limbo where her only joy was Michael, his infectious smile and gurgling greeting when she came in from work. She forced herself to eat proper meals, knowing how important it was for Michael's sake that she stay healthy, and she kept the small mobile home immaculate.

Although she'd sold her car when she went to Spain and couldn't now afford to replace it, she took Michael out for daily airings in the second-hand stroller she'd bought at a thrift shop. Sometimes she just took him for a walk and other times they went to a nearby park to play on the grass.

Often, despite her resolution to put the past behind her, she couldn't help comparing the mobile home to what they had left behind, and there were times when she wondered if she had the right to deprive Michael of what was his by birth. Then she remembered her own childhood, the feelings of rejection that had plagued her so often, and she was sure she had done what was best. Her son would have few material advantages with her, but he would have the security of knowing that he was loved and accepted. With his stubbornness and intelligence, he would make his own way in the world. It wasn't the worst way to go.

Although she had half expected Laurens to make some effort to find her, if only to settle the matter of an annulment, she heard nothing. Even if he'd had second thoughts about his latest accusations and tried to get her to return, she would have refused. She'd never doubted his physical desire for her, but that wasn't enough. Whenever something—or someone—aroused his jealousy, he would revert to his old distrust, and she would be forced to prove herself all over again. She would always be on tenterhooks, wondering what would trigger his suspicions the next time. She couldn't live like that. She had too much pride, too much self-respect.

Nor did she want Michael to grow up in an atmosphere of distrust. Better that he have few material things than to live in luxury with a father who doubted that Michael was his son.

The days grew into weeks, and Thanksgiving came and went. Mayi often thought about Tia Petra, who loved Michael as if he was her own son. After some thought she finally wrote Tia Petra a brief letter, saying that she and the baby were well; she enclosed a snapshot of Michael, knowing that the older woman would treasure it. She also wrote to the Bilbaos, saying only that she thought of them often and that she missed the village and the people who had been so kind to her.

But she didn't explain why she had gone away, and she didn't include her address in either letter. That part of her life was over. To keep the pain alive by retaining any ties with Zubilibia could only make it harder to put the past behind her.

She often wondered about Engrace, who was suffering her own exile. Although she too must be yearning for the valley, she had Luis, her husband, to comfort her. Had their baby been born yet? If so, Engrace would have something else to sustain her and make up for what she'd lost.

Just after the New Year, Mayi changed jobs. Through one of the other keno runners she learned of an opening for a language teacher in a small private school. She applied for the job and was hired. The pay was much less than what she earned at the casino, but the job had several advantages. For one thing, it would give her experience for future résumés; for another, it was day work, with weekends free. Part of her duties consisted of tutoring newly enrolled students to bring them up to the classroom level, so her hours were flexible and she had a couple of afternoons off a week in addition to her free weekends.

When she had saved enough money she put the down payment on a car, a twelve-year-old Ford, which immediately expanded her world. Now she could take Michael on excursions into the mountains. She renewed a few old friendships and even made a couple of new friends among her co-workers. Although she was invited out to dinner by the vice-principal of the school, a widower in his early forties, she declined with the excuse that she was married, a condition she wasn't even sure was still true.

Having learned how to be frugal at an early age, she could cope much more easily with the lack of money than she could with the spells of despair that still haunted her. Michael's eyes had darkened to the same amber-flecked brown as his father's, and sometimes when she was looking at him she wished he had inherited her eyes so she wouldn't be reminded of Laurens so often. But she tried to take each day as it came, making adjustments to her new life, planning for the future, and eventually she achieved a certain plateau of peace.

The first time she laughed spontaneously at some of Michael's clownish antics was a landmark for her new life, and from then on it was easier. Knowing that she was a single parent with a child to raise, and that her life must go on not only for Michael's sake but for her own, helped. As the weeks went by she even began to hope that at some point she would be able to view her year in Zubilibia impersonally and come to terms with the past once and for all.

LAURENS STOOD BY THE LIBRARY WINDOW as he so often did these days, staring out at the mountains that loomed behind the villa. Because he was alone, he didn't try to hide behind the mask of indifference he wore in the presence of others.

Although it was late March, the wind that blew so constantly this year still held an icy tinge as it whistled up a dirge against the stone walls of the villa. Already the snow had disappeared from the mountain peaks and the first spring flowers were appearing in the haunted meadow, but Laurens knew that this year winter would remain in his heart. He didn't need the mirror in his dressing room or his aunt's worried looks to tell him that the past months had aged him. There were new lines in the face he shaved each morning, and his eyes had a bleak, frozen look even when he smiled.

But on the outside he presented a good face. He worked harder than ever, putting in long hours at his desk or at the winery or at his office at the co-op, even though some of it was make-do work. Only when he was alone did he allow his facade of normalcy to slip a little.

A knock sounded at the door, and he adjusted his expression before he called out, "Come in." He was not surprised to see it was Tia Petra. She was bringing him an afternoon snack, something she had started doing these past weeks. When he saw the pastries and buttered scones, a brief amusement stirred. Food was always Tia Petra's solution to any problem, which was strange, since she ate so little herself and was so thin.

"I thought you might like a cup of coffee and something to eat," she said brightly, and to please her he smiled and told her that he was a bit hungry.

"What were you looking at when I came in?" she said.

"I was checking up on Topet," he lied, wondering what she would say if he told her he'd been staring into space, thinking about a girl with fiery hair who had taken away his heart as well as his son when she'd left him. "He seldom comes out of his doghouse these days until late afternoon."

"He misses her, you know," Tia Petra said abruptly.

Laurens had every intention of ignoring the remark, just as he did any attempts to bring Mayi into conversation, but instead he found himself saying, "They took to each other right from the start. I was sitting on the hill behind the haunted meadow the day the two of them met for the first time. Topet had followed me there, but Mayi couldn't see me because the sun was shining in her eyes. She was running through the grass and Topet took out after her like a puppy. Later, I heard her tell him that she'd never had a pet—"

"Why don't you go after her, Laurens? Why do

you torture yourself so? She loves you. No matter what came between you two, I'm sure she still loves you."

"Once she did. But after what I did to her—I can't believe that she could forgive me for what I said."

"Do you want to tell me about it? Would that help?"

He turned brooding eyes upon her worried face. "It wouldn't help, but maybe it would make you understand how hopeless the situation is." He paused a moment, then said painfully, "I accused her of having an affair with Nicky Carrera. I was crazy with jealousy because I found them together in the grotto. I—I misunderstood something that I saw, and I said something unforgivable. I asked her if Nicky was Michael's father."

She was silent for a moment. "She'll forgive you if you go to her. She's a very forgiving person."

He shook his head. "Maybe, but she'll never return to Zubilibia. I failed her once too often. This wasn't the first time. Our whole marriage was built on sand...."

He told her about Mayi's friendship with Pio then, and as he heard his own voice, measured and unemotional, stating the facts that had once seemed so condemning, he realized that he no longer believed that Mayi was the woman Pio had loved. The facts were the same—the letter from Pio, the insurance, the other damning evidence. But now he knew that it was impossible for the woman he'd married, that he loved, to be the woman Pio had called "my lady." Whoever that woman had been didn't matter now. He no longer felt any hatred for her. All the destructive emotions had been burned out of him. *Leave her to heaven,* he thought, *or to her own hell.*

But the knowledge had come too late. How could he go to Mayi and ask her to forgive the unforgivable? She had done the right thing when she'd left him, and if it meant that he must live out his life with this shadow in his heart, it was only fitting. He hadn't measured up. He, who had so much pride, had failed Mayi in the worst way a man can fail a woman. He had taunted her for being a bastard, and then he'd told her he believed that their son was another man's child.

When he was finished, Tia Petra sat for a long time staring at him. He read disbelief in her eyes—and then pity.

"You've made mistakes," she said at last, "but I'm sure Mayi will forgive you. She loves you, and your son needs you. Find her and tell her what you've just told me. Tell her that you've paid too high a price for being inflexible. When she finds out that you've made peace with Engrace, she'll believe you."

"I doubt it. I was so bitter when I learned that Engrace had eloped with Luis that I accused Mayi of planning the whole thing, of going to Guernica with me in order to keep me busy so they could get away without my interference. She denied it, but I refused to listen. When I got Engrace's address out of Constancio and went to see her in San Sebastián, she told me that Mayi had begged her to go to me, to tell me the truth and try to get me to accept Luis into the family. That's one more thing she would have to forgive.''

"You've changed, Laurens. Before you met Mayi, you never would have gone to Javiar Hiribarren to ask him to end the old feud. It wasn't easy for you—I know what it cost your pride. Mayi will see that, too.''

"You still don't know the whole story, Tia Petra. I once told Mayi that I wanted her to stay away from Engrace because I was afraid she would corrupt my sister. At the time she knew that Engrace and Luis were having an affair, that my sister wasn't the innocent I thought her to be. She could have thrown it in my face, got some of her own back, but she didn't. It must have hurt her badly. How can I ask her to forgive that?''

"I didn't say it would be easy, not for a stiff-necked man like you,'' Tia Petra said, her tone dry. She hesitated, then gave a tiny shrug. "I received a letter from Mayi. I've been debating whether to show it to you.'' She took an envelope from her smock pocket and handed it to him. "She enclosed a photo of Michael. The postmark on the envelope is Reno, Nevada. In her letter she says—well, you can read it for yourself.''

Laurens's hands were unsteady as he opened the envelope. For a long time he stared down at the snapshot of Michael, at his lopsided half smile, before he unfolded the piece of notepaper. The letter was short, written in Mayi's neat, well-rounded handwriting.

I'm sure that Laurens has forbidden you to speak my name, just as he ordered us not to talk about Engrace, but I know you must be wondering what happened and worrying about your great-nephew, too. Which is why I want you to have this snapshot. I'll write you from time to time and send more pictures.

I wish with all my heart that it could have been different, that we could have worked it out. I loved Laurens, no matter what he believed, but he didn't love me, and I couldn't go on living with a man who only tolerated me because I was his wife. If I had continued to believe it was best for Michael, I would have stayed anyway, but my son's welfare must come first. I know this will seem mysterious to you, but it isn't my place to tell you the whole story. Perhaps, someday, Laurens will—at least his version of the truth.

If things were different, Michael and I would have lived out our lives in Zubilibia. Since that is impossible, we must make a new life for ourselves. Time has a way of healing wounds—or so they say—and I'm sure they're right, because my own wounds are already beginning to heal. I know that in time I'll be able to put Zubilibia and Laurens out of my mind—and my heart, too.

Goodbye—and good luck. I miss you very much.

Laurens folded the letter; his throat was so dry it was hard to speak. "She's better off without me. To try to find her, to rake everything up again just when she's getting along so well without me, I can't do that to her, Tia Petra."

His aunt made an exasperated sound; she reached forward and tapped his hand with her finger. "You're a fool, nephew. You aren't thinking straight. Look closely at the letter. Don't you see those smudges at the bottom of the page?"

"I don't understand—"

"Ah, men. They can be so dense. Those are dried tears. A woman would see that immediately. When Mayi wrote that letter, she was crying. Probably because her eyes were blurred with tears, she didn't notice that one tear had smudged the ink. Does that sound like a woman whose wounds are healing?"

Laurens read the letter again. For a long time he stared at the smudged ink. When he finally looked up, Tia Petra had left the room, and he was alone with the letter that could mean everything to his future—or nothing.

CHAPTER SIXTEEN

IT HAD TURNED HOT overnight, which was not uncommon in early June in the high, dry basin that housed Reno. The dusty streets of the small mobile-home park where Mayi and Michael lived were baking in the heat of a blazing sun that blistered the unprotected skin and assaulted the eyes of anyone unwary enough to go out without sunglasses.

It was Wednesday, one of Mayi's days off from her summer job at the casino, and she sat at the tiny table in the kitchen, her head on her arm, a glass of iced tea in front of her. A slow, ineffectual stream of air from a revolving fan blew across her exposed neck, and she mentally cursed the failure of the mobile home's antiquated air-conditioning unit.

She was wearing only a thin cotton robe, and her hair was piled on her head for coolness. She felt somnolent and dull-witted. The heat had made Michael fussy, and it had taken her a long time to get him settled for sleep. In half an hour or so the sun would drop behind the row of mobile homes on the other side of the street, and she longed for darkness, even though its coolness might be more of an illusion than reality.

She got up to check on Michael, something she did far too often. Although she knew it was unwise to keep such a constant watch over him, she lived with the terror that something would happen to him, and at times she longed to be able to share her responsibility with another person, a longing she knew was unrealistic.

Even now thoughts of Laurens still slipped uninvited into her mind at odd moments. Sometimes it was the way his lips twitched slightly when he was amused by something she'd said and was trying not to show it, sometimes it was simply how safe she'd felt when he'd put his arm around her in his sleep. Would it always be this way? Would she never be free of him?

Outwardly she had coped reasonably well. When the school had closed for the summer, she had gone back to work at the casino, and luckily Mrs. Oldsfield, her babysitter, was amenable to watching Michael at night again. Although her salary as a keno runner was considerably higher than a teacher's pay, she had put in an application for a teaching job with the Reno school system well in advance this year because she was looking ahead, thinking of the future. She was determined that when Michael grew up, it would be as a teacher's son, not the son of a keno runner. He would never have cause to be ashamed of her, and she wouldn't lie about his father, either.

She would tell Michael that Laurens was an honorable man, but that the gap in their different cultures had been too great for her to bridge, and she had decided that he would be better off living with her in the United States.

And if Michael asked why his father never came to see him, never wrote to him, or called him on the phone, she would tell him that she hadn't wanted her son to grow up with divided loyalties. He would probably resent that and blame her for depriving him of a father, but at least he would retain some of his illusions. When he was older, if he wanted to go to Zubilibia to see Laurens, she wouldn't try to stop him. Laurens's version of the truth might hurt him—or perhaps it would make him stronger. Either way, it was too far in the future to worry about now.

Mayi bent over Michael, her smile tinged with sadness. He was lying on his back, his hands above his head, and was wearing only a diaper. He looked so angelic with his flushed cheeks and his damp hair curling around his face that it was hard to believe he had a healthy temper and could be very stubborn about getting his own way. *Like father, like son,* she thought, and a familiar pain went through her, making her wince.

She turned away from the crib, wondering if it would always be this way. Just last week a man had spoken to her as she was hurrying through the coffee shop with a stack of keno cards and money. In that split second before she'd turned she'd felt a blazing moment of hope, but of course the man had been a stranger, wanting to place a bet. Gradually, though, she was overcoming this tendency to see Laurens in every dark-haired man, to hear him in every deep male voice.

Mayi returned to the kitchen to replenish the ice in her glass of tea. She rested her head on her arms and dozed off. When she awoke, her arms were numb, but the sun had dropped below the horizon, and already the air was cooler. She pulled aside the curtain so the kitchen would catch the evening breeze. Although still warm with day heat, the stir of air was welcome against her damp skin.

She went to take a long shower, one of the few luxuries she allowed herself now that she was saving every extra cent toward the day when she could make the down payment on a home for Michael and herself. Even if she had to work at two jobs, Michael would have a real home.

She came out of the shower, not bothering to towel herself dry; the air would do that for her. For a while she sat in the dark, brushing out the tangles in her hair and tossing the ends until they were dry. She had just about decided to turn on the lights and fix herself a salad and a sandwich when the shrill ringing of the doorbell startled her.

Mayi was sure it must be Mrs. Oldsfield, who sometimes dropped by for a chat on Mayi's night off, and she slipped back into her thin robe again, not bothering with a bra or panties. But when she opened the door, it was a man's shoulders that were outlined against the streetlight.

"Hello, Mayi," Laurens said. "May I come in?"

Her first emotion was shock, then joy—followed quickly by wariness. But she stepped aside, mutely allowing Laurens to enter her home and come back into her life.

As he brushed past her, she caught the familiar odor of his shaving soap and suddenly the desolation was back, as sharp and immediate as the day she'd left Zubilibia. She leaned against the door, fighting both tears and anger that he had dared come there and disrupt the peace she'd fought so hard for.

"I wasn't sure if you would let me in," he said.

"And if I'd slammed the door in your face, what would you have done?" She was proud that there was only a polite curiosity in her voice.

"I would have tried again and again until you did."

She snapped on a lamp and turned to stare at him. His eyes were red-rimmed and his face was haggard, as if he'd been ill. She knew she should have felt pleased, knowing that he had suffered, too, but she only felt sad.

"Did you come here to see if Michael is beginning to look like the Pelentes? Well, he doesn't. He looks like me."

"But he has my eyes, Mayi. You knew he would, didn't you? That's why you painted him that way."

She bit her lip, remembering the pastel she'd been doing for Laurens's birthday the day she'd left Zubilibia. She had been sure that Michael's eyes would turn brown and that they would have the same golden lights that made Laurens's eyes so startling. Was *that* why Laurens was there—to get his son?

"You can't have him, Laurens," she said, and despite herself her voice was shrill. "This is *my* country. Your laws don't apply here. I'll fight you through every court in the land and I'll win, because no judge would—"

"I don't want to take Michael away from you, Mayi. That's the last thing I'd do."

She sagged in relief, and unexpectedly the tears she'd been holding back escaped and ran down her cheeks. She fought against them, only to lose the battle. Somehow she found herself in Laurens's arms, her face buried in his chest. He was rocking her gently back and forth as if she was a child who had been hurt.

Briefly she felt comforted, but it couldn't last. She pulled away, not looking at him. She had done so well these past months, seldom relaxing her guard or feeling sorry for herself. Why had she let go now and shown weakness in front of Laurens? Would he try to take advantage of it? If he did he would find out that she was a fighter, that she— only what exactly was she fighting? Hadn't he already said that he wasn't there to take Michael away from her?

"If it isn't Michael, then why are you here?" she asked.

"Because I couldn't stay away any longer. I told myself that you'd never forgive me, but logic

doesn't mean much where the heart is concerned—
something you once tried to tell me. I came here to
ask you to return to Zubilibia with me, to be my
wife again.''

He paused and she knew that he was fighting his
own battle to keep his voice under control.

"I found out a lot about myself these past
months,'' he went on. "I love you, Mayi. You're in
my blood, in my heart. If you'll come back to me,
I'll make any concession—and do everything within my power to make you happy.''

Mayi read the desperation in his eyes, and she
knew that she had won. It was something she had
dreamed about during her more bitter moments, to
see Laurens humbled. So why did she feel so rotten? Was it because she hadn't ever, even in her
worse moments of despair, wanted him to suffer as
she had? What she wanted was the man she'd first
fallen in love with—strong and proud and confident....

Most of all she wanted their marriage to succeed,
and for that to happen, something in addition to
love was needed—simple, unqualified trust. She
loved Laurens, wanted him, but she couldn't live
with his distrust, no matter how willing he was to
try again. Eventually his doubts would tarnish their
love and ruin things between them again. What she
needed was to know that Laurens believed her in
spite of the evidence against her.

Ironically, it would be easy now to prove her innocence. When she'd returned to Reno and taken

her possessions out of storage, she had found the note Pio had written her in a footlocker along with other papers and souvenirs. She'd kept it as a remembrance of their friendship, and as she'd read it again, she'd realized that it was a silent testimony to the truth.

It was so obviously the letter of one friend to another, not a love letter. There was no way the recipient of the letter could be the woman Pio had called "my lady."

"Are you saying that you're willing to forgive me for what you believe I did to Pio?" she asked carefully.

"There isn't any question of forgiving you. I'm sure you couldn't be that woman. The woman I married and lived with could no more be the woman Pio described than—than Tia Petra. The real question is, can *you* forgive me for my lack of faith?"

She hesitated—but only for a moment—before she held out her hand. For a long time he stared into her eyes, and then he took her hand and squeezed it tightly. But he didn't kiss her, and she knew he sensed that she still had reservations.

"I have a letter that Pio sent me just before he was killed," she said. "Do you want to see it?"

"No, it isn't important."

"Are you afraid that it's a love letter and it might prove I'm the woman Pio wrote you about?"

"I'm not afraid. Even if it was, then I'd have to believe that Pio was out of his mind when he wrote it."

"I want you to read it anyway, just to—to clear the air. Then we never have to talk about it again."

"Very well, if that's what you want. But first I want to see my son. I've missed him—God, I've really missed him, Mayi!"

Silently she pointed to the bedroom, but she didn't follow him. Instead she sank into a chair, watching the bedroom door. It was several minutes before Laurens joined her; his face had a drawn look that brought a lump to her throat.

"He's a beautiful child," he said simply.

"Yes, he is. The letter's in the kitchen. I think you should read it—just to make sure."

As she led the way to the kitchen, she had to smile; now that Laurens was in it, the room seemed suddenly to have shrunk in size. Laurens reached out and touched the corner of her mouth. "I've missed that most of all. I used to try to be funny, you know, just to see your smile. Why are you smiling, anyway?"

"I was thinking how different this is from the kitchen at the villa—and how small it seems with you here."

He looked around as if he was only now aware of his surroundings. "It doesn't matter. Places don't, you know, not when you're unhappy."

She nodded. She would be happy anywhere with Laurens, but not until she was sure the past was buried.

She told him why Pio had written her the letter,

and though Laurens listened silently, she had the feeling that his attention was elsewhere.

"I'm sure that Pio must have been in love with someone when I first met him," she added. "There was so much sadness in him, and once he said something about love being hell. I should have remembered his letter earlier, but I was so confused that— I was so sure, you see, that Pio must have been suffering from delusions. But now I'm convinced there really was a woman. I didn't meet Pio until the second semester when I asked permission to audit his class. Earlier, I'd had a conflicting schedule, an English class I needed."

She paused, regretting that she hadn't been experienced enough to sense Pio's unhappiness. "Maybe the woman he fell in love with was a student or a teacher or someone he'd met off campus. He must have been crushed when she threw him over, but one thing I'm sure of—he was getting over it. He didn't deliberately drive his car off the highway. He wouldn't have asked me to marry him if he hadn't intended to take me home with him. He never pretended to love me. He told me that he would be a good husband, that I'd have a home and security, and he did want children. I'm sure that had a lot to do with his proposal."

She got Pio's letter from a drawer and laid it on the table in front of Laurens, but he didn't touch it. He watched her, his face sober, until she finally asked him why he wasn't reading the letter.

"I don't need to. Why are you so determined

that I read it, Mayi? Don't you trust me when I tell you that all that jealousy and suspicion is behind me?''

His words echoed through her mind, stirring up memories of other confrontations they'd had, and suddenly she knew that he was right. He had once lost his faith in her, but now she was making the same mistake. If she believed him, why was she insisting that he see the proof of her innocence?

A flush swept her face, and she looked at him with stricken eyes. He reached across the table and grasped her hands tightly between his.

''Listen to me, Mayi. You're only human, just as I'm human. We'll make a lot more mistakes in the next fifty years. But if we never lose sight of our love for each other, we'll make it. I'm not the man I was a year ago, but one thing is the same. I love you with all my heart. In fact I fell in love with you so quickly, so hard, that it scared me. The intensity of feeling that Pio described was so similar to how I felt about you that I made a terrible mistake and assumed that we both fell in love with the same girl. I was so afraid of being hurt, the way Pio was, that I ended up opening all the avenues to pain. I've tried to make amends—for one thing, I've made peace with Luis's family. The strange thing is that the Hiribarrens have been wanting to put aside the old feud for a long time. Engrace and Luis are back in Zubilibia, living with his family on their farm. I visit them and the baby often.''

''The baby?''

"A girl. Her name is Petra Mayi Hiribarren. That should cause a bit of confusion at family gatherings."

She smiled at his wry tone. "Family gatherings—that sounds wonderful, Laurens."

"I want you there beside me—you and Michael." There was a question in his eyes as he watched her.

"And Pio's death—are you satisfied that it was an accident?" she said, evading his silent question.

"I know it was. The witness who reported the accident finally stepped forward. It seems the man had been drinking that night and was afraid that if he got involved the police would test him for alcohol content. But he was a good enough citizen to call in the accident. Pio was just ahead of him on the highway that night. A deer dashed across the road in front of Pio's car. He was going so fast that when he cut his wheel sharply to avoid the deer, the car went over the shoulder of the road and into the ravine. The witness said he'd been having nightmares about it, which is why he finally stepped forward, but I suspect it was the reward I offered and the promise of anonymity."

"I'm glad. This will be a comfort to Tia Petra and Engrace," she said.

"And I'm glad I made peace with the Hiribarrens. It was time to let the past die. Tradition is important because it's the mortar that's held the Basques together so many generations. But we've always been versatile and adaptable, taking what we want from other cultures and discarding the rest. So changes are good, but only by degrees.'' Again there was a wryness in his voice.

She met his eyes, and when she saw the hunger there, it sparked off her own long denial. She gave a small cry and then they were both standing, and she was in Laurens's arms.

As he cupped his hands around her hips and lifted her so that he could press his face against her breasts, she was sure that her flesh was melting, her bones dissolving. He could have taken her there, on the kitchen table, and she wouldn't have cared, but he carried her into the living room and laid her on the shabby couch, then knelt beside her. When he kissed the hollow at the base of her throat, her pulse leaped, and he laughed and kissed it, too.

Gently he pulled the end of her robe ties. The robe fell open, exposing her nude body to his hungry eyes. He touched the tiny bell around her neck.

''You still wear it, Mayi,'' he said.

''I've never taken it off.''

''We've wasted so much time—so much time,'' he groaned, and buried his face in the softness of her breasts.

She knew how much he wanted her, so she was surprised when he pulled away, his eyes haunted.

''Is it too soon? I don't want to rush you, Mayi.''

But she didn't want to wait, not even another minute. She wanted him now, wanted the ardent lover of their wedding day who had been so tender, even though he'd been almost crazy at the sight and touch of her.

She sat up, smiling into his eyes. He sucked his breath in sharply as she began to unbuckle his belt. Item by item she undressed him, and when she saw the naked beauty of his strong, masculine body, saw the proof of his need for her, she pressed herself against his heated body, mutely urging him to take the gift she so freely offered him.

He kissed her—on her lips, her breasts, on the sensitive places he knew so well, and every kiss intensified the mindless desire that had been unappeased for so long. He stretched out beside her on the sofa, but before he kissed her again, he asked, "Are you sure, Mayi? Because if I take you now, I'll never be able to let you go again."

"Yes—oh, yes, Laurens! I want you—I'll always want you," she said. With a groan, he lowered himself into the cradle of her arms, and she knew that she was where she belonged.

CHAPTER SEVENTEEN

IT WAS ALMOST JULY when Mayi and Laurens and their son returned to Zubilibia.

Mayi had wanted to show Laurens the mountains of Idaho, that raw, stark land that had been her own birthplace, and he had suggested that they spend their honeymoon there. "It isn't every couple who get to take their son along on their honeymoon," he said, his eyes crinkling at the corners and earning him Mayi's kiss.

The two weeks had been ecstatically happy, a time of healing, of getting to know each other again, of becoming a family. Laurens had loved the lofty mountains, the deep valley, the solitude of the cabin they had rented, and she delighted in introducing him to the breathtaking scenery, the small, unassuming towns and the friendly down-to-earth people of her native state.

But more and more, as the days passed, Mayi found herself yearning for Zubilibia, the one place where she truly felt at home. Much as she loved her own birthplace, she knew that for the rest of her life the home of her heart would be Navarra.

Two weeks after they came to Idaho, she packed

their suitcases with eagerness and anticipation, and during the plane trip to Spain, she found it hard to contain her impatience. Sensing her feelings, Laurens held her hand tightly as the plane they'd hired for the last stage of their journey circled for a landing. Mayi, her son sleeping in her lap, stared down with hungry eyes at the emerald-green valley and the brown tile roofs of the village.

There—that patch of green edged on one side by neat shops, at the other by a few handsome houses—was the village square where she and Laurens had danced for the first time. That sturdy house with its reddish brown balcony, which was a bit larger than its neighbors, must be the Bilbaos' pension. As for that patch of white just off the square, that was the sun, reflecting off the whitewashed walls of the pelota court. And the church— even from such a distance, its stone walls and lofty roof had a permanent look, as if it had been there forever and would still be there for centuries to come.

Mayi's breath escaped her in a long sigh as the plane flew low over the sprawling villa, then settled down on the meadow that served the valley as a landing field. Now that she was there, she felt a strange reluctance to move or speak, as if her voice might break the spell and everything would dissolve like the mystical village of Brigadoon. She was afraid that she would awaken to find that it had all been a dream and she was back in that shabby mobile home in Reno....

Then Laurens was taking Michael from her arms, holding their sleeping child against his strong shoulder. He smiled down at her, that special smile that always seemed to come from deep within him, and she knew that this wasn't a dream. Finally she had what she'd always yearned for—a home, a family, rewarding and worthwhile work as a teacher, and most important of all, a man to stand by her side, to share the burdens as well as the triumphs of life, to be her companion through all the years to come.

"Come, Mayi," Laurens said softly. "We're home now."

His strong hand helped her to her feet; a minute later he followed her off the plane. As they greeted Manuel, then got into the Jeep, she couldn't help remembering the night she'd returned from Guernica, and she shivered a little despite the warm day.

"Excited?" Laurens said, and she pushed the memory away and smiled at him, nodding. "Well, you aren't the only one. I feel as if I've been away for a year. I love travelling and we'll do a lot of it in the future, Mayi, but coming home—well, it's special."

"Special," she echoed. "Very special."

He laughed and kissed her, his lips lingering on hers, and the promise in his touch warmed her; she felt as if all she had to do was spread her wings and she would be able to fly. The thought of what Laurens—and the smiling Manuel, who was loading their luggage into the Jeep—would think if she took off into the sky like a snow dove made her smile. But when Laurens gave her a questioning look, she told him it was a private joke and didn't explain.

Michael awoke as they were climbing the front steps of the villa. He yawned, his expression so comical that they were both laughing as they came into the coolness of the front hall. Tia Petra, looking smaller than Mayi remembered, was just coming down the stairs. Her cry of joy when she saw Michael filled Mayi with guilt.

Michael eyed the strange woman for a long moment, and then his mouth turned upward into his radiant smile, and his chortling laugh, so like Mayi's, filled the hall. Although she obviously couldn't wait to get her hands on her great-nephew, Tia Petra prudently held back and contented herself with a dry "Well, you're a handsome one, young man, just like your father."

But Michael would have none of that. He waved his hands, demanding imperiously to be held, and Tia Petra's gray eyes filled with tears as she took her nephew in her arms at long last.

Mayi turned away, not wanting them to see her own tears. A moment later, when a door opened and Engrace flew into the hall, she found herself the recipient of a hug so vigorous she was afraid for her ribs.

"Thank God you're back," Engrace said in her ear, her voice low. "I've been so worried about Laurens. He's been like a ghost this past year—"

"I know—and I'm sorry," Mayi said contritely. "I never should have left."

"Well, it all worked out for the best. And I have you to thank for making Laurens more—more tolerant."

"You and Luis are happy?"

"Oh, yes, although we have our little differences of opinion," Engrace said, laughing. "And wait until you see our Petra Mayi—she's sleeping now but she should be awake shortly. Tia Petra says she's the image of me at that age. Thank the saints she didn't inherit the Hiribarren nose," she said, rolling her eyes so comically that Mayi had to smile. Marriage, it seemed, had brought Engrace out of her shell, or perhaps living with a big lively family had done that.

Later, after the greetings were over and family and village news had been shared, Mayi asked about Topet. He had been on her mind for the past hour, but she'd been so afraid the news would be bad that she had postponed asking the question.

"He's as well as can be expected for such an old dog," Tia Petra said, smiling at her. "He should be back in a little while. He goes to the meadow this time every day. I think he's looking for you, Mayi."

Mayi swallowed hard, fighting the mistiness in her eyes. "I think I'll go to meet him," she said, rising.

"I'll come with you—if Tia Petra will keep an eye out for Michael," Laurens said.

They were silent as they strolled toward the meadow. When they reached the stone wall that surrounded the grassy field, Laurens stopped her. "I've been wanting to do this all morning," he said. He bent his head and kissed her, and she clung to him, the old magic starting up in her heart.

A sound came from behind them, and they broke apart. A golden head poked up through the high grass, which was still green from the spring rains, and Topet, his nose lifted into the wind, stood quivering before them. He gave an imperious bark, as if demanding that they identify themselves, and Mayi knew that he was completely blind now.

She knelt and held out her hand. "Argus," she called, her mind slipping back to the first time she'd met him in this same meadow.

For a moment he stood like a statue, and then he was bounding toward her as if he were still a puppy. With a joyful bark, he cavorted around her, forgetting his dignity, and she flung back her head laughing.

"I'm home for good, Topet," she told him joyfully. "This time I'm home for good."

After Topet was curled up in the grass, sleeping, Laurens put his arms around Mayi. "That first day, when I saw you racing across the meadow with Topet at your heels, I thought you were the most exciting woman I'd ever seen," he said, his voice husky with desire. "Even when we're old and gray, that's the image of you I'll always carry in my heart. I want you, Mayi, and I'm not sure I can wait until tonight to make love to you.''

"Then why wait?" she murmured, sinking down upon the fragrant, sun-warmed grass. "Make love to me here in the haunted meadow where it all started, and maybe we can dispel the ghosts once and for all."

Laurens kissed her, his lips sun-warmed and comforting. As she returned his kiss, she knew that she would never forget this day, and as they renewed their love for yet another time, ten angels entered into Mayi's heart.

Begin a long love affair with

HARLEQUIN
SUPERROMANCE.™

Accept LOVE BEYOND DESIRE **FREE.**

Complete and mail the coupon below today!

FREE! Mail to: Harlequin Reader Service

In the U.S.
2504 West Southern Avenue
Tempe, AZ 85282

In Canada
P.O. Box 2800, Postal Station "A"
5170 Yonge St., Willowdale, Ont. M2N 5T5

YES, please send me FREE and without any obligation my
HARLEQUIN SUPERROMANCE novel, LOVE BEYOND DESIRE. If you do
not hear from me after I have examined my FREE book, please send me
the 4 new **HARLEQUIN SUPERROMANCE** books every month as soon
as they come off the press. I understand that I will be billed only $2.50 for
each book (total $10.00). There are no shipping and handling or any
other hidden charges. There is no minimum number of books that I have
to purchase. In fact, I may cancel this arrangement at any time.
LOVE BEYOND DESIRE is mine to keep as a FREE gift, even if I do not
buy any additional books.

NAME _____ (Please Print)

ADDRESS _____ APT. NO.

CITY _____

STATE/PROV. _____ ZIP/POSTAL CODE

SIGNATURE (If under 18, parent or guardian must sign.)

SUP-SUB-33

This offer is limited to one order per household and not valid to present
subscribers. Prices subject to change without notice. Offer expires April 30, 1985

134-BPS-KAS4